P9-DDG-861

A GATHERING OF SHADES

ALSO BY DAVID STAHLER JR.

Truesight

A GATHERING OF SHADES

DAVID STAHLER JR.

HarperTempest
An Imprint of HarperCollins*Publishers*

Library of Congress Cataloging-in-Publication data
Stahler, David.
  A gathering of shades / David Stahler Jr.— 1st ed.
    p. cm.
  Summary: Having moved with his mother to a remote corner of Vermont
after his father's death, sixteen-year-old Aidan learns much about his family,
including that ghosts inhabit an ancient orchard on the family farm, sustained
by his grandmother.
  ISBN 0-06-052294-1 — ISBN 0-06-052295-X (lib. bdg.)
  [1. Ghosts—Fiction. 2. Grief—Fiction. 3. Farm life—Vermont—Fiction.
4. Moving, Household—Fiction. 5. Vermont—Fiction.] I. Title.
PZ7.S78246Gat 2005   2004021498
[Fic]—dc22   CIP
                                               AC

Typography by Sasha Illingworth
1 2 3 4 5 6 7 8 9 10

First Edition

For my parents, Rena and David,
with love and gratitude for the roots they gave me

PROLOGUE

The sun still had a ways to go before setting, but in the shade of the orchard it felt like dusk already. The old woman, having wandered down from the house an hour ago, smiled in the coolness of the shadows, and for a moment just listened to the brook that now, in the heat of solstice, had slowed to the murmur it would hold for the rest of summer. Wearing a cotton dress, white with blue flowers, she looked as weathered as the old wooden chair she sat in, slicing off bites of pear with a jackknife, taking time to lick the juice that trickled down her wrists and lay along the blade. A few red pearls of blood from the prick on her fingertip mingled with the juice, giving it a coppery tang, but she didn't mind. She chewed the fruit slowly, as if it were a meditation, offering none to the figures that had gathered around her, that sat close by or stood, leaning against the apple trees. She knew they would refuse. Besides, they had already had their treat.

"So they're coming tonight, you said?"

"By Jesus, Smitty, you don't miss much, do you," the old

woman replied, and everyone laughed.

"Well, Eloise," Smitty said, sinking his massive bulk down within a checkered wool jacket. "I thought that's what you'd said, but you know I don't remember so good no more."

"Never did, even before," a girl called over to Smitty. She stuck her tongue out at him and grinned. Her T-shirt read "Nirvana."

"How'd you know, Eve? You wouldn't know."

"Christ, Smitty, everyone knows," another woman injected from across the circle. She reclined regally in the grass, her antique dress folded around her. "Every time Bobby stops by, he tells us how dumb you used to be."

Again, laughter as all the others joined in.

"Quiet!" Eloise barked, and all laughter ceased. "Marie— all of you—that's quite enough of that, eh? I didn't invite you here to listen to you bicker or pick on poor Smitty. Smitty, my dear, I'm sorry. I shouldn't have started it. And in answer to your question—yes, they ought to be here in an hour or so."

"Coming for good, are they?" an old man in faded overalls asked from beneath the low-hanging limbs.

"I guess maybe, Alton," Eloise said. "But who's to say."

"Suppose we won't be seeing much of you then," he replied. A quiet murmur of doubt rippled among the group, a snowy set of whispers that could have been mistaken for a rustling of leaves. Eloise shivered at the collective sound of pessimism; no matter how long in their company, she knew even she would never get used to that sound.

"Now, I said no such thing. Perhaps I won't be down as often. Then again, you never know. I'll certainly try, for all our sakes. Besides," she added in a gentle rebuke, "let's not be selfish, eh? They're in bad shape, I suspect. They may need me even more than you do."

Her words seemed to satisfy them, and the rustling passed.

"You're quite right, Eloise," a man with graying hair said. He wore a blue military coat with tails and brass buttons. He gave the old woman a curt bow and she nodded, smiling, in reply. "As we all know, there are things worse than death."

They all looked away, with a silence that implied assent.

"All right, enough gloominess," Eloise said. "I can't hardly remember a summer evening so perfect. Let's just enjoy it together. It's what we're here for, isn't it? Drink up, my dears, drink up!"

She gestured to the center of the circle, where a granite basin supported by an ornate pedestal stood, the hub of their wheel. The liquid within reflected the gold of the sky, and for the second time that evening, they gathered around it to quench their thirst.

ONE

Aidan swallowed back the sour taste in his throat as they neared the accident up ahead. He hadn't seen it happen—the steel twisting, the fiberglass panels cracking, the windows fracturing. All in the crush of an instant. And then the letting go, the settling of pieces, shards raining down to mingle with roadside trash. But what he hadn't seen he could imagine—a sight that flashed through his mind each time an ambulance or cruiser picked its way, wailing, through the maze of cars heading north out of Boston.

They had been close. Not close enough to see it happen, not close enough to make out the bodies, to know for sure if they had lived or not. Not close enough to avoid the ensuing jam of cars as everything came to a halt, but close enough so that as they approached the scene, it was still a scene. Sitting with his mother up in the cab of the U-Haul, their Accord trailing along in tow, Aidan looked out over the cars. It felt strange to be so high, to be peering down from a position of privilege. Until now he had been enjoying the perspective; its

1

novelty had made the normal crush of afternoon traffic less tedious. But now, gazing ahead to the flashing lights and haze of smoke, it was as if he and his mother were stranded on some floating raft, a lifeboat being ushered toward fresh destruction by a wave of sedans.

I won't do it. I won't be like them, he told himself. In the end, he did it anyway. He became like them—just another rubbernecker, compelled to stare by that bizarre mix of fascination and horror. To look away felt somehow wrong, unnatural in spite of his hatred for the programmed response. The burned and broken husks—four cars in various states of wreckage—lay interspersed with perfect, gleaming cruisers, fire trucks, and ambulances. Though there was movement at the site, a calm had settled in. Men in uniforms paced slowly or stood around, some speaking in clusters, others looking at the wrecks or staring back at the faces of passing commuters. They seemed to be waiting for something to happen, but everything already had: the victims had been extracted, packaged, bundled, and shipped, ferried out to whatever hospital was close at hand, both the living and the dead. All that remained was the cleanup.

This was the effect. What had been the cause? He wondered. A momentary lapse of concentration? A bumped elbow, a mistimed step on the brake, a drift into another lane? That was the way these things went. Something small, trivial, petty, would blossom into disaster, alter some lives unexpectedly and forever, leaving others intact and oblivious. Most of life's accidents had their roots in the stupid and the mundane.

"You don't have to look, you know."

Her words broke the spell of his gaze. He turned to his mother in the driver's seat, looking small behind the wheel, her arms reaching out and up, her legs stretching to work the pedals. She sat upright in the seat, staring straight ahead, eyes never deviating from the line of brake lights flashing into the distance before them. She was pretty and—as his friends constantly reminded him—looked a good deal younger than forty. Her dark hair, cut short, and her petite frame implied fragility, but Aidan knew they merely disguised the toughness of a rural-grown girl. Except for now, of course. For in spite of the stiff pose and resolute stare, he had heard the trembling in her voice, could see the eyes that blinked too much.

"Just don't even look at it, Aidan," she said, her voice firmer now.

But it was too late—he had already absorbed the ugliness of the scene, a cruel compensation for that other accident neither of them had been there to see.

"Shit," she said, perhaps at the traffic, perhaps at the accident, perhaps at the heat that was everywhere—pouring in through the open windows and through the blasting vents of the van, the one with the air conditioner that didn't work. Or maybe it was just a general curse. Aidan didn't say it, but he shared the sentiment.

They had finally passed beyond the wrecks, and the traffic

was breaking up. Suddenly there was open road, the cars accelerating into their own spaces, as if they had been held at the starting line and the green flag now waved, setting them free to tear away to their homes, the accident already forgotten.

"God, it's almost six-thirty. We're going to be so late," she said.

"You're the one who wanted to leave today. Friday afternoon, first day of summer. Stupid."

"I know," she said, chafing at his resentment. "You wanted one more night with your friends. One more night to do whatever it is you do," she said, casting a sidelong glance in his direction. "I'm sorry, Aidan, but today was the right day. Summer solstice—the longest day. First day of our summer vacation. It had the right symbolic resonance."

He sighed. She was such an English teacher sometimes. He reached down and switched on the radio—at least *it* worked—and tuned in FNX, cranking the volume so that a wash of distortion and heavy beats filled the cab, competing with the roar of wind from the open windows. He didn't have to look to see her grimace, and it satisfied him to add her annoyance to his own. Normally she would have turned the music down or off altogether. This time, she didn't. She let him sink back into the sullen defiance he'd been bearing since this morning, when they'd started loading up whatever belongings hadn't been sold before heading off in the sluggish van for northern Vermont.

"Vermont?" Mitchell had asked.

Aidan thought back to last night, when he had gathered with a few friends for one final get-together, a "going-away party," as his friend Andy had called it. They met where they always met—High Rock, an aptly named landmark in the town forest—for the usual beer and cigarettes. Aidan had been silent most of the night, listening to the voices of Andy, Mitchell, Jonesie, and Mike rising in the dark as the glowing embers of their smokes flared from time to time, bobbing up and down like fireflies on speed.

"Yeah, dumb-ass," Aidan joked, finishing his beer, "Vermont. How many times do I have to tell you?"

"Whatever," Mitchell quipped back. "I don't even know where that is."

"Jesus, Mitch," Jonesie said, "it's a goddam state. It's right above us, for chrissake."

"No way, dude," Mitchell replied proudly, "that's New Hampshire."

"Yeah, but next to that is Vermont. You know—skiing, maple syrup, that kind of crap."

"Whatever," Mitchell reiterated. "New Hampshire, Vermont—what's the difference?"

"Not much," Aidan said, cracking another beer.

"You're lucky, Aidan," Mike said. "We go up there every year during winter break. My uncle's got a condo at Killington. Wicked skiing."

"I don't ski," Aidan said.

"Besides," Andy broke in, "Aidan's going farther north than that. He's going to . . . what did you call it?"

"The Kingdom," Aidan replied.

"The Kingdom? What the hell does that mean?" Mike asked.

"Beats me. That's just what they call it."

"So does that mean you'll be *king*?" Mitchell said, snorting.

"Yeah, that's funny, Mitch," Aidan retorted.

"If he's king, he gets his pick of any hottie he wants," Jonesie offered.

"They don't have hotties up there, do they, Aidan," Andy said. "Didn't you tell me Kingdom girls have half the teeth and twice the ass of Boston girls?"

"Something like that," Aidan laughed.

"That's okay," Mitchell said. "Who needs girls when you got sheep around, right Aidan? I'll bet you got *lots* of sheep up there."

They all burst out laughing. Everyone except Aidan.

"So why do you have to go, anyway?" Mike asked.

"I don't know. Gotta sell the house. We got family up there. It's my mother's decision, not mine. You want to know, ask her," Aidan snapped, lighting a cigarette. The sudden bitterness in his voice brought a lull to the conversation. Andy broke the silence.

"A toast!" he cried, raising his beer in the darkness. "To our pal, Aidan, future redneck—"

"And sheep lover!" Mitchell added, to snickers. They all took long swigs. Aidan tossed back with the rest of them, half choking as he chugged the remainder of his third beer.

"Drink up, boys!" Andy croaked. "For tomorrow we may die!"

At Andy's words, the group went silent once more. Someone gave a nervous cough.

"Sorry, Aidan," Andy murmured.

A second later someone farted and everyone—Aidan included—broke out laughing once again.

Aidan smiled at the memory, then fell back into a scowl when he caught his mother casting another glance in his direction. Along with a mild hangover, he had been nursing his resentment all day, all month in fact, ever since she had told him her decision to sell the big house in the nice suburb that they could no longer afford on her salary alone and move north. She had always been so cautious, so predictable, that the decision threw him for a loop, made a confusing world even more confusing. But today especially, he had worked his resentment into a quiet rage, ignoring nearly every question, every attempt to elicit a response. He had finally been able to cut himself off entirely. And after a while, her resignation—a "fine, be that way" attitude—suited him.

And so he had barely said a word. Neither had she, for that matter. They now crossed the border into New

7

Hampshire, the traffic swelling again as the four lanes of I-93 shrank to three, then two.

"You hungry?" she asked a half hour later, not waiting for him to answer. "I'm hungry. We'll stop in Concord. You know that place? That diner? We'll stop there." His response was to fiddle with the radio. They were at the Concord toll-booth now, and the Boston station was breaking up. Soon, he knew, there would be no good radio, nothing but top-forty crap, easy listening, and country swill. And even those stations would become fewer the farther north they went.

They wandered up the highway that cut through the state capital, getting off at the diner next to the interstate. Aidan was too hot to be really hungry, but it would make a nice change from the monotony of the road and would prolong the inevitable arrival.

They went inside and took a booth. Like most diners, it was dedicated to the past and filled with memorabilia. But what confused Aidan, what irked him even, he now realized, was its lack of focus. It offered no monolithic tribute, but a hodgepodge of American pasts all competing with one another. Whereas most diners lived in the 1950s or some other particular era, this one presented a bizarre assortment of periods. Elvis and Marilyn competed with Rosie the Riveter, GI Joe, Jimi Hendrix, and the Eagles for wall space. Racks of old LPs and newspapers from the past fifty years were jammed between the booths. Even the menu lacked any sort of consistency; fried chicken, meat loaf, burgers, and other traditional diner fare rubbed elbows with spaghetti, burritos, and pork lo mein.

He had loved stopping here as a kid on their trips north. The posters, postcards, and knickknacks, the mini-jukeboxes in each booth, had all dazzled him. Now, at sixteen, Aidan felt overwhelmed by the accumulation of time, by the barrage of history that rolled itself into a tacky ball of the past. And there was something else here that bothered him. He couldn't figure it out, but she reminded him.

"God, it's been a while. The last time we were here . . . "

"Dad was with us," he said, filling in her pause as he realized.

"Right," she said, sliding down the booth to nestle in the corner.

Aidan glanced at her a moment, could see the sheen of oil and sweat on her gaunt face as she pushed the hair back from her forehead. *She looks tired*, he thought. He started to reach across the table for her hand, then checked himself, turning back to his menu before she could notice. The waitress came; they ordered. In spite of having not been hungry, he got a fish sandwich, extra tartar sauce, fries, and chocolate milk. She ordered grilled cheese and water.

They ate in silence and returned to the road in silence. Even the radio was mute, switched off at Tilton. He leaned against his door, watching the landscape become more green and rugged as they traveled farther north and the evening sun settled farther west. He watched the familiar exit signs come and go. Ashland, Plymouth, Campton, and still they didn't talk. The White Mountains loomed before them, growing with every mile. They had just passed Lincoln and were entering the Notch when she finally spoke up.

"You do realize, Aidan, that you've become nothing but a stock character. A stereotype—poster boy for the angry youth of America. Look out folks: he's lean, he's mean, he's got an attitude. He'll ignore you to death and amaze you with his disaffectedness—"

"Shut up, Ma!" he finally snapped. For a moment they just sat still, glancing at each other. He broke the pause first and punched the dash in front of him. What pissed him off the most was that she was right, as usual. He was acting like a jerk, the classic moody teenager, but couldn't she understand why?

North of the Notch, as they rounded the bend toward Franconia, she again broke the silence. Her tone lacked its earlier bite.

"Still thinking about it, aren't you."

"About what?"

"The accident," she answered. "You're back on it. Don't worry, I'm there too."

"Not really. Not today's," he said.

"I didn't mean today's. But seeing those wrecks certainly brought it back—for you too, I'm sure."

It came pouring out before he could stop himself.

"I just keep seeing him in one of those cars. How he must

have looked when they pulled him out and how those cops must have just stood around afterward waiting for some stupid wrecker. And the people going by—they just looked, slowed down and gawked like I did today. They didn't know him or even really care. He probably died with some jackass in his BMW watching."

"You can't think about your father that way. No one looks good when they die. You have to remember him the way you knew him. Think of something before, something happy—doesn't matter if it was last year or five years ago. It's what I do. I try to do that."

"I guess," he whispered.

He didn't tell her that it was getting harder to remember what his father looked like, beyond some generalized impression. It was as if, with each passing month, his father was fading away, piece by piece. At first he had seen him everywhere. Every time he closed his eyes he was there, showing up every night in his dreams. But lately all he could manage were momentary fragments, like disjointed clips from movies, millisecond loops that degenerated into random bursts of facial features—a grin here, a wink there, a turning of the head as the face disappeared from view, the echo of a voice. How long would it be before even these disappeared? It terrified him. He had tried to find a picture this morning in the hope that it might bring back something concrete, but everything had been packed away.

Still, maybe she was right. He closed his eyes and tried

recalling some moment of the three of them together. That last summer on the Cape when they'd stopped for a picnic on the beach near Chatham Light. Planted on one corner of the blanket, he could see his mother, he could even see himself, but when he looked around, sure enough, his father was gone, the empty space leaving Aidan with a hollowness that flooded all over again with grief. *Shit.*

"It's hard, I know," she said. "That's why we're going, Aidan. A chance to start over. A chance for you to learn something about your roots. A chance for me to get back to mine. I need this, Aidan."

"I don't," he replied.

He hated everything about this move. He hated leaving behind the friends he'd made these past two years in Needham, not to mention those he still kept in touch with from Quincy, Franklin, Mansfield, all the towns they'd lived in around Boston, moving every few years to ever-wealthier suburbs with each big promotion his father received. He hated leaving the big house on Sizemore, where the homes all mirrored one another in size, shape, and patterns of color and materials, all variations on the common dream of middle-aged lawyers, doctors, systems analysts, and corporate managers like his father. His mother hadn't particularly cared for the new house or for the neighborhood, in spite of its luxury ("McMansions," she'd snorted derisively the first time they drove down Sizemore Street), but for his father it was a dream come true, a tangible reflection of everything he'd strived to attain, the antithesis of everything he'd struggled to leave behind, most notably the Kingdom.

The Kingdom was the Northeast Kingdom, a long-standing name for the corner of Vermont tucked away between Quebec in the north and New Hampshire in the east, the poorest region of a poor state. His father, Tim Dunkley, and his mother, Patrice Boisvert, had grown up there as neighbors on adjoining farms. A year apart in age, they had been childhood playmates–turned–high school sweethearts, or something like that—Aidan had heard the story before but had never really paid much attention. All he knew was that his father disdained the Kingdom ("A squalid backwater," he called it), had left as soon as he could, and avoided going back as much as possible, only begrudgingly agreeing to the occasional visit to placate Aidan's mother.

And that was the other thing. It wasn't just that he hated leaving Massachusetts behind; he hated coming here, a place his father had so eagerly left and seemed to despise so much. And now he was being forced to settle here for good, stuck on a mountain in an old house with only his mother and grand-mother for company. He had never liked that rickety farm-house with its moldy smell and the attached barn that sagged so severely it threatened to collapse at any moment and bring the house down with it. And while he didn't exactly dislike his grandmother, Eloise Boisvert—that wiry woman every-one called Memère (the French-Canadian slang for "grandma"), with her glacier eyes that seemed to look right

13

through you—he had never warmed to her. She wasn't a proper grandmother—some sweet old lady who sat quietly in the corner knitting an ugly sweater—or even a grouchy, bitter grandmother whose endless complaints could be easily ignored. No, Memère had an intensity, an unabashed frankness, that unnerved him. He always had to be on guard around her—the way she smiled at him, as if she knew some secret about him that he didn't know himself.

All he wanted was to have his old life back. It had been a good life, a comfortable, easy life. Of course, it hadn't been perfect; there were the fights about Vermont and sometimes about money—his mother feared they lived perpetually above their means, his father derided her fears as mere Yankee stinginess. Nor was Aidan a perfect son, slipping at times into what his mother referred to as suburban punkdom. Still, though they may not have been entirely happy, they were happy enough, and he'd never thought much beyond it.

And then it all went away, disappeared one cold November night last fall. It was a week before Thanksgiving, a school night, and Aidan had gone to bed. His father had been working late with clients from out of town and had taken them out afterward for dinner and drinks in Boston as he usually did. It was just another night, no different from any other. The next thing Aidan knew, his mother was waking him. It was nearly two in the morning and she was crying. She was telling him about a visit from the state police.

She was telling him there had been an accident on the turnpike. Several people had been killed and one of them was his father. He could only listen to her cry for the next hour while she held him. Sometimes he felt like he had gone to sleep that night and had never woken up, that he was still asleep and the last seven months were a dream he was having still.

After that night nearly every aspect of Aidan's life seemed a struggle. Winter had been darker and colder, spring had come late, and when it came held no pleasure. He fought with his mother, his teachers, even his friends over trivialities he couldn't understand. For the most part—after the initial trauma had been absorbed, after the ensuing rites of mourning had been observed—life without his father wasn't hard, which, in a bizarre paradox, made it all the harder. For it wasn't as if it were some brutal horror, some peril against which he could struggle and be heroic. It was just a series of days occupied by minor losses, by a constant readjustment of little thoughts, by the banishment of old assumptions about the way life was supposed to be.

They crossed the Connecticut, the river that formed the border between New Hampshire and Vermont, made their way up the long hill—their U-Haul chugging in low gear past the Welcome Center—and cleared the top of the valley where the first real view of the Kingdom opened up. It was late now, and the clouds hung low. Within the gap between the mountains and the clouds, the sun was slipping down to the horizon, casting streaks of meltcolors across the sky. In the distance the familiar profile spread before them. They could see the Willoughby Gap, with Mount Hor and Mount Pisgah forming either side, sheltering the vast lake for which the gap was named. To its right the bubble of Haystack protruded from the ascending slope that rose to become Bald Mountain. Between Aidan and this line of mountains lay rows of hills and valleys, and beyond it more layers. Somewhere their mountain, a little mountain called Harper, was nestled, hidden behind the larger peaks of the undulating landscape.

"There it is," his mother said. He could hear the excitement, even a tinge of pride, in her voice as the panorama came into view. "We should make it to the farm in less than an hour. Look at the green, Aidan."

It was green. And it was beautiful. Aidan felt it. But it was an alien beauty from an alien land where he didn't belong.

The U-Haul began to pick up speed now that they had cleared the rise and were heading toward St. Johnsbury. I-93, a highway that began in Boston, was coming to an end. Soon they would switch over to 91, continue north to Lyndonville, where they would leave the highway for good, and begin delving deeper into the hills along the winding secondary roads. Then they would leave all blacktop behind, be left with nothing but a gravel road as they drove the last stretch up the mountain. It was evolution in reverse, civilization in recession. His father had been right.

Aidan looked one last time at the mountains before they slipped behind the near horizon. The last time he had seen this view—the last time he had been to the Kingdom—it was Thanksgiving and they had come to bury his father before the ground froze for winter. Then there was no green. The hills were gray, so was the sky. The wind was chill, the grass was long yellow from the killing frosts of October, and everything was dead.

TWO

Darkness was settling in by the time they pulled into the driveway. There was no lamp to illuminate the yard; what light there was shone weakly from the downstairs windows of the house. As they stepped down from the cab, Aidan was surprised by the contrast. The shrill rhythm of the U-Haul's engine, the vibration of the road, were now replaced by what seemed at first to be silence, though with concentration the ear realized that the hush was in fact the mild drone of crickets, their chirps woven together into a sound that almost wasn't there. The air was cool and clear—the pinkish orange haze that brooded over the entire Boston region most summer nights didn't exist here—and though the sky was still lit a deep navy blue, stars shone from all its corners. Already he could see more stars than in even the darkest Boston sky, though, like the crickets, they took time to make their presence known.

They waited for a moment for Memère to come out and greet them. When she didn't show, his mother went up onto the porch and called out, but no one replied. The house seemed to be empty.

So much for the warm welcome, he thought. He had expected to find her waiting. In spite of himself, a tiny hope welled up. *Maybe she moved. Maybe she died and no one told us.* The words just popped into his mind, followed by a guilty thrill.

"No one's here," he quipped. "Guess we better go."

"Don't start, Aidan," his mother warned. She sat down on the porch steps. Aidan joined her. They sat in silence for a few minutes until a voice called out in the dark.

"There are the travelers!" Memère pronounced, as if she had just summoned them. She came up out of the shadows from the lawn below.

"Hello, Mama," his mother said, rising from the steps and going out to meet her in the driveway with a hug and a quick kiss. "What were you doing out there in the dark?"

Even in the dusky yard Aidan was sure he saw the old woman stiffen for a moment. "Aidan, come here. Give Memère a kiss," his grandmother called out to him, ignoring her daughter's question. He got up and went to her.

"Hello, Memère," he said, kissing the soft cheek she offered.

"Welcome home," she said. Then, as if reading Aidan's mind, she squeezed his hand. "I was speaking to Patrice. I know this isn't your home. Not yet."

Typical, Aidan thought. *No embarrassment, right to the point.*

"It is his home, Mama," his mother interjected. "He's happy to be here. Right, Aidan?" Her tone was neutral, but Aidan knew the prompt carried an implied threat.

"Yup," he said.

"Really? Sure about that, are you?" his grandmother asked with what seemed to be genuine surprise, though in the dark Aidan couldn't tell for sure.

"Of course," he said.

"Well, that's odd," she responded. She shrugged her shoulders. "Anyway, enough talking in the dark. Come inside so I can actually see your faces."

His mother and Memère moved toward the house, but Aidan hung back.

"Ma, I think I'll go for a walk. I need to stretch my legs after the long drive."

"Aidan—" she said with that tired tone of frustration. She didn't need to finish the sentence.

"Let the boy go, Patrice," Memère broke in. "It's a fine night for a walk. Just stay close, dear. Better to reacquaint yourself with the place in the light of day, eh? You never know what you might bump into out there in the dark."

"I won't go too far," he said, and turned away from the house.

Aidan crossed the broad lawn that sloped down away from the house. He was wearing his Tevas, and the dew felt cool against his feet. He passed the garden, barely visible in the fading light from the house, and slipped through a hedge of young poplars. The house was nearly out of sight.

This should be far enough, he thought. He took a pack of Camel Filters out of the pocket of his shorts, removed one and lit it, waving the match out and throwing it off into the grass. Exhaling, he looked up at the brightening stars. The Milky Way was beginning to emerge as the sky slipped into black. He took another drag and stepped aside to avoid the cloud of smoke that hung and curled in the still air. Though he was pretty sure his mother knew he smoked, she hadn't said anything yet, and he felt a compulsion to hide the fact from her as long as possible. If she didn't know and found out, it would just be one more disappointment.

Not that she could say much—she herself had resumed the habit a few months ago after having quit for over two years. Like Aidan now, she had hid it from him at first. But he knew the signs, having himself become a secret smoker. It was stupid; he knew it and surely his mother did as well, but under the circumstances certain things could slide—they would have to make allowances for each other. In fact, in Aidan's mind, at least, it was something that bonded them in a time when not much else did, when each had slipped into his and her own private grief, leaving them unable to deal with each other's. In some respects, their smoking was like their grief: a habit indulged on the sly, each party aware but pretending to be ignorant of the other's secret, shared relief in the pretensions of normalcy that allowed them to get through the days.

He smoked quickly, finished the butt, and stamped it out. Reaching back into his pocket, he took out a piece of cinnamon gum and popped it into his mouth, chewing intensely to rid the odor of cigarettes from his mouth. It was a futile gesture—he knew his body, especially his hands, must reek of smoke—but it was all part of the ritual. His eyes had adjusted to the dark now, and he looked around before turning back. He had left the lawn and crossed down into the edge of the orchard, as Memère always called it. The dozen or so apple trees that still remained loomed, their shadows scraggly and overgrown in the dark, black against the lighter shade of sky. The grass was tall here—at late June knee-high—and saplings had begun to encroach along the borders. As a kid he had been frightened of the place; it had felt too old, and he an invader, disturbing its silence, disturbing the quiet of its trees that lay in rows like graves grown wild, growing into one another and filling the spaces in between with leaves and spiky branches.

He remembered coming here once in the fall with his parents to pick apples. Most of them were wormy and misshapen, only good enough for sauce and pies, but a couple trees still provided apples that could be eaten right from the tree, their flesh pink, sweet, and unblemished. He had climbed into one of the larger trees, high up, reaching out for the perfect apple, when the bough snapped and he had fallen, banging against the limbs on his way down before dropping into the grass with a thud. He had broken his arm and had to wear a cast long past Halloween. Immediately after the fall, he remembered feeling more shock than actual pain, disbelief that he could be too heavy for the tree, that it would betray him so suddenly. He remembered his parents carrying him back to the house. Though he didn't cry—at least not then—his mother did, and it comforted him. His father only smiled and told him that everything would be okay, and he believed him.

"Bastard."

The sound of his own voice startled him, and he glanced around, guilty in the dark. He rubbed his forearm against the memory of pain as if, for a moment, it had broken all over again. *I didn't mean it!* he thought. He wanted to call it out, but the thought of hearing his voice again in the night was too much. He turned and cut for the lawn.

He had just passed the garden when a chill overtook him. It started in the base of his spine and crawled its way up, like a pack of spiders racing toward the hollow in the back of his neck, culminating with a ringing in his ears. He pulled to a stop, closed his eyes, and shivered, trying to work the sensation from his body. Opening his eyes, he gasped.

A man was crossing the lawn, cutting between Aidan and the house, walking slowly, a dark figure that seemed to disappear in and out of shadow.

Aidan's heart began to pound, pushing a sense of euphoria through his system to mingle with the terror as he peered into the gloom. Now that his eyes had adjusted to the dark, the house lights seemed glaring and intense, obscuring everything around them, and he struggled to make sense of the shape. Who could be wandering this time of night? *Go after him*, he told himself. *Do something! Say something!* But he was frozen. All he could do was watch as the shadow, flickering in and out of view, headed for the pines at the edge of the lawn and then disappeared into the trees.

Aidan made for the house, his heart still pounding, fighting back the urge to run for the porch. Approaching the spot where the figure had disappeared, he glanced over at the pines.

Don't be a wimp.

Aidan forced himself over to the edge of the lawn. He stopped to listen but could hear nothing—his pulse was pounding too hard. He stepped closer to the trees, now only a few yards away. He took cautious steps, but the throb did not respond to slower movement. If anything, it beat harder.

The shrubs exploded, knocking Aidan to the ground in fear. He looked up in time to see a deer leap from the bushes through the air. It landed with a thud of hooves and bounded off across the lawn down into the orchard.

For a moment Aidan just lay there in the dark, absorbing the rush of adrenaline, feeling the whole of his body as it lay stretched across the earth. Then he began to shake, his relief finding itself in laughter. He gave in to the giddiness, allowed it to drain the tension, and then stood up and headed for the porch with quick steps.

In spite of the laughter, doubt began creeping in as he

replayed the moment in his mind. He knew that what he had seen had to have been the deer, that he had simply spooked it on its passing through, and that the figure of the man had simply been a trick of the half-light, the playing of country shadows in his suburban mind. Still, when he closed his eyes, that ambling shape kept returning, walking before him, silent and out of reach, yet somehow familiar in its movements, as if he had seen that gait before.

Approaching the porch, he could hear the voices of his mother and Memère in the kitchen, coming through the screen door. He crept up the steps and paused beside the threshold.

"I wish he'd just come back already," Aidan heard his mother say.

"Once he comes inside, he knows that's it for him. It's final," Memère replied.

"You're right, Mama. He's having a hard time. Be gentle on him this summer. You can be when you want to."

"Il est toujours un enfant, n'est pas?" Memère said, breaking into French as she sometimes did with her daughter, who usually resisted responding in kind.

"Yeah," she replied. "He's still a child in some ways. All the more reason to go easy."

"Everyone has to grow up sometime, Patrice. Boys have to become men. And girls must become women."

"What's that supposed to mean? Don't forget, I'm forty now."

"Hasn't my youngest come home to the nest? She wants

Mama to take care of her, to make everything better?"

"You know it's not like that."

"That's right, I forgot. You've come back to take care of me. Crazy old Eloise, right?"

"That's right. Like it or not, I'm about the only thing standing between you and the Pine Knoll Nursing Home."

"That may be. Your brothers would have to knock me out and tie me up to get me away from here. They know it and so do you," she said. "But I appreciate the sentiment on your part. And the effort. As for Aidan, I think I've got just the thing for him."

There was a pause. His mother said something he couldn't make out.

"We'll help each other. How's that sound?" Memère said. "And we'll help Aidan. Don't worry, Patrice. Everything takes time. Even death."

There was a long moment of silence. Aidan heard his mother make a strange choked sound. She was probably starting to cry. He didn't want to hear any more. Slipping away from the door, he retreated to the bottom step of the porch.

For a long time he sat there, just listening to the crickets, to his mother saying good night, to Memère heating up a kettle on the stove. *So she thinks I'm still a kid?* he thought, recalling his grandmother's words. Well, she was right about one thing—he hadn't realized it until she said it, but once he went into that house, it really was over. His old life would be laid to rest. Still, it didn't seem true. Just like his father's death—none of it was true.

He buried his head in his hands. What a long, strange day it had been—numbly loading up the truck for hours in the heat, the accident, the long drive, and then to arrive here, a place of strange shadows and silence. And Memère coming up out of the dark like that. Aidan lifted his head, remembering his mother's query. What *had* she been doing out there?

Memère was at the kitchen table drinking tea when he finally came through the door, squinting into the light.

"Your mother's gone to bed. Poor thing's exhausted. You must be too, eh?"

He looked at her for a moment—there seemed to be other questions in her eyes—and then turned away, shoving his hands into his pockets.

"I'm a little tired," he said.

"See anything out there?" she asked, getting up from the table.

"The stars are nice. And I saw a deer."

"*Ah, oui. Les chevreuils.* Christly things have been getting into my garden. Game warden says he'll let me shoot them if they don't stop chewing off the tops of my beet greens."

Why don't you just build a fence? Aidan thought but didn't ask.

"Your mother brought that in," she said, pointing to Aidan's bag sitting at the foot of the stairs. "Your room's on the left. Same as always. Everything should be clean."

"Thanks, Memère," he said. "See you in the morning."

She intercepted him as he turned toward the stairs. He stepped back nervously.

"I left something for you, upstairs on the bed. Just a little present," she said.

"Thanks, Memère," he answered, stepping around her to the foot of the stairs. She stopped him again, this time moving close and taking a sniff. Aidan resisted the temptation to squirm as he felt, for the second time that night, his heart begin to pound.

"It's a book, Aidan. You don't have to read it, but you might like it. Something to keep you occupied this summer, eh?"

"Okay, maybe I will."

"Bon," she said with a quick smile, and let him go. He watched as she turned away and went back to the kitchen table, back to her cup of tea. He picked up his bag and headed upstairs.

The flight of steps creaked, the upstairs hallway creaked, everything creaked in the old house. Compared with the modern expanse of his home on Sizemore (*former home,* he remembered), this place was cramped and dingy, with low ceilings, narrow halls, and tiny rooms with tiny windows. Worst of all, the place had the smell of old. It wasn't that it was dirty—Memère kept a clean house—it was just that everything, the upstairs especially, had that musty quality, like the odor of old encyclopedias sitting in a library basement. During past trips, it had been a tang that would linger in his nostrils for days, even after he had gone home to Massachusetts.

He stepped into his bedroom, the one he always stayed in when they visited. His parents would sleep in his mother's old room, and he stayed here in what his mother referred to as "the boys' room," for it had always belonged to one combination or another of his uncles. He flipped on the overhead just long enough to switch on the bedside table lamp; he preferred the glow of the smaller light that made the room seem less sterile and cramped. Under the overhead light—a glaring metal-rimmed thing straight out of the fifties—every corner of the rectangular space was barren and exposed, somehow still frozen in the past, haunted by the ghosts of children who had become adults long before he even existed. In the orange light of the lamp, it became his room. He set his bag over by the bureau and sat down on the metal-framed bed. It creaked, of course. Up near the pillow, he saw the book Memère had spoken of.

He picked it up and was surprised to discover that it was a brand-new paperback, unblemished, with crisply cut corners. For some reason, he had expected her to give him something in hardcover, likely something old and used. He looked at the cover. *The Odyssey* it said at the top, with "Homer" in large letters underneath. He had heard of it; he knew it was Greek, a story from mythology. So it was something old after all. He tossed it onto the side table and got undressed.

He slid into bed and nestled into the sheets. In contrast with the house around him, they smelled fresh. He looked over at the thick volume next to him on the table and picked it up again. It wasn't like an ordinary paperback, some pocket novel he might once have picked up at a drugstore or train station. It was larger and its pages were thick, substantial. He opened it to a random page and groaned at the lines of varied lengths. It wasn't a novel at all—it was poetry, something his mother loved and he hated. He suddenly noticed a slight bulge near the middle of the book and opened it to discover a bookmark had been placed inside. It was pewter and tiny, in the shape of a dagger, flat and thin. There was no verse scrawling down the page that had been marked, only a title: "Book XI—A Gathering of Shades." He closed the book, opened it again, and flipped to the first few pages. Coming across the table of contents, he scanned the titles of the twenty-four books. They were strange, though somehow inviting in their vagueness and tone of gravity: "Death in the Great Hall," "Father and Son," "One More Strange Island," "The Songs of the Harper." Maybe he'd try it after all. He snorted derisively as his eye caught the title of the second book—"A Hero's Son Awakens."

He closed the book again, put it aside, and switched off the light. He buried his face in the pillow. He fell into a deep and dreamless sleep.

THREE

Someone was calling his name. A light voice, distant and singsong, beckoning. How long had she been calling? He opened his eyes to bright light in the windows and buried his face back into the pillow, trying to remember where he was.

"Time to get up, sleepy," his mother said, standing in the doorway.

"What time is it?" he asked, opening his eyes again.

"Almost noon. I let you sleep in. Figured you could use it."

"Thanks," he mumbled.

"Come downstairs. Memère made you breakfast. Crepes."

"Crepes. Right."

She left. Aidan got out of bed, put on the same shorts from yesterday and a fresh T-shirt, and headed downstairs.

He took his time going down, gazing at the collection of photos that lined the stairway. They ranged from the very old—tintype-looking things, yellowed but strikingly crisp, populated by strangers in antique clothes bearing family

features that made them eerily familiar in spite of their age—
to more recent prints. He paused by a picture of himself. He
was about five in the photo, smiling on a swing, forever
frozen in the air at the pinnacle of the backward rise just
before the plunge. He remembered nothing about that day.
He couldn't even tell where the snapshot had been taken.
Lingering over the image for a moment, he tried to find some
connection to himself in the picture, but the boy was as much
a stranger as the ancestors from a century ago.

He skipped over a wedding photo of his parents and went
to a portrait of his grandfather. Pepère had died five years
ago, dropped dead on his way in from the barn. In the picture, taken only a couple years before his death, he was smiling, leaning on his maple walking stick. He looked as if he
had just come from the woods, and he probably had. Aidan
closed his eyes, and the image turned to movement as Pepère
came toward him from the photo, a quiet, gentle man, so different from his wife. Pepère used to take him for walks on the
mountain, ambling beside him and pointing out features in
the distance. Opening his eyes, Aidan left the photos behind
and continued down the stairs.

The kitchen was transformed by morning light streaming in. Bottles in the windows glowed blue and brown against
the green of the birches in the backyard, and the smell of
coffee hung in the air. The picnic table that occupied the
center of the room was clear except for the end, where a place
had been laid out. Memère was at the stove, humming the

anonymous tune she forever seemed to hum, always slightly different but always still the same song. If it had any words, Aidan had never heard them. He could see his mother out on the porch, a mug in one hand, a cigarette in the other, reading a magazine. As he sat down at the end of the table, Memère came over, skillet in hand.

"Sweet dreams?" she asked, slipping a pile of crepes onto his plate.

"Didn't have any dreams," he said.

"Too bad," she replied. "I'd hate to sleep without them. Otherwise, sleep is just killing time, eh?"

"I guess so," he said. He poured maple syrup over the crepes and began shoveling them in. They were sweet, made sweeter by the syrup, and still hot from the stove. They were different from the thick pancakes his father used to make. Memère's crepes were light, eggy, almost slippery going down. Though he would never admit it to her, he preferred the crepes. From the corner of his eye, he could see her watching him, a smile creeping across her face.

"You eat like a good boy," she said. "Like a pig, of course, but that's how boys are supposed to eat. You remind me of your uncles. *Petits cochons.* All of them, by Jesus."

The screen door slammed as his mother came in.

"Patrice," Memère called sharply, "outside with that!"

"What?" his mother said, confused. Memère gestured with a finger to the lit cigarette until her daughter did an about-face and returned to the porch.

Aidan paused at the exchange. It was strange to see his mother being scolded as if she were some naughty child. It made her seem like someone else.

"You don't like Ma smoking?" he asked.

"Smoking? She can smoke or not as she likes. But not in my kitchen, please. That goes for you too, mister man," she said, causing Aidan to choke on a mouthful of crepes. His mother came back in as he was recovering.

"Aidan, your uncles are coming today," she said.

"Which ones?"

"Memère said Richard called yesterday and was going to make a special trip over this afternoon. Said he had to meet with a client in St. Johnsbury and wanted to stop by after." Richard, Memère's oldest son, was a lawyer in Burlington.

"Be just as fine with me if he turned back for Burlington and skipped us altogether," Memère snapped.

"Well, Mama, I want to see him, all right?"

"Go ahead. See him. But he's on my shit list right now," she muttered. Aidan wondered what Richard could have done to get on that probably lengthy list.

Aidan's mother ignored her. "Donny also called this morning. Said he'd be over later too, after chores. Said he wants to talk to you, Aidan."

Uh-oh, Aidan thought. He had a sudden sinking feeling, as if the crepes in his belly had turned to lead.

"What about?" he asked. In truth, he didn't dislike Donny. It was just that they never had much to talk about.

His father's younger brother hardly spoke to anybody, let alone his nephew.

"He didn't get too specific, but I think he might want you to help out a bit this summer."

Aidan groaned. Donny had inherited the farm, though whether he ran it out of a sense of duty or a genuine desire to tackle such an enterprise, he kept the knowledge, as he did most things, to himself.

"Watch it," his mother snapped. "It wouldn't hurt to help a little, get some good exercise—it would be good to get a job for the summer anyway. Besides, it might be nice to spend some time with your uncle. Get to know him better."

"Yeah, great," Aidan sneered. "A summer shoveling shit with Uncle Donny. I can already imagine the incredible conversations we'll have."

"That Donny's a hard worker," Memère said. Aidan cringed. It was the perpetual standard of character in the Northeast Kingdom. "He's a good boy. And smart. He'll surprise you, Aidan."

Aidan bit his tongue. The last thing he wanted to do was spend the summer farming—a job he had no interest in, which he knew nothing about—with a guy who hardly spoke. Aidan sensed the irony here as the future began hurtling down on him like a meteor from the sky. *What would Dad think?* he wondered.

"Fine," he said at last.

"Good," his mother said, sounding mollified. "I've got to

head down-street to Maxfield and run some errands. Your uncles should be here around three or three-thirty. Until then, you can do as you please. The boys can help us unload the U-haul before supper, and I'll go return it in the morning."

"Sounds good," he said. He finished his crepes and headed for the porch. Glancing back from the doorway, he could see his mother roll her eyes as if to say *See?*

"You weren't any better," he heard the old woman say.

He let the screen door slam behind him.

Aidan stopped and turned around, hands on his knees, bent over to catch his breath. He had climbed the upper pasture and hit the second meadow road that divided the field above from the one below. He was taking "the tour," as Pepère had called it. It was no formal path or road, simply a general way that took him up the mountain, among the various fields and woodlots, forming a loop that ended back at the farm. If it could even really be called a farm. Memère and Pepère hadn't been farmers, not by trade. Pepère had worked for the railroad in Island Pond as a young man and later as a machinist at a shop in Lyndon. They'd had a few milking cows, some chickens and pigs for slaughter, and a large kitchen garden, but that was about the extent of it.

The real farm belonged to his father's family, directly below the Boisvert place. The Dunkleys' operation, while not huge, was big enough to keep the family afloat, though barely, and often only with the help of a little logging on the side. The Dunkleys maintained about a hundred head of milkers, a mix of Holsteins and Jerseys that pastured up and down this side of the mountain, though mostly down below on the Dunkleys' land, closer to the milking barn. These upper fields, which were part of the Boisvert place, were reserved as hayfields. Donny hayed these fields now. Like his neighbor Robert Boisvert up above, Jack Dunkley had passed away suddenly. Aidan had never been told the exact circumstances of his grandfather's death; all he knew was that there had been an accident, that it was gruesome, and that it involved a tractor. Aidan was only five at the time. He had never thought about Grampa much, partly because he could hardly remember him but also because his father had never talked about him or seemed to want to, and Aidan had known well enough not to ask.

His heart having returned to a normal pace, he stood and surveyed the landscape. He was two-thirds of the way up Harper Mountain, though it wasn't exactly a mountain in Aidan's mind. It was barely higher, if at all, than the hills around it. Perhaps it was the unique structure of the mountain; while the surrounding hills seemed connected into contiguous masses, weaving along in ridges like giant snakes, Harper rose alone, a gently slanting monadnock independent of the land around it.

Harper had two distinct sides—one civilized and cultivated, the other wild. This southern face, though sparsely settled, was mostly open land, dotted with scatterings of maple, pine, and white birch, capped by a steep slope thick with fir and spruce tangled in with yellow birch, beeches, and pin cherry. Looking up, one could imagine these woods growing like a head of hair on the mountain, wrapping around to the north and riding down the back side all the way to the bottom.

The base of the southern side was a different story. There the slope became so gradual it was nearly level. Donny maintained several cornfields along this stretch by Mallard's Run, a river that skirted the entire southern face of Harper, cutting off the mountain from Maxfield Center, a village of about five hundred. Aidan could see the river from here, could make out the village on the other side, and the hills that spread in layers, growing darker and hazier as each gave way to each into the distance. Two hundred miles beyond them lay the pieces of his old life—the bustling highways and malls, the gleaming towers of Boston, the house on Sizemore.

He stopped climbing and followed the meadow road that cut across Harper's face, but he hardly noticed where he was going. All he could think about was how at this time yesterday he was loading boxes into the truck, still on the street that calmed with its stately order. What did it look like today? Probably the same. A truck was still there, only now the boxes were coming out. New owners were moving in, strangers occupying his house, his world. And what were his friends doing? Andy, Mitch—he could see all of them sitting around Mike's pool, blasting tunes, talking about girls. He imagined an empty chaise lounge where he would be reclining now. Or maybe it wasn't empty. Like his house, maybe it had a new occupant, someone who had taken his place as life moved on without a beat. Most of all he wondered what his father would be doing now if the universe had followed its proper course. It was Saturday—he would probably be working. But maybe he wouldn't be. It was a sunny day, blue sky with few clouds. Maybe he would say the hell with work and take them all to the beach. They would sit in the sand, listen to the surf, and forget about everything.

And then Aidan was there. The meadow road ended, cut off by a gravel road that led to the cemetery. Occupying barely a quarter acre, Southlook, as the sign by the gate called it, contained about a hundred graves. There were probably no more than a dozen names among them—Mathewson, Allard, LaCroix, families who had settled on Harper and farmed its southern side or logged its northern face, families who, in some cases, no longer existed. Most of the gravestones were old—made of dark slate, others bright marble, rectangles that rose straight from the ground without a base, some at slight angles, graves so worn the names and dates, carved in a spidery script, could just be read.

But not all the graves were old, and not all of the names were unfamiliar to Aidan. He hesitated before the gate, looking back and forth between the valley, which was now dark in the shadow of midday clouds, and the cemetery where the sun was still shining, lighting up the graves against the overgrown tufts of green. He swore and kicked the ground. He should have remembered he would end up here. And now he had to make a choice. He should go in—it was the proper thing to do, wasn't it? One was supposed to pay respects. Still, he hesitated. He wasn't prepared. He hadn't been planning on it. He should come back, maybe with his mother. He started down the hill. And then he stopped.

"Goddam it!"

He passed through the gate and headed for the back, cutting left between the last two rows. He passed his grandparents. First his grandmother: Grace Francine Dunkley. She'd died of an embolism when Aidan's father was five. His father had mentioned her only once, and that was to say he remembered little about her. Next Grampa: John Matthew Dunkley, a man Aidan remembered mostly for his scratchy face, always in need of a shave.

And then, there he was: Timothy John Dunkley. The headstone was made of black marble, simple and unadorned. Aidan could see his legs reflected in its sheen. The grass at its base was the same as all the other grass around it, the scars from the sod cut last fall having already healed. It was as if he had been there forever.

"You're not supposed to be here," Aidan said.

He had never understood why his mother decided to bury his father here in this cemetery on the mountain, in this land he had hungered to leave and had never wanted to return to, buried beside a man he always seemed to have disdained. They had never reconciled, and yet here they were, side by side. He was sure his father would have hated it. He had wanted to tell his mother as much when the arrangements were being made, but things then were hard enough already. His mother claimed that that's what his father would have wanted, but Aidan knew better. He felt like he was the only one who did, the only one who had realized the truth: that funerals and everything that came with them were for the living, not the dead, that the living remembered the dead the way they wanted to and not always how they actually were. That seemed to be the way memory worked, maybe even the way it was supposed to. Except for Aidan.

She should have buried him in Massachusetts, not here. Then we could have left him there. Everything about this move confused Aidan. He still believed she had brought them up here to escape the pain of her husband's absence, to leave behind the house, their friends, the places, everything that reminded her of him. This is how they would deal. In spite of the fact that Aidan didn't want to leave, in some ways it might work for him—everything he associated with his father lay south. But how could this help her? There must still be so many memories of him here for her, how could she ever escape? And why have him laid to rest here, why bring him back? None of it made sense.

Yet here he was. Right beneath him, right now.

"Come back," he whispered.

It was an old refrain, one he'd spoken many times during the first few months after the accident, spoken in the middle of the night when he'd woken from a dream, his sheets drenched with sweat. He hadn't wished it for a long time, had tucked it away in the dark corners of his mourning. Now it rose again, ripe and unbidden.

A sour tang crept into the back of his throat. He grimaced. There it was—the taste of grief, horrible in its familiarity. He swallowed hard, but it didn't go away. It usually didn't. Not for a while. *I should've kept walking*, he told himself.

He tried swallowing again, and as he did his body twisted as if moved by some force beyond his will. It was that spidered quiver, the same one from last night. But this time there was no ringing in his ears. It was a different sound. Somewhere a child laughed, high and trembling. Then it was gone, leaving nothing but the shivering of leaves.

He glanced up at the maple that loomed over the back of the cemetery. Its branches shook in the wind.

He turned and left, picking up speed in spite of the weakness in his legs. The sound of his steps bounced off the flat stones around him, echoing whispers that drove him toward the exit.

"Hey!"

Coming out of the gate, Aidan jumped at the sound of a girl's voice. He had been focused on the ground and hadn't even seen her where she sat nearby, perched on her bike. For a moment he just stood there staring, his heart still pounding. His face flushed, and he cast a quick glance back at the grave-yard.

"Hope I didn't startle you," she said when he didn't reply. Her voice was light and high in pitch, but strong, devoid of airy affectation. Her hair, the color of sand, was collected in a tight bun against the back of her head, a single strand float-ing along her cheek. She wore a red tank top and shorts. A single silver bracelet on her left wrist flashed in the sun, and from where he stood he could see the sweat glistening on her tan shoulders and neck.

"No. Not really," he said, looking down.

"You know someone?" she asked, nodding toward the cemetery.

"No," he said, his voice just above a whisper.

"My name's Angela," she said.

"Hi, Angela."

She laughed at the reply. There was no irritation in her laugh, merely amusement. "What's your name?" she demanded, breaking into a smile.

"Aidan," he said. For a moment neither spoke. She just continued to stare with that same smile on her face.

"A bit hot for biking today, isn't it?" he said at last to break the silence, and winced inwardly. *Smooth, Aidan. Real smooth.*

"I don't mind it," she said. "Besides, this isn't real heat. At least you can breathe up here."

"You're not from around here?"

"Just moved up a week ago from Connecticut. New Haven—on the Sound."

"Oh," he said.

"What about you?" she asked. "What's your story?"

"I live down below," he said, and gestured toward the farm. "My mom and I moved up from Massachusetts. Near Boston."

"Oh yeah? No kidding. I go to Andover. You've heard of it, I guess," she said. He nodded. His father had tried to talk him into applying to the fancy prep school north of Boston, but he'd resisted, not wanting to leave the new friends he'd made in Needham. "Well, I don't know if I'm going back," she continued. "My parents want me to, but to be honest, I'm a little tired of the scene. Besides, it's too much work."

"Too bad," he said. "Now you'll be stuck up here."

"You don't like it here?"

"You do?"

"Yeah. I mean, look around"—she waved her arms—"it's beautiful. And no assholes trying to show everybody how great they are every second of the day."

"Is that why you moved up here?"

"My parents wanted to. Said they wanted to get away. Get back to the earth or something dumb like that. Relive their glory days as hippies. But I have my doubts—there's a bunch of guys in our house right now installing central air."

"Right. But there isn't really anything to do around here. It's kind of boring."

She shrugged her shoulders. "It's what you make of it, I suppose."

"I guess," he replied. There was another long pause.

"Well," she said at last, "I should be going. Maybe I'll see you around?"

"Maybe," he said, trying to convey certainty in his voice.

With a quick wave, she turned and sped off down the hill. He watched her go. Only after she had disappeared did he realize he'd forgotten to ask her where she lived.

FOUR

It was nearly two by the time Aidan made his way back to the house.

"Memère?" he called out in the kitchen. No one answered.

He poured a glass of juice, went onto the porch, and looked down across the lawn. In the glare of the afternoon, it seemed so much larger than it had in last night's darkness. For a moment the walking figure flashed through Aidan's mind, disappearing once more into the bushes along the edge. Memère was down in the garden on her knees, bent over a row, weeding. He hovered on the porch and gazed south. Above the tips of the apple trees in the orchard he could see the hills out across the river valley, but that was all. Nothing human seemed to exist; there was no sign of civilization—no houses, no roads or power lines, no highways or malls. He was stranded. This farm was an island, this mountain was an island, and the bridges had been burned behind him, the lifeboats sunk.

"Aidan!" Memère called out. *"Ici! Aidez-moi!"* Her voice was made thin by the distance. Still, the barking tone came through.

He couldn't speak French, but he figured she wanted him to come down there. He emptied his glass before strolling to where she waited, still on her knees.

As he made his way across the grass, he looked around at the lawn ornaments scattered about. There were the standard flamingoes, their pink bodies floating on plastic stilts. Nearby a little village of gnomes, frozen in the laughter of their own private joke, huddled around a pillar that cradled a purple globe, a glass sphere that reflected back the faces of the gnomes, twisting their smiles into manic glee. A wooden cutout shaped and painted to look like a fat woman bending over, her bloomers decorated with hearts, stood amid a cluster of bird feeders and foil pinwheels that spun when the breeze was right. Separated from the crowd in an implied deference to piety sat the quintessential Kingdom relic—bathtub Mary (a less refined version of Mary on the half shell), the Virgin standing in the shelter of an enamel tub sunk halfway into the ground. Aidan remembered how his father would always joke at the lowbrow collection and at the passion with which his mother-in-law cared for her treasures. "It's a Quebecois tradition," his mother would respond defensively.

Memère was holding out her hand as Aidan approached.

"Help me up, would you, dear?" she asked. She groaned

as he pulled her to her feet. "Knees give out once in a while. Christly weeding always does it to me. The downside of old age."

There's an upside? Aidan wondered. "What do you do when no one's around?" he asked instead.

"Oh, I usually just crawl my way back to the house."

"How can you if your knees don't work?" he challenged.

"I'm joking, Aidan," she said, frowning. "Jesus, you're a serious kid."

"Oh," he said faintly.

"No, I can get up. Just takes me longer, that's all." She held on to his arm as they made their way back to the lawn. She was breathing heavily, and Aidan could see a trickle of sweat beneath the wide brim of her hat. "Took the tour, did you?"

He nodded.

"Did you stop in and see your father? You went by there, didn't you?" she asked, looking away as she spoke.

"I went in. Just for a second."

"Good for you, Aidan," she said, turning back to him. To his relief, she dropped the subject. "Let's go up to the house. I'll make you something."

"I'm not hungry, thanks," he replied.

"All right, then." She stopped to gaze at the bird feeders. Most were nearly empty. "Time to fill the feeders again. They go through the stuff like you wouldn't believe."

A bird, nearly the size of a robin, black with a brown

head, swooped down to one of the tube feeders and began picking at the remaining seed.

"Shoo!" she screamed. She picked up a little stone and chucked it at the bird, which took off for the trees. Aidan jumped back in alarm.

"Don't you *want* the birds to come?" he asked as she stooped for another pebble in anticipation of the bird's return.

"Not that one," she snapped. "You know what that was? That was a goddam cowbird. You know what they do, don't you, is they go and lay their egg in another bird's nest. Push out one of the other eggs and slip theirs in. Their egg hatches first and crowds out the others. Then some respectable bird ends up raising one of those god-awful ugly things and lets its own babies starve." She laughed. "Kind of smart, if you think about it. Still, I usually shoot 'em when I can. Got to give the others a chance, you know. Nature's cruel, Aidan. Never forget that."

"I know," he said.

"Course you do, dear," she said, nodding. She took his hand again and they walked back to the house.

Aidan was helping his mother bring in the groceries when a pickup came growling up the driveway. He stopped to watch as the blue Ford, its body rusting from the bottom up, pulled off to the side of the driveway. His Uncle Donny got out and ambled over. At first glance one would hardly have guessed that this man and Aidan's father had been brothers. Aidan's father had been tall, of fair complexion and with sharp features, while Donny was shorter and broad shouldered, with dark hair like Aidan's. His face and arms were rugged and tanned. He wore a dirty T-shirt, stained blue pants, and rubber boots, and Aidan could tell he'd just come from the barn, for aside from the dirt, he carried that tang of manure that made Aidan's nostrils flair and tickle. But it wasn't just in their physical appearance that the brothers varied. Aidan noticed how they carried themselves differently. Aidan's father had always had a bouncy gait, an air of confidence and energy that was infectious to anyone in his presence. "Life of the party," Aidan's mother used to joke. Donny was no slouch, but he walked with a heavier step that hovered somewhere between calmness and resignation, never settling on either one.

"Aidan, hi," Donny said shyly, breaking into a smile. Aidan took a sharp breath. Here the brothers did converge—both had the same smile. Aidan had never noticed it before and was struck by how such different faces could be rendered so alike by a single movement of the mouth. And there was the voice, too. They spoke with the same tone and inflection, though Donny still possessed the heavy Vermont accent that Aidan's father had made a conscious effort to shed years ago.

"Hi, Donny," Aidan replied. "Ma!" he shouted. "Donny's here!"

Aidan's mother came out from putting the groceries away. She smiled when she saw Donny and bounced down from the porch. She came over and gave him a hug, which he stiffly returned.

"Jesus, Donny," she laughed, "you stink."

Donny took a step back and flashed that same smile. Aidan wondered if his mother also noticed the resemblance.

"Sorry, Patty," he said. "Just finished chores. Should've showered. Didn't even think of it." Patty was what both he and Aidan's father always called her. Everyone else called her Patrice.

"Don't worry about it. You know I've never minded the smell of manure. It's a good smell," she said.

"I guess," he said. "Can't hardly smell it no more, so used to it."

Memère came out onto the porch carrying a tray with lemonade and glasses. Putting the tray down, she beckoned and they came up, settling into the frayed wicker chairs scattered across the deck. Memère poured each of them a glass before finally perching on the swing that hung from the ceiling of the covered porch.

"So, how's farming?" his mother asked.

"'Bout the same. Hanging in there," Donny said.

"Is Aunt Sherry coming over?" Aidan asked, trying to think of something to say.

"Nope," he said.

"Aidan," his mother broke in, "Donny and Sherry got divorced three months ago. Donny, I'm sorry—I forgot to tell him."

"That's okay. You know, I've been thinking 'bout it some, and I figure it probably should've happened a long time ago. Can't say I miss her much, truth be told. Mostly I miss her help in the barn. But she didn't like farming—wanted us to go someplace different. I told her I couldn't, and so she left. That's 'bout all there is to it. There weren't no hard feelings between us, then or now."

Aidan's shock at this rare monologue from his uncle made him forget his embarrassment at having raised the subject to begin with. So Sherry was gone. Aidan didn't feel any real sorrow over her absence—she was even more laconic than her husband. At least Donny smiled once in a while.

"You were too good for her, Donny," Memère said. "I never liked that sullen girl. Her mother was the same way—always looked like she'd just eaten a turd."

Aidan nearly sprayed lemonade all over the porch.

"Mama!" Aidan's mother gasped.

Donny only smiled faintly and shrugged. "Thanks, Eloise," he said. "But Sherry weren't that bad. Just a little shy, that's all."

There was a lull. Again Aidan's mother spoke up.

"So Donny, you said you wanted to talk to Aidan?"

"That's right," Donny said, sitting up. He paused, as if rehearsing the speech in his head one more time. "Like I said, it's been a bit harder managing things since Sherry left. I had one guy working for me, but he quit last week. I was thinking, if you weren't too busy, maybe you could help. Wouldn't need you all day or even every day, but maybe you could help out with the milking from time to time. Help out in the fields, especially."

Aidan glanced over at his mother. She was staring at him intently. So was Memère. Reading their looks, he knew what reply was expected.

"Sure, why not?" he said.

"Good," Donny said. He leaned back in his chair. "I wouldn't really need you right away. You just got out of school, right? Could use a break, I bet. I'll be starting with the rowen in a week or so. I can use you then."

"What's rowen?" Aidan asked.

"Second cutting. First cutting's hay; second cutting's rowen. That's just what they call it."

The crunch of gravel was all that betrayed the Saab convertible as it cruised up the driveway and stopped in front of the porch. The car was neither silver nor gold, but somewhere in between. Uncle Richard got out with a smile, still in his suit. Heavyset with graying hair, he bounced up onto the porch and came straight for Aidan, tussling his hair the way he always did. It was one of those gestures of affection that Aidan had responded to as a child, but that over the last few years had become a bit annoying.

"Aidan Maiden," he said, still grinning. He made up names for everybody.

"Hi, Richard," Aidan said. "How was the meeting?"

"Good—it's a big case. Big money."

"Aren't you going to say hi to your little sister?" Aidan's mother said, getting up from her chair.

"Itsy Patritsy," he said, turning to face her. He pinched her cheek.

"Ow," she said, knocking his hand away, but they both laughed and embraced.

"I'm glad you made it up here with no trouble. Hey, Donny," he said, nodding to where Donny still sat.

"Rich," Donny said, nodding back.

"How's the farm?"

"Good. Thanks for asking."

"Of course." Richard turned to his mother, moving back and forth on her swing. She was staring intensely at him, her eyes narrowed into a glare. "Mama," he said, "I see that look. Still mad, eh?" He bent down and gave her a kiss before she could duck.

"Damn straight I am," she said. "And you know why, don't you!"

Richard turned to his sister. "I tried to talk Mama into selling the farm and moving down to Maxfield. There was an opening at the Cullingford Inn. It's a nice place, Patrice."

"I know. She told me all about it. But it doesn't matter. Aidan and I are here now. We can take care of the place."

"I'm here too," Donny offered.

"That's right," Memère said. Aidan watched her eyes flash at Richard. "He stops by more than all of my own children put together."

"He *does* live next door, Mama," Richard said. "Come on,

give me a break—I just worry about you, that's all."

"You just want to get me off this place so you and your money-grubbing real-estate friends can get your hands on it!"

Richard laughed, but Aidan could see he was getting angry. "Mama, that's ridiculous, and you know it. This is a nice spot to live, but it isn't worth much."

"Oh really?" she snapped. "Well, what about the other side of south face? What about Parrish Road? You've seen them new houses springing up like milkweeds? Goddam flatlanders."

"I've seen them, Mama." He sighed. "Look. You won, okay? Patrice is here, Aidan's here, everything's the way you want it. Just remember, I'm not the only one in the family who thought it might be nice for you to be someplace safe where you can be taken care of and have some company."

"I've got all the company I need right here on this mountain!" she snapped. She got up and went inside, letting the door slam behind her, leaving Richard with a pained expression. Donny looked over at Aidan and raised his eyebrows but said nothing.

"Don't worry, Richard. She'll get over it," Aidan's mother said.

"I know," he agreed. "I just don't like her questioning my loyalty, that's all. It's not easy being over on the other side of the state thinking about her here alone. I suppose it's just as well you came, though it's not fair that you should have to be stuck up here."

"You mean with her?" she said. "She's not that bad, you

know. I hope I'm as steady when I'm her age."

Richard snorted. "You think so, Patrice? To be honest, I don't believe Mama's as stable as you think she is. She seems tough enough on the surface, and maybe for a few days everything'll be fine, but you wait." He looked back toward the door and lowered his voice. "I spent a week with her this spring. Gretchen and I both took a week off and came up to stay with her. Three different times that week, I caught her talking to herself. And it wasn't like she was 'talking to herself'—Lord knows we all do that. No, she seemed to be talking to someone else, like she was having a goddam conversation, but nobody was ever there. Once I found her down in the orchard, talking and laughing—it was creepy, Patrice. My own goddam mother creeping me out. I finally confronted her the day before we left. I couldn't stand it anymore, so I asked her. 'Who're you talking to, Mama?' I said. You know what she told me? 'The dead, Richard. The dead.' And then she started laughing. I shit you not, she started laughing!"

It was Aidan's mother who laughed now. "Richard, wake up! She was pulling your leg! God, if you had the same look on your face then that you have now telling me, it's no wonder she said that. She saw you coming a mile away."

Richard shook his head. "You can shake it off if you like. But I know what I heard, and it wasn't playing. But that's okay, Patrice. You'll see." He was silent a moment, looking at her. "What about you? Are you okay?"

She smiled. Aidan could see it was her stiff smile, the smile she gave lately when someone asked how she was doing. "I'm fine. We're both doing fine. It's been tough, but things are getting better." Aidan had heard these same sentences a million times. Did they sound robotic to everyone or just him?

"Good. I'm glad to hear it," Rich said.

Why? Aidan wondered. *Why is everyone always glad to hear it? Why should we be fine?*

"I miss him like hell, Patrice. Everyone does."

"Thanks," she said.

"Just call me if there are any problems," he said. He took a card from his jacket pocket. "I know you've got our home number, but here's my cell in case you need anything. Don't hesitate to call. I'll come over as quick as I can."

"Actually," she said, "how about right now? Aidan and I could use some help unloading the stuff in the van. I've got to drop the truck off in the morning."

He looked at his watch. "Sorry, sis. I'd love to, but I've got to go. I've got to be back to Burlington by six. Gretchen and I have a dinner party tonight. Besides, I really can't get this suit dirty."

"Classic," she said.

"I know," he said in mock shame, "I'm terrible." He gave her a kiss and headed for the car. "Listen," he said, getting in. "I want you and Aidan to come visit when you get a chance. Gretchen would love to see you. We've got a pool. Maybe

Aidan could stay extra, visit a little while. What do you say, Aidan?"

Burlington, on the western side of the state, was the closest Vermont came to a real city. It was small, but it was still a city. "Sure," he said.

"All right, Richie Rich—get out of here before he jumps in the car and takes off with you," Aidan's mother said. She laughed and grabbed Aidan in a headlock. Richard smiled and waved, backed the car around in the driveway, and sped off.

Aidan watched the curl of dust rise up from the gravel and hang in the air after Rich had disappeared. The cloud drifted down across the lawn, where it melted into nothing. When he turned around, he saw Donny already had the back of the U-Haul open and had begun taking boxes out. Aidan watched as his uncle and his mother each took the end of an armchair. It was the one his father had fallen asleep in every night while watching TV. It was leather. Black. They carried the chair out and placed it in the shade. A look from his mother broke Aidan from his spot, and he joined in the work. It only took about half an hour. There wasn't much: a few pieces of furniture, boxes of clothes, dishes, and other smaller items, some of Aidan's things—his computer, stereo, TV, bike, snowboard, and other "toys"—and boxes and boxes of his mother's books. All the big items—tables and chairs, appliances, couches, beds—had already been sold off piece by piece over the last few weeks.

Partway through, Memère came back out on the porch.

She just watched and said nothing. Aidan glanced at her from time to time. She was strangely quiet and serious, and her gaze kept drifting out and away, as if she were searching for something in the distance. Aidan thought of what Richard had told his mother. In spite of her skepticism, Aidan was inclined to believe his uncle. He wondered when he would start seeing the signs. Maybe he had already and just wasn't familiar enough with them to know it. Memère caught him staring and returned the gaze. He went back to work carting boxes.

In the end they put most of the stuff in the barn—cleared the stale and dusty hay away in one corner and piled everything against the dirty wall. There would be time later to sort through and decide what to bring in. After Donny and his mother left, Aidan stared for a moment at the pile of belongings. It was all that remained of his old life. His eyes lingered on the leather chair next to the pile of boxes. It sat by itself, empty and unburdened. *It shouldn't be left out here*, Aidan thought. *It'll spoil in the barn. All the dust.* He resolved to steal a sheet after dinner, come back out, and cover it.

The shadows were growing long as Aidan undid the latch and swung open the barn door. The black chair was nearly invisible in the barn, and it took his eyes a moment to adjust before spotting the dark mass in the corner by the boxes. Going over to it, he snapped open the sheet he had swiped from the linen closet and let it float down over the chair. He spread out the corners and stood back. The chair was now a white blob, glowing against the darkness, almost hovering, like some crude Halloween ghost. The air in here reeked of mildew and made his nose prickle. For a few minutes he just stared at the covered chair, not wanting to leave. How many nights had he come downstairs long after dinner to see his father in that chair, having just gotten home from work, a stiff drink in one hand, watching the news or maybe a Red Sox game if they were winning?

His skin prickled. This time he was ready for it. He braced himself as, for the second time that day, a tingle ran along in his spine. Again, a child's laugh sounded in the distance.

"Who's there?" he called, but the voice had already faded.

He crossed to the threshold and peered out into the empty yard. A wind had stirred, setting the wind chimes hanging from the porch roof ringing. He hadn't noticed them before. The chimes rattled, laughing against the breeze.

You're an idiot, he thought, embarrassed by his fear.

There was a sharp crack of the screen door slamming. He ducked back inside the doorway and glanced out. Memère had just left the porch steps and was making her way across the lawn toward the garden. Aidan figured she was going back down to weed again, but she didn't stop at the garden. She continued straight past it, pausing only briefly before passing into the tall grass in the direction of the orchard. A moment later she disappeared, swallowed up by the poplar saplings. He waited, expecting to see her reemerge, but she didn't. It was only later, long after the sun had set, that he happened to spy her from his bedroom window scuttling back up to the house, her light dress floating in the twilight. Through the open window he could hear the sounds of her humming, a distant song rising in the night.

FIVE

Lost in the ticking whir of the bike's tires, Aidan coasted toward Mallard's Run, toward the bridge that would take him back onto the mountain. He closed his eyes, relishing the hum of his tires against the pavement, the sound of civilization. In another minute it would be replaced by a jarring buzz as the road switched over to gravel.

It was Saturday. His first full week in the Kingdom was drawing to a close, and Aidan was doing his best to enjoy his only real taste of summer vacation, his last few days of freedom before being roped into serfdom. Though he wasn't sure what to expect, he figured the coming weeks would be long, full of sweat and backbreaking toil. After all, that's how his father had always characterized farming. "Worse than slavery," he'd said once. "At least slaves have the luxury of not caring. A slave doesn't have to worry that the results of his drudgery will crumble apart at any second."

After Donny's and Richard's visits last Saturday, Aidan had spent the next day moping around the house, arguing with his mother and evading Memère. After that he spent most of his time avoiding the place altogether. The first few days he renewed his exploration of the mountain, circling out to the far reaches of the farms. He went in different directions this time, careful to avoid Southlook, mostly hoping to run into Angela again. They had spoken only for a few minutes, but her image kept returning; sometimes it was just the flash of her bracelet or the strand of hair against her cheek, or the way she had laughed at his awkwardness. He even ventured over to the other side of the south face on the off chance of discovering where she lived, but after finding no trace of her, he gave up.

On Wednesday he grabbed his bike and headed into Maxfield. He tried hanging out in the town green the way he and his friends used to back in Needham, but it wasn't the same. The only other people in the park were a trio of mothers with their little kids, lounging on a blanket near a fountain, and a bunch of old people huddled on a pair of nearby benches who gave him dirty looks, as if they were wondering why he wasn't somewhere being productive, the way a young man should.

And so he spent the rest of the week avoiding both the mountain and the town. Instead he went for long bike rides, taking the winding routes out of Maxfield in all different directions. Wherever he went, everything looked the same— the same hills and ridges, the same farms, the same little sur- rounding villages with their white churches and mini-marts.

Only Harper seemed to stand out, a single mountain rising alone, always in the distance, always calling him back. None of it really mattered. With his tiny headphones stuck in both ears, he pedaled to the rhythm of the music, oblivious to even the massive logging trucks that hurtled by, lumbering north toward Quebec. When he came to the rare stretches of straight road, he would close his eyes and—for the briefest moment as the beats pulsed in his ears—feel like he was back in the city.

He now crossed over the bridge and had begun pedaling back up the mountain when the sight of Memère ahead made him pause. He gave a quiet groan—ever since Uncle Richard's warning, Aidan had been avoiding her. When he was around her, he felt constantly on edge, watching the old woman through a lens of suspicion, scrutinizing every move for signs of senility. He thought about taking off, but looking around he realized it was too late—there was nowhere to hide.

She was walking along with a smile stretched wide across her face, wearing the flowered cotton dress he always saw her in—*Does she have a whole closet of them, or does she always wear the same one?* he wondered—and carrying a maple staff that was nearly as tall as she. She came to a stop as he pulled up, removing a handkerchief from her pocket to wipe the sweat along her brow.

"What are you doing, Memère?" he asked.

"Walking, dear," she replied.

"I mean," he stammered, "where are you going?"

"Into town. I need to pick up a few things at the hardware store."

"You're walking *there*?" he asked. He couldn't believe it—from here it was at least two miles to town, not to mention the steep walk back up the mountain. "Why don't you just have Ma drive you?"

"Patrice is busy. I didn't want to bother her. Besides, I always walk into town. It's good exercise. Good for the bones, eh? And it's a beautiful day, isn't it?"

"I guess," he replied. "What's with the stick?" he asked to change the subject.

"This?" she said, hefting the polished staff with a grin. "This is my companion. I never go to town without him."

Oh, God, he thought. *She's nuts. Totally crackers, just like Richard said.* "Your companion, huh?" he said, not knowing whether to laugh or feel sad, or even scared. "I suppose you have a name for him, then?"

"As a matter of fact, I do, smart-ass," she quipped. "It's Herbert."

"Herbert? Why Herbert?"

"Why not?" she said, and chuckled. She began tracing lines in the gravel with her staff. "So, Aidan," she said, "what do you think of the book I gave you?"

"I haven't started it yet," he replied.

It wasn't true—he *had* begun reading it. He'd grabbed it a few days ago before heading out to explore. He wasn't even sure why. It just caught his eye on the bedside table as he was dressing, and he stuck it in his pack. He didn't get very far that morning—just a page or two—but as the days went on, he found himself stopping more and more often to read. Sometimes it was only for five or ten minutes while he had a smoke. Other times he would settle into the shade of a tree to read and be shocked to find an hour had passed. By last night he had managed to cover the first eight books.

He liked sections of it—the detailed descriptions of treasures and weapons, the strange rituals of hospitality—and had even gotten used to the rhythms of the verse. But other parts of the story confused him. What initially threw him were the first four books. He had been under the impression that this was an epic about the hero Odysseus, but for the whole first part of the story, Odysseus was nowhere to be found. Sure, everyone talked about him, but that wasn't the same. Aidan kept looking for the moment when the champion would step into action. When he finally did come into the story, he didn't exactly strike Aidan as the greatest of heroes—at least not the ones he was used to seeing in movies and video games.

First Odysseus was sitting on the shore of an island bawling his eyes out over not being able to get home to his wife, Penelope, which was just plain stupid in Aidan's mind. Kalypso—the goddess who had kept Odysseus on her island for years—had offered him immortality if he would remain, but he had refused. Who wouldn't want to have never-ending sex with a beautiful goddess? Who wouldn't want to live forever? Then the hero was getting trashed out at sea by the god Poseidon, washing up battered and half dead on the shore of some island, where it took a young princess to help him out. When Aidan left off, Odysseus was in the great hall of a king, blubbering again as a harper sang some old war song. If this was what heroism passed for in ancient Greece, he would take Schwarzenegger any day.

But there was something else that troubled him about the story, something that made him wonder about Memère. The main character at first wasn't Odysseus but his son Telémakhos. As with Odysseus, Aidan wasn't too impressed with him. He seemed to just sit around and mope. It was only because of the goddess Athena that he finally got off his rear and did something. Was this Memère's way of trying to tell Aidan something? Maybe his mother had put her up to it— this was just the kind of thing she would do.

And then there was the issue of the father. Telémakhos's grief for what he believed to be his father's death hit a little too close to home. The fact that Odysseus was still alive, that the son's later search for his father *wasn't* pointless, only made it worse.

All in all he couldn't understand why she had given him this book to read—it didn't seem like the thing a grand-mother would give, even one like her. Maybe this was why he was lying to her now about not starting it. If he said he had, she might want to talk about it. Who knew what she might say?

"I suppose you're wondering why I gave it to you," she said.

How does she do that? he wondered. "I guess."

"When I was younger than you," she said, "I had some trouble in school—not with learning, mind you, but with behaving. I was a little pain in the ass, to be honest. One day teacher got so angry she grabbed the thickest book off the shelf and slammed it on my desk. 'Eloise,' she said, 'since you can't contain yourself, maybe this will shut you up. There'll be no recess for you until you're finished.' It was *The Odyssey.* I spent the rest of the year reading that book, and let me tell you, I hated it. Of course, I didn't learn my lesson, and the next year, same thing. By the time I graduated eighth grade, I'd read that christly book five times.

"Funny thing is, every time I read it, I hated it a bit less. After a while I grew to love it. Something so vital about it. Hardly a year's gone by where I haven't read it at least once." She turned and looked away, back toward the mountain. "That book's changed my life in ways you couldn't imagine," she murmured. She turned back to him. "It's helped me through some tough times, Aidan. Maybe it'll do the same for you."

She went back to tracing patterns in the dirt. He watched her for a moment, trying to see if there was any sense to her designs. "Well," she said after a moment, "I must be off. Come on, Herbert," she said, hoisting the stick and laughing again. "*Au revoir*, Aidan!"

He watched her go for a moment, then shook his head and continued up the road.

His legs were still shaky later that evening as he rocked back and forth on the porch swing, waiting to be called in for supper. It had been a long ride, but he didn't mind. The only bad part was the long and jarring ride up the washboard dirt road to the farm at the end, where, like tonight, he would have to face yet another dinner making conversation around the table with his mother and Memère.

"Supper's ready!" Memère shouted through the screen door.

"Right," he called back. He rose slowly, taking heavy steps toward the kitchen. He wasn't very hungry. A knot had settled in his stomach as he thought once more about next week. It was even worse than the end-of-summer blues. He had always dreaded going back to school, but at least then he'd been able to see his friends. Now even that was gone. And so, as they gathered around the kitchen table and Memère placed dinner before him, he found himself snapping in a way that startled even him.

"What is *that*?" he demanded, pointing to his plate. On it sat a large piece of pie. But instead of fruit, it was filled with a consistent brown mass of what looked like hamburger. At his tone, both women froze.

"Aidan," his mother said with her trademark sigh, "don't be rude. Just try it."

"Well, what is it?" he asked again.

"*Tortière*. Pork pie. Pepère's favorite," Memère said, sitting down across from him. "You don't *have* to eat it, Aidan, for Christ's sake," the old woman added, watching him poke at it with his fork.

"Well, what else is there?" he asked.

"Nothing!" Memère replied, laughing.

Aidan bridled at her teasing but, after a tentative sniff, took a bite. He could feel both their eyes on him as he chewed. It was still hot and didn't taste at all like he had expected. The sweetness of the pork mixed with a strange blend of spices and, to his surprise, was delicious.

"It's not bad," he murmured, taking another bite, trying not to show them his delight.

They ate for a while in silence. As Aidan took another slice, his mother spoke up.

"So I've hardly seen you today, sweetie. What've you been up to?"

"Nothing," he replied. "If you haven't noticed, there isn't a hell of a lot to do around here."

"Well, you'll be busy enough in a few days," she retorted.

"Thanks for the reminder." He looked up to see Memère's eyes narrow at his abrupt reply. He gobbled down the rest of the *tortière* and stood up from the table. "Thanks for supper, Memère," he said, and headed for his bedroom before his mother could ask him any more questions.

He shut the door, then flopped on his bed and looked

around the room. He had everything just about set up now. Posters of bands with weird names his parents had always picked on him for liking—Guided by Voices, Archers of Loaf, Spoon—decorated the room along with all the other teen accessories he'd accumulated while out shopping with his friends. His computer was put together over on the desk, though without an Internet connection he didn't seem to have much use for it—all his games had been played to exhaustion. He had asked his mother several times that week to get him an account, but she kept putting him off. If he were able to go online, he wouldn't feel so isolated, so cut off up on this mountain. He could have at least some connection to the outside world. Best of all, he could start e-mailing his Boston friends again.

His stereo had also been set up, but he hadn't used it much either. He'd listened to his Walkman plenty out biking, but somehow it felt weird to play his music in this house, as if it belonged to another place or time, was part of another life. Most of his CDs still lay in the box he'd packed them in. Instead, he ended up spending much of his time perched on the window seat, looking out over the yard as the shadows grew steep and the sun took its time fading into the long summer twilight. He would sit and listen to his mother and Memère do the dishes down below him in the kitchen. Sometimes they spoke amid the clinking of plates and silverware, their voices sounding muffled through the ceiling. Sometimes they didn't speak at all.

He heard the porch door slam and went over to the window. Memère was leaving the house, as she did every night after finishing the dishes. Aidan watched her as she took her time crossing the lawn, stopping to examine her ornaments for any signs of wear, checking the garden farther down for evidence of predation. It was like a little ritual, every night the same. As always, she reached the end of the lawn and, with a look back to the house, slipped through the hedge, passing out of sight into the orchard. By now he knew she would be gone for an hour or two, coming back long after the sun had set and the light was faint.

His mother, meanwhile, would sit at the table out on the porch, chain-smoke cigarettes, and—in a recent development that surprised Aidan a bit—drink a glass or two of wine. Aidan would go down from time to time to get something from the fridge or maybe watch a little TV, and whenever he passed, he would watch her through the window. Several nights he could see she was writing. She had paper and pen, and next to her wine bottle was a pile of paper that had been ripped into shreds. Once he saw her finish writing on a page, look it over, and then tear it up. Other nights she would crumple the paper instead, roll each sheet into a neat wad, compact, like an egg.

Tonight was no different. After Memère had gone, he drifted back downstairs, coming out on the porch just as she finished tearing up a sheet. She smiled when she saw him and put the pad over the pile of torn paper. He was going to ask her what she was writing, but her smile—the sad smile of vulnerability he had first seen last November—put him off.

"Where does Memère go every night?" he asked instead.

"She goes for a walk. She says a walk after supper keeps her going. Besides, it's cooler this time of day."

"You don't go with her?"

"No. She doesn't ask and I don't really care to. Maybe you should."

"No thanks," he said. He paused for a moment. "I think Uncle Richard was right," he said offhandedly.

She looked at him sharply. "About what?"

"About Memère. About her being, you know . . . " He made a twirling motion with his finger alongside his head.

"Your grandmother is *not* crazy, Aidan."

"Are you so sure? I'm not." He recounted the afternoon conversation with Memère to his mother.

"So what?" She laughed. "You're just seeing what you want to see, Aidan. Just believing what you want to believe."

"Still," he said, shaking his head, "maybe she would be better off somewhere else. Someplace comfortable, where people could take care of her . . . "

"You mean people in white coats? In a place with rubber rooms? I hope you're joking." Her eyes narrowed, and for a moment her face looked just like Memère's had at dinner. When she spoke again, her voice was cold. "I know what this is about. Forget it. We're here for good, Aidan. Get used to it."

"And what if I don't?" he retorted.

"Then you'll just stay miserable, I guess. But I don't think you will. In fact, I think what's bothering you is the possibility you won't."

His face reddened. He whirled around and stormed back inside, letting the screen door slam behind him. Grabbing the cordless phone and his mother's address book from her purse hanging by the door, he stomped up the stairs.

Back in his room, he looked up his Uncle Richard's phone number in the address book and dialed. It rang three times, four times, five. *Come on, come on*, he thought. On the sixth ring, Richard answered.

"Hello?" his uncle said. His voice sounded abrupt, almost annoyed. Aidan hesitated.

"Richard?" he said at last.

"Aidan Maiden. How's it going, chief?" His uncle's voice warmed.

"All right, I guess."

"Can't be that good if you're calling me so soon. Life in the Kingdom getting to you? Or is it sharing a house with two women?"

Aidan laughed. "Both, you could say. Hey, listen, I was wondering if I could take you up on your offer. You know, come and visit for a while."

There was a pause on the other end. Aidan could hear his uncle talking to somebody in the background. A dog was barking. Richard came back on. "Sorry, Aidan. What were you saying?"

Aidan repeated his question. There was another pause, but this time the line was quiet. "Well, I'm in court just about every day next week, kid. And the week after that, Gretchen and I are taking off to California for vacation. And after that, I'm not sure what's going on."

"Oh," Aidan said, trying to hide his disappointment.

"I know. I'm sorry, Aidan. But listen, call me in a month. We'll work something out. Besides, your mother might not be hot to let you go so soon after moving in. Give it some time."

"All right."

"Good. Speaking of your mother, put her on. I'll talk to her."

"She's not here right now," Aidan replied.

"Well, tell her I said hi, okay?"

"I will. Thanks, Uncle Richard."

"See you, kid."

Aidan hung up. Even though Richard was his mother's brother, he reminded him more of his father. The same cordiality, the same excuses.

He sank into the corner of the room and tossed the phone aside. For a minute he just sat there, staring at it on the floor next to him. Reaching over, he grabbed it and dialed the number of his friend Andy back in Massachusetts. He had held off all week, as if calling right away might seem too needy or somehow desperate. But at this point, he figured he was both. He had to talk to someone. Andy was the first guy he'd met after moving to Needham—he'd lived three houses down—and was as close to a best friend as Aidan had.

The phone rang. Andy's mother answered. After a quick exchange, she called for her son. A moment later Andy picked up.

"Aidan, what's up?" Andy said brightly. Aidan hesitated at the sound of his friend's voice. Though it had been barely more than a week since they'd last talked—that Thursday night before the move—it felt like ages ago.

"It's so boring up here, Andy," Aidan said. "There's nothing to do."

"That sucks, man," Andy replied.

Aidan went on to describe the mountain and what he'd been doing all week. It didn't take long. He finished by describing his grandmother—what Uncle Richard had said about her and about her evening disappearances. So far it was the only really interesting thing that had happened.

"Your grandmother sounds tweaked. You really think she's nuts?"

"Well, she's different. I mean, she's been cool to me so far, but I don't know."

"Hey, you should follow her. See where she goes at night."

"Maybe," Aidan said. That actually wasn't a bad idea—it would beat sitting around in his room. "So what's up with you, anyway? How is everyone?"

"Good. You know, the same. Actually, I was just getting

ready to head out. Becca's having a party at her house."

"Weren't you trying to hook up with her?"

"Well, yeah, that was last week. I've been hanging out with Rachel the last few days. I'm heading out to pick her up. She's actually waiting for me right now."

"Oh, okay. Listen, Andy, you should think about coming up this summer to hang out. Maybe we could do some mountain biking or something."

"Yeah, that sounds cool. All right, gotta go. We'll talk later."

"Sure. Say hi to everyone for me."

"No problem. Take it easy, Aidan."

And then he was gone. Aidan heard the click. He held the receiver to his ear, listening as click followed click before finally giving way to dial tone. An image of Odysseus alone on the sea, choked with salt water as Poseidon cast him between the waves, suddenly rose out of nowhere. Aidan hung up the phone and tossed it on the bed beside him.

He wandered over to the window and stared out. The sun had set, and the blue sky was darkening. Sometime later Memère emerged from the trees and began walking slowly up the lawn. As he watched her head toward the house, he remembered Andy's suggestion. Where *did* she go each night? Tomorrow he would find out.

SIX

Aidan brushed aside the poplar branch and took another step. A twig snapped beneath his foot and he dropped into the grass, his heart beating. Had she heard him? He was sure he was far enough behind—he could catch only glimpses of her as she slipped between the trees, and only by freezing into perfect stillness could he even faintly hear her. And besides, she was old—old people had trouble hearing, didn't they? Maybe, but she wasn't like other old people; she missed nothing. She was sharp, like the blade of the jackknife he knew she carried in the pocket of her dress. He waited another thirty seconds before getting up again. Sunset was probably twenty minutes away, but the dew was already gathering in the shade, threatening to soak his shirt, leaving him cool. It felt good—today had been the hottest since coming to Vermont. A layer of evening mist, only just visible, was starting to take shape. It would build and thicken all night, leaving everything wet by morning.

I can't believe I'm spying on my grandmother, Aidan

thought. *This is what I've sunk to*. For a moment he moved outside himself, imagining the scene from above. It seemed so silly, him stalking in the grass in pursuit of an old woman who moved freely along, a smile surely on her face. He also felt guilty being so surreptitious, but there was a certain elation that came from the fear of being caught. The guilt, the thrill, the realization of the absurdity of it, all came together, and before he knew it, a snicker began to work its way out. A moment later he was shaking, hand over mouth, fighting back the laughter that threatened to give him away. Finally the wave subsided. He continued creeping along.

Aidan went another thirty feet or so past the first set of apple trees and paused as a new sound caught his ear. Music. She was singing. He could hear her high voice, faint and distant, working away at the wordless song she always sang. He crept closer through several more rows, and the singing sounded nearer. Still he couldn't see her. He went farther, past more trees. A new sound was now woven into her song, the sound of running water. A brook had added its music to her own. He stepped closer through the grass and, catching sight of her once more, ducked behind a tree.

She stood in the middle of a clearing, as if the apple trees had moved back to form an imperfect circle. The clearing wasn't empty. He could see something standing near the center, a statue of some kind, though Memère was blocking the view. She stepped aside for a moment, and he realized it wasn't a statue at all, but instead what appeared to be a birdbath—a shallow basin atop a short pillar of stone—like the ones he'd seen in parks around Boston. A wooden chair, bleached by cycles of rain and sun, rested nearby with a blue glass pitcher on its seat. As Aidan watched, Memère, still humming, walked over to the chair and took up the pitcher. She filled it with water from the brook, came back, and emptied it into the basin. Then she stood back and looked at the sky. The sun was no longer visible in the clearing. The clouds above were streaked with pink and gold against the blue. Memère placed the pitcher down at the base of the pedestal. The humming stopped. Everything was still.

A breeze from nowhere picked up and washed through the orchard, shuddering the leaves into a single whisper, pushing the mist along before it. Aidan could sense the goose bumps forming along his back and arms, and he shivered from the breeze as a prickle of anticipation ran across his body. The breeze disappeared as quickly as it had come. A sudden urge to flee seized him. He felt he had intruded upon something he shouldn't see, but he couldn't even begin to understand why; the weirdness of the scene pushed all other thought from his mind and made his grandmother a stranger. He turned away, tensed to bolt, but she began to sing again, and he felt compelled to turn back to the clearing once more and watch from his place in the shadows.

She took something from the pocket of her dress. Aidan could barely see it at first, it was so small. He realized it was a needle and gasped as she pricked the tip of her index finger without the slightest grimace of pain. Returning the needle to her pocket, she squeezed the finger, holding it out over the basin. Aidan watched as the drops of blood trickled into the pool without a sound. A moment later she turned from the pedestal and, nursing her finger, went over to the chair and sat down. She didn't move. She seemed to be waiting.

Richard was right. She really is crazy. Somehow he had thought it would feel good to discover the truth, but as he saw her sitting there, leaning back against the chair with a smile, he felt only sadness.

He'd had enough and turned to leave when another breeze, this one more urgent, cooler, swept over, tossing the tree limbs above him. Again the breeze faded fast, but as the rippling of the grass and leaves slowed, another movement caught his eye. He ducked back down and watched them as they emerged from the other side of the clearing.

A man came first. He was old—at least as old as Memère—and dressed in overalls with rubber barn boots like Donny's. Behind him came two middle-aged women. One was in a pale-blue dress, wearing black horn-rimmed glasses and looking like she'd just stepped off the set of a *Leave It to Beaver* remake. The other looked oddly familiar; Aidan could swear he'd seen her somewhere before. She had on a dress, cinched at the waist, so long it disappeared into the grass. Her hair was pulled back into a bun that sat high upon her head. Behind them traipsed a scruffy man in a red-and-black-checkered wool jacket that barely contained his enormous gut. Beside him walked a strikingly beautiful girl about Aidan's age. Her hair was dyed jet-black in total contrast with her pale skin. Her nose and eyebrows were pierced and she wore a Nirvana T-shirt just like one Aidan used to wear back when they were his favorite band.

Others came behind them—eight in all—each dressed differently from the rest, as if they had all just come from some bizarre costume party. They were virtually silent as they drew closer, with only the faintest rustling of the grass to betray their presence. They crept forward with slow, shy movements, like wild animals unsure of their surroundings, ready to flee at a moment's notice. Strangest of all, there was an indefinite quality to them all, a washed-out element—as if they'd been left out in the rain too long—that seemed to blur the edges of their movement. Aidan couldn't make sense of it. It had to be a trick of the shadows, a distortion of the mist that hung in the air, meager and thin.

As they moved farther into the clearing, forming a semicircle around the birdbath across from Memère, Aidan stared in wonder. Forgetting for a moment how they got here or where they had come from, he tried to figure out *why* they were here to begin with. He couldn't come up with anything that made sense. Was his grandmother directing a play? Part of some theater group in town that had decided to practice here? Why would she keep something like that secret? It was the only thing he could think of, but even this idea was absurd.

Memère spoke up. "Okay ladies and gents, step right up. One at a time, please."

One by one the people came forward, stepped up to the basin, leaned over and took a drink, each one bending down to touch his or her lips to the water, where Aidan's grandmother had dropped her blood. Some took long, thirsty gulps, while others only sipped. Regardless, as they stood up, there was a sharpening to their look and a flush of color, not just in their faces but through every part of them from head to foot, as if they had become more present. They took turns and didn't rush, each person finding some spot to settle in the clearing after drinking.

Aidan watched the ritual unfold with a growing sense of horror. Then it occurred to him—not only was his grandmother crazy; she seemed to be involved in some satanic cult, the kind he'd seen stories about on the news.

When they had all taken a turn and found their places, the last to drink—a man maybe fifty years old, wearing a long blue coat with brass buttons that looked like part of some officer's uniform—turned toward Memère.

"Once again, Eloise, our thanks. As always, you produce a delicate and delicious brew."

"*Merci*, Jackson," she replied. "You surely do know how to flatter an old woman."

The woman in the long dress spoke next. "So Eloise, tell us about your day."

"It was hot today, and I don't mean maybe," she replied.

"Though I suppose you wouldn't care too much about that. Let's see . . . well, I worked in the garden a bit this morning. Beet greens are ready. I picked a few and washed them for supper."

"Oh," the woman with glasses gushed, "how I loved those. I remember the sweetness of the beets, like little rubied candies at the ends of the greens. And that earthy taste, especially when mixed with a little vinegar."

"That's right," Memère said. "That's exactly right. 'Course, they're not doing as well as I'd like. They don't seem to grow as big now as in years past. And those goddam deer keep eating off the tops of some."

"They was in there last night. Two of 'em," the fat man in the wool jacket said.

"True, Smitty. I saw the tracks this morning," Memère said.

"Well, Eloise, I told you before," the first woman scolded, "if you'd simply move the garden closer to the house, by the barn where I used to have it, then you wouldn't have this problem."

"I know, Marie," Memère acknowledged. "But I like my garden in the sun. It's too dark over by the barn."

The woman shrugged as if to say *Suit yourself*. Listening to them talk, Aidan felt even more confused than before. Is this what people in cults talked about? There was a lull in the conversation. Everyone sat quietly, looking down, luxuriating in the sense of peace that seemed to fill the air. Only the old man in overalls was looking up. He turned his head, surveying the clearing, before resting his gaze directly on Aidan. For a moment their eyes locked, and a slight smile crept over the man's face. Aidan ducked farther behind the tree, his heart pounding.

"You can tell the young fella to come out. He don't need to be shy," the old man said.

"Who?" Memère asked sharply. She sat forward and looked about, though none of the others in the circle seemed alarmed. They simply looked at one another and smiled. Aidan clung more tightly to the tree.

"Come out, come out wherever you are!" the girl chanted, clapping her hands.

"Come out, Aidan. Come out! Come out!" the rest joined in.

Hearing them call out his name sent a shiver of goose bumps across his skin. *How do they know who I am?* he wondered. For a moment he thought of running. But like before, something compelled him to stay. Some strange mixture of fear and curiosity, the same he'd felt that first night pursuing the figure on the lawn, kicked in and kept him from going. He stepped out from behind the tree and came into the clearing.

"Merde!" his grandmother said. Her face bore a mixture of anger and embarrassment when she saw him emerge, but her look softened as he came over and stood beside her.

"What's going on, Memère?" he whispered, avoiding their gazes. "What are these people doing here?"

"So you see them, do you? Interesting." She paused for a moment, staring out at the assembled group. "Well," she said at last with a sigh, looking up at him, "no point, I suppose, in pretending things are other than they are." She gestured to the others. "These are my friends, dear," she said. She turned back to the group. "Everyone—this is my grandson, Aidan."

Everyone in the group rose to their feet and slowly began moving toward Aidan and his grandmother, pulling in closer and tighter. Their faces were serious but not severe. Their eyes never blinked. Aidan stepped closer to his grandmother. She patted his hand, which was gripping her shoulder.

"Don't squeeze so hard, child," she said. "They won't hurt you."

"Who are they?" he asked again.

"I told you, they're my friends. They live here on the mountain."

"He knows who we are," the man with the officer's jacket said. "Don't you, Aidan?"

Aidan shivered. He thought back to that first night, to that flickering figure in the dark, and to the strange noises and chills, like the one he was having now. He thought back to what Memère had told his uncle when he had asked to whom she was talking. "The dead, Richard," she had said. "The dead."

"You're dead," he whispered. "They're ghosts, Memère."

"I know, dear," she replied.

"But that can't be," he said. He felt weak. His knees trembled, his head spun. *This is a dream*, he thought. *I'm still dreaming.* It was the same dream he'd been having since the night his father died.

Memère stood up and took his hand. "This is Jackson," she said, pointing to the man with the long coat. "He used to live down below where your father grew up. He led a battalion in the Civil War," she said with an air of pride, then added in a loud whisper, "He got shot. Never made it home, poor thing—his body, anyways."

She proceeded to run through the group, telling their names, when and where they'd lived on the mountain, and sometimes even how they'd died. Smitty was the heavy man in the wool hunting jacket. He used to log and drive a wrecker. Alton was the old farmer in boots and overalls who had farmed the other side of south face. Beside him was his wife, Esther, a plump woman who looked young enough to be his daughter, having passed away a few decades before her husband. Wilma wore the blue dress and glasses. She'd succumbed to cancer in the sixties. Eve, the punked-out girl, grew up not far away on Parrish Road and was a relative newcomer to the group. Daniel was the first one to settle on Harper Mountain back in the 1700s. He wore knee-high breeches and still had on the new suit coat he was wearing the day his favorite bull gored him.

"And this," Memère said, pointing last to the distinguished-looking woman in the long dress, "is Marie Boisvert, your great-great-aunt."

A chill ran through Aidan as he suddenly realized where

he'd seen her before—the photo on the stairs. Her hair was the same, even the dress—it was all the same.

"He's cute," Eve whispered, stepping closer to him with a wicked grin.

"Now you leave him alone and mind your manners, young lady," Memère snapped, and shooed her away. Eve stepped back, pouting.

"Why are you here?" Aidan asked, his voice trembling.

"We come here every night," Esther said. "Your grandmother takes care of us. She feeds us."

"No. I mean, why are you *here*," he spread his arms wide, "on earth, still walking around?" He looked from face to face, but each one turned away, their expressions sad despite their smiles. He turned to his grandmother, his face now as pale as the ghosts'.

"They're waiting, Aidan," she replied.

"For what?" he demanded.

"To move on. When the time is right. When they're ready."

"To go where?"

"I've asked them before, but they never answer. Some things they tell me, some they don't. Either they can't or don't want to. They can be shy, and a bit peculiar."

Aidan shook his head. "This is ridiculous, Memère. Ghosts are just in stories and cheesy horror movies. They don't really exist."

"That's right, Aidan. Yet—here they are," she said.

Aidan turned back to the silent crowd that had begun to withdraw to their original places. They seemed to be brooding.

"They don't like it when you say things like that, dear. It hurts their feelings," his grandmother added in a whisper.

Aidan exploded. "This isn't funny, Memère!" he shouted at her, jerking his hand away. She flinched and stepped back. Her smile faded. He looked around. The others were still staring at him, but they seemed unperturbed by his outburst. *This is a joke*, he thought. *Some elaborate joke they're playing on me.* "The dead don't come back!" he cried, this time at everyone, and rushed over to Daniel, who sat closest to him. The man got up and backed away as Aidan approached. *I'll put an end to this right now*, he thought. *I'll teach them to play with me.*

"Aidan, no!" Memère shouted.

Aidan lunged forward to grab Daniel, but instead of grabbing him his hands passed through the surface of his body. The world dissolved into slow motion as his hands disappeared. Aidan felt as if he'd suddenly plunged his arms into a swift icy current—a substance that wasn't solid, wasn't air, but something in between. Aidan and the man looked at each other in mutual shock, both gasping at the sudden joining of each other's presence.

Aidan pulled away at last. His whole body shook, and he looked at his grandmother in disbelief.

"Come here, sweetheart," she said, stepping forward to hold him.

"No!" he screamed. He stumbled backward into the grass, picked himself up and fled.

The dead don't come back! The dead don't come back! Over and over the words repeated in his head, a rhythm that beat in time to his running and the pounding of his heart. He sprinted up the lawn, past the leering gnomes, past the Virgin with her arms stretched out in benediction, past his mother on the porch who was rising to her feet asking what was the matter. He rushed up the stairs past the portrait of Marie and into his bedroom, where he slammed the door and locked it.

He could hear his mother pounding on the door as he curled up on the bed and shut his eyes. He ignored her questions, pulling the sheets up around him in spite of the stuffiness in the room after the day's heat. Eventually she went away, and everything was quiet.

For hours, it seemed, he lay there trying not to think of what had happened. The more he tried, the more he saw their faces, the more he felt the icy touch of something from another world. He finally gave up trying, and only then did he fall asleep. For the first time in months, he saw his father in a dream—all of him, clearly. They were together in his father's car on the highway driving toward some distant city. Once in a while they would look at each other, and every time his father's face was smiling.

SEVEN

Aidan woke to pale light at the window, meager and thin in contrast to the brighter glow that had greeted him on waking late every morning last week. Looking out, he saw only a veil of fog obscuring the outside world. He could barely distinguish the far end of the lawn, and the trees at its edge came and went, offering the only means of discerning depth in the uniform mist. Today was his first day working with Donny, and he dressed in old clothes suitable for spoiling in the barn. Putting on his watch, he discovered it was only six o'clock—he usually wasn't up for at least four hours. There was a dim rattling of dishes from downstairs but no voices. Memère was awake. His mother must still be sleeping. He took up his book, settled into his spot on the window seat, and waited.

An hour passed, then another. Aidan read the account of the Lotos Eaters. They were kind. They didn't mean to hurt. They only offered the lotos plant to exhausted men, who then ate and forgot whatever they still remembered of their homes. Odysseus tied his men weeping to the benches of his ship and sailed away, a cruel but loving leader.

The fog was breaking now. From time to time the sun appeared, discernible through the filter of mist, perfect in its roundness, a golden coin. Trees, too, were starting to appear, emerging from the wall and staying, not hiding back in fog when he looked the other way, like earlier in the morning. He read now of Polyphemos, the one-eyed giant, ripping apart the bodies of men, drinking their blood, laughing at the terror of their surviving friends trapped in a cave with death. Still the kitchen below was quiet, aside from the occasional rustle from Memère, and still Aidan waited. After last night's sleep and now in the wan mist, the orchard was far away, and maybe yesterday had never even happened. Nothing had happened. He could pretend that it had just been another part of his distant dreams that each morning evaporated faster than the fog.

The hallway creaked. There was a light knock at his door.

"Aidan, it's ten past eight. You'd better get up," his mother said.

"I'm already up," he called back. He expected to hear her leave, but the hall was silent.

"Are you okay?" she asked. "You seemed upset last night."

He felt like talking to her right now about as much as he did his grandmother. He could only be safe with the two women together. "I'll be right down," he said.

"Fine," she said. He paused, listening to the stairs creak as she went down to the kitchen.

Setting aside the book, he turned back to the window one last time. The mist was gone now here on the mountain, and the sky was clear. Down in the valley, though, it still lay thick and white, a bright sea all around, flat out to where a ridge broke through, the nearest green island.

The stairway smelled of bacon. Memère and his mother glanced up at him as he came to the bottom step and into the kitchen. He smiled briefly and sat down to his place, where a cup of coffee waited. He wondered who had poured it. Both women gazed expectantly at him. He just looked down at the table and fixed his coffee—lots of cream, even more sugar. Memère finally got up and went to the stove, returning with eggs and bacon. She set the plate down before him, her back to his mother, and when he gazed up she widened her eyes for the slightest moment and pursed her lips. She wanted to talk. He looked back down at the table and began eating with quick bites, scrambling to finish the plate.

"Nervous?" his mother asked him.

"About what?"

"Work. The farm. You've never really had a job before."

"I did—last summer, remember?"

"I'd hardly call that working. You spent more time lying around the Johnsons' pool than actually cleaning it."

"I'm not nervous," he said. "I'm just not too excited, that's all."

Memère went back to the stove and returned with another plate. She set it before her daughter and sat down next to her.

"Thanks, Mama. But after this no more, okay? I've got to start eating lighter in the morning—I never even ate breakfast until last week."

"That's the problem. That's why you look so skinny. And pale. What happened, anyway? You used to be so robust. You practically lived outside—I used to have to drag you in by the ear at night to get you to come in. The little Indian—that's what we called you."

"Yeah, I was a girl then, Mama. That was before I knew about things like skin cancer. And cholesterol," she said, and pushed the plate away, having taken only a few bites. "Besides, what about you? I don't see you eating."

"I already ate," she replied. "I always feed myself first. Then I can take care of the others."

"How maternal," Aidan's mother snapped. Memère grabbed her daughter's chin and turned her head to face her. For a moment everything stopped. Aidan watched, his fork frozen halfway to his mouth, as a look passed between the two women. Then Memère let go and her daughter turned back to the table, drawing the plate to her. She took a few more bites of egg and toast before speaking again. "Anyway, Aidan, I was thinking last night. I'll call around today and try to find an Internet provider. Get you back on the Net."

"Thanks," he said.

"Aidan," Memère said, "before you go, I could use some help in the garden, eh?"

He knew what she was up to. "I really should go. Donny said he wanted me there at nine."

"That's okay. I can help you, Mama," his mother offered as Memère opened her mouth to speak. Aidan breathed a sigh of relief and got up from the table.

"Thanks for the breakfast," he said, and headed out the door.

"Say hello to Donny!" his mother yelled after him as the screen door slammed.

Aidan grabbed his bike and sailed down the driveway, shivering in the morning air. He kept his eyes straight ahead and down, avoiding the fields and trees to either side. Who knew what he might see there. He was taking the long way to the farm—it was shorter just to cut down through the trees below the house, but that would take him near the orchard. Besides, on his bike it was just as fast, maybe faster, to stick to the road, and he could nearly shut his eyes, hear only the drone of his tires as he coasted down the mountain. This way maybe he could avoid them.

This is silly, he thought. *I can't do this forever.* He forced himself to look up and around. A light breeze was sifting the leaves on the poplar trees that lined the road to his left, and the grass on both sides sparkled in the sun where the dew still lay, but he saw nothing else—there were no figures emerging from behind the trees or rising up from the ground. Still he shivered at the idea of what could be waiting around every corner, what might have always been there, and when he looked out again for the briefest moment, he imagined he saw them—Smitty, Alton, Eve, and all the rest watching him from wherever they spent their days. They flashed in and out of sight, their blank faces quickening his pulse.

He left the main road and turned up the lane that led to the farm. Enormous maples lined both sides of the road, their arching foliage casting the long drive into shadow, a tunnel whose light at the end opened to the yard. Donny's truck was in the driveway, along with several tractors in different stages of repair surrounded by tools, giant tires, and pieces of equipment. Donny's place seemed even more run-down than Memère's. At least Memère kept her house and yard neat and well ordered, right down to the placement of her gnomes. Here was a different story. The unpainted milking barn—a long, single-storied building attached at a right angle to the house—had a couple broken windows along the far end. Its roof sagged in the middle, and the facing side was a patch-work of materials: wide vertical boards, squares of chipboard, vinyl siding, even a few shingles in one corner. Whatever lay at hand seemed to have been nailed on. The white house was in somewhat better shape; it was in bad need of a paint job, but its various parts were more or less intact. Only a single black shutter hung partially detached, sloping in to block the window.

Getting off his bike, Aidan took the place in. Behind the

milking barn he could make out several other outbuildings and a squat gray silo. A few cement bunkers stood to the side of the milking barn, some filled with manure, others with chopped corn.

"Been a while since you been here, ain't it?"

Aidan turned from the barn to the house. Donny was standing, mug in hand, in the doorway of the mudroom that connected the house to the barn.

"A few years."

"Your dad didn't like visiting this place much." He left the doorway and came down to where Aidan still straddled his bike.

"I don't know. I guess not," Aidan replied.

Donny smiled—that same shy smile from a week ago. "I seen you checking the place out. Not much to look at, I know."

"It's not that bad," Aidan said.

"Goddam dump is what it is. Too bad—used to be a beautiful farm back when I was a kid. Oh well, that's what happens when you're a one-man operation—certain things go by the wayside, aesthetics being one of 'em."

Aesthetics? Aidan wondered. That sounded like a word his mother might use. "Why don't you fix it up, then?"

"Give me fifty grand and six months and maybe I could. As it is now, I don't even have enough time to scratch my ass, and I can barely make payments on this Christly equipment that breaks down if you so much as look at it funny." He paused, seeming to check the bitterness creeping in. "But hey, I'm keeping the place going, even if it don't look like it." He turned and headed for the barn. Aidan leaned his bike up against a tractor tire and jogged to catch up. "Let's put you to work," his uncle said.

"Are we going to milk the cows?" Aidan asked.

"Nope. Already been done—finished about an hour ago. I milk at six. Six in the morning, six at night, twice a day, three hundred and sixty-five days a year."

They went inside. After the brightness of the yard under mid-morning sun, the barn was like a tropical cave. Its windows were few and far between and were so dirty they blocked much of the light, and the air was humid and charged with the odor of manure mixed with the sweetness of hay and, most of all, raw milk. Metal pipes formed stalls that lined both sides of the barn, and a wide central aisle ran the length of the building.

"So what *do* you want me to do?" Aidan asked.

"Well, I'm just about ready to start baling rowen—if the weather holds—so I'll need you for that. But first I got to clear some space out in the hay barn. That's what you can do today."

There was a squish. Aidan looked down to discover his foot in the middle of a pile of manure. It was dark and fresh, oozing up around his sneakers. He lifted his foot and tried to shake, then scrape, it off. Donny laughed as Aidan's face curled into a look of disgust.

"Shit," Aidan said.

"That's right. Get used to it. A pair of these might be useful," Donny said, pointing to his own rubber boots, which rose halfway up his calves.

"How can you stand it?" he asked, still trying to scrape the manure off against the edge of the concrete walkway.

"You mean the shit? It makes the corn and the hay grow. It helps feed these cows so they can produce milk. And more shit, of course."

They exited the rear and headed for the largest of the makeshift barns out back, its long, vertical boards aged myriad shades of gray. The skeletal frame of a hay elevator ran at a sharp angle from the ground up to a large opening on the second story. Its metal structure was built around a conveyor belt that wasn't so much a belt as a single chain armed with spikes that grabbed the bale and carried it to the top. The front of the barn sported a tall door suspended along the top by wheels set into a metal track. Donny threw back the latch and slid the door open a few feet, and the two of them squeezed in.

It seemed even darker here than in the milking barn, but the moisture was gone, as was the rankness of manure, and the only smell in the dry air was the aroma of hay tinged with dust. Donny pushed the door all the way open to let in more light, and the shadows retreated to reveal stacks of bales lining the back walls. The second story came out only about three quarters of the way, making it more like a loft. It, too, was loaded with bales. Donny pointed to a ladder that ran up the wall to the edge of the loft above.

"You can go up there and start throwing down hay to make room for the rowen. Come back down from time to time and stack what you've tossed down against the wall here. But there's a trick to it—I'll show you."

Aidan watched as he climbed the ladder. He threw down about a dozen bales, which Aidan dodged as they hit the hay-covered floor with a whisper. He came back down and showed Aidan how to stack them, almost like bricks, so they would lock together and stay firm against the walls.

"You're going to have to get yourself some of these," he said, tossing a pair of gloves to Aidan. "You can use mine for now."

"You're going?" Aidan asked in alarm as Donny headed for the door.

"Goddam right I am. I've got to get up and ted them fields above your grandmother's. I just mowed them yesterday, and the grass needs to be turned now while the sun's hot. If this weather holds up, we'll be baling tomorrow."

"Oh," Aidan said.

"Christ, don't look so friggin' upset. I'll be back in a few hours, and then you can go for lunch. This should be enough to keep you busy till then."

He turned and left. Aidan watched from the doorway as he headed back into the milking barn and disappeared. A few minutes later Aidan heard the stuttering growl of a tractor starting. He put on his gloves and turned back to the hay.

He climbed up to the loft and set to work. The bales were heavy, and he struggled at first to find the strings that held them together, and then to fit his gloved fingers underneath to get a hold. He worked steadily, trying to lose himself in the effort. But try as he might, he kept returning to last night. He could no longer pretend that it had never happened, nor could he pretend that the strangers in the orchard with Memère were anything other than what they claimed to be. The icy touch of Daniel had been no trick. The ghosts were real.

He tried to remember everything he knew about ghosts. They were scary. They haunted the world, the places where something terrible had occurred or where they didn't want the living to be. Problem was, these features didn't seem to match what he'd seen last night. Those spirits hadn't seemed angry or upset. The worst he could detect was perhaps the slightest sadness, but even that could have been mistaken for the solemnity of ritual. Still, who knew? His grandmother seemed on friendly terms with those figures, but even she didn't seem to understand much about them. There were too many questions. Weren't ghosts the echoes of those doomed to wander the earth, spirits wracked with pain? Weren't they being punished for unforgivable crimes or for failures from their past life? Weren't they tortured souls? Could they go anywhere? Be anywhere? Right here, right now? Worst of all was the silent question he knew was there, the one he refused to listen to, itself a ghost of thought: If these spirits were real, couldn't there be another one among them? One who also suffered? Couldn't his father be one of *them*?

The questions kept circulating through his mind, an unending series of doubts and fears that he kept pushing back only to push back again as they returned, just as his eyes kept darting toward the darkened corners of the loft in spite of his efforts to fix them on the hay. And though the loft was choked with heat radiating down from the tin roof of the barn, he could feel the goose bumps on his arms rise with every brush of sound against the rawness of his senses. In the light rustling of the bales, he heard the swish of his feet in the grass echoing off the gravestones as he fled Southlook a week ago. This hay was not the thick green grass of the cemetery in need of mowing. It was grass that had long been cut, dried, and pressed, but the sound was still the same.

Glancing at his watch, he realized nearly an hour had passed, and he stopped and looked over the edge. He had thrown down too many. He descended the ladder, waded around to the back of the mound, and began piling bales, struggling to do it the way Donny had shown him. It was slow going. Already his arms ached and his eyes stung from the sweat. Worst of all, he itched all over from the chaff, which seemed to have found its way into every opening of his shirt and pants. No wonder his father had hated this work.

He finished piling the bales, but a few of them had

broken and there was now a pile of loose hay almost knee-high in the middle of the floor. Dry or not, it seemed impossible that so much grass could be packed into the oblong bales. It was already eleven-thirty and Donny would be back soon. He looked around for a pitchfork or a rake, anything to shift the pile over to the corner, where it could be missed in the shadows.

As he searched along the edges of the barn, his foot struck something small but hard buried in the hay. Reaching down, his hands closed on metal, and he pulled the object out of the chaff. It was a tractor, a toy tractor, not like the green John Deere tractors Donny used, but an older model. Instead of tires it had spiked iron wheels. It had once been painted red, but most of the paint had been chipped away, exposing the dull die-cast metal. This wasn't like the Tonka toys he'd played with as a kid—this was old but toughly made, heavy in his hands despite its small size.

How long had it been buried in the hay? He spun one of its wheels, watching the spikes blur, and tried to imagine a little boy pushing it through the dirt. It must have been his father's.

"That used to be mine."

Aidan's heart surged at the sound of that voice behind him. He froze, watching the spinning wheel slow as the seconds ticked by until it finally stopped.

"You can have it if you want. After all, it was your father's first."

"Oh," Aidan said. His body relaxed as he realized who it was behind him, and he turned to where his uncle stood in the doorway, a dark silhouette against the outside glare.

Donny came over, reaching out for the tractor, and Aidan placed it into the rough hand. Turning sideways to the door, his face half in light, his uncle held the tractor out between them, looking down at it without a word. Aidan tried to read his face but couldn't tell what emotion, if any, ran beneath the blank expression. Donny looked back up and, giving the toy back to Aidan, smiled.

"Where'd you find it?" he asked.

"Over there, under some hay," Aidan said, pointing toward the wall.

"Christ knows how long it's been there."

"You lose it?"

"Forgot about it, more like," he said. "I remember the Christmas Dad got this for Timmy. I was so goddam jealous. He gave it to me later on after we'd both played with it a few years—said he didn't want it anymore. Guess I didn't either too much after that. Funny how it's that way sometimes with older brothers." He stared down at the toy, which Aidan turned now in his hands. "We used to play right out here with it—smooth out a spot on the ground and make little piles of chaff and dust. Had a little rake, too, we'd pull behind, pretend to push the hay into rows."

He looked back up at Aidan. "One of the only toys Dad ever got us growing up. And even that was made for working."

"I don't want it," Aidan said, holding it out again. Donny nodded and took it from him. With a quick step and a hop he hurled it up into the loft above. It disappeared into the dark. Aidan kept waiting for the clunk of it striking a wall, but there was no sound.

"Guess it's lost again. Maybe this time for good," Donny said. He looked around, surveying Aidan's work.

"I broke a few bales," Aidan said.

"Don't worry about it. Everyone does."

"I don't know if I piled them right."

"You did fine, Aidan." He went over to the opposite side from where Aidan had found the tractor and took down two pitchforks that hung against the wall. He gave one to Aidan and began forking up hay and pitching it over to the side. Aidan joined him. It took them only a few minutes to move the pile.

"I know what it's like to lose a father," Donny said as they finished. Aidan winced at the comment that came out of nowhere. He had hoped that if anyone would avoid mentioning it, Donny would.

"You miss him," his uncle offered. Aidan said nothing as he placed his pitchfork back against the wall. His uncle changed the subject. "You want some lunch? I don't got much besides peanut butter and jelly. Or you can go home if you want, come back in an hour."

"No. Peanut butter and jelly's fine."

"Good."

They left the hay barn and headed for the house. Again they went through the milking barn—the shortest way—and as they emerged on the other side Aidan stepped up next to his uncle.

"Do you? Miss him, I mean."

"My father?"

"No. Mine," Aidan said. They had reached the doorway of the mudroom.

"Timmy?" he said, pausing on the threshold as Aidan pulled up short behind him. "I've been missing him since I was sixteen." He pointed behind Aidan. Aidan turned around, looking for whatever his uncle was pointing at in the cluttered driveway.

"June eighth, 1979. I stood right here by the door as he walked by me over and over, loading his shit into an old truck Dad just bought him for graduation. He didn't say nothing. I didn't neither. Then he was gone. Nothing much has changed since."

He went inside, leaving Aidan staring at the yard.

Aidan sat in the window seat, looking down across the lawn. Memère was puttering at the edge of the garden, inspecting the tomatoes, taking her time as she meandered toward her evening rendezvous in the orchard. Twenty-four hours ago the world had been a different place. Twenty-four hours ago—what seemed like years—he had stood hiding behind a tree, watching as she passed before him into the mix of saplings and tall grass. Tonight he knew where she was going, and what she was going to do. Perhaps she was taking her time on purpose, waiting for him to join her. But he wouldn't go.

Reaching the edge of the lawn, Memère paused at the mouth of the path and stared back up to the window where he sat. Even at this distance he sensed her pale eyes penetrating his window. It was that same gaze he had felt last night from the ghost named Alton, those same old eyes calling him out from hiding. He was sure that he was veiled by the reflection of the sun against the glass, that she was only guessing he watched. Nonetheless, he looked away. When he turned back, she had disappeared.

With Memère safely gone, Aidan went back downstairs. Coming into the kitchen, he paused, drawn by the sunset. He pushed open the screen door and hovered in the threshold. The sun was now low in the western sky, swollen and inflamed in the summer evening, coming in under the roof and bathing the entire porch in light. His mother sat at her usual after-dinner post, the table before her bearing the ashtray, the ruffled papers. The glass of wine was gone tonight, replaced with a heavy tumbler. The ice cubes in the glass had nearly melted, and the caramel drink glowed in the light. Even in the masking shade of sunset, he knew the color of scotch. It was what his father used to drink in the evening, every night before bed.

His mother glanced up at him as he stepped out, giving

him a quick smile before turning back to the sky.

"Quite a show," she said, gesturing toward the ball now dipping into the farthest row of hills beyond Maxfield.

Aidan sat down in the swing. Its chains creaked in time with his groan. She laughed at his display.

"Sore?"

"Arms mostly," he said.

"Donny called while you were in the shower. Said you worked hard today. He sounded pleased."

Aidan smiled and glanced over to her, but her eyes still followed the sun. "It weren't too bad," he said, doing his best impression of his uncle.

"He's all Kingdom, that's for sure," she said with another laugh. "Still. Don't let him fool you. He graduated at the top of his class. Got offered a full ride to UVM just like Dad. Only he didn't have to go asking. They came after him."

"Why didn't he go?"

"I never asked him. Your father was furious, though. I'm sure you can imagine."

The sun was sinking fast now, its movement visible, though it seemed to be the hills that were really moving, rising up to eat the light. An impulse seized Aidan as he swung. He got up and walked over to the table. Reaching behind her, he took one of her cigarettes and lit it, exhaling above her head, his smoke mixing with her own. He could see her stiffen. He waited, but she didn't speak or even turn. He went back to the swing. The sun was gone now and the porch darkened while the sky continued to burn. For a while they sat in silence.

"You just missed Memère," she said at last. "She went for her evening walk."

"I figured," he said, flicking ash onto the porch.

"You should go with her some night. It would be nice for you to spend some more time with her. She won't be around forever, you know."

"I guess," he said. He closed his eyes, seeing the circle of shadows in the orchard, imagining her grasping the pitcher this very moment.

He went back to the table and crushed out what was left of the cigarette into the crowded ashtray. He looked down at the papers on the table, trying in the growing twilight to make out what she had written. He couldn't really see much—the page was full of lines of writing, but each had been scribbled out. Written in, scribbled out, all the way down the page. He suddenly thought of Odysseus's wife, Penelope, weaving her tapestry by day, unthreading the rows by night in a desperate effort to hold her suitors at bay on the outside chance that, one day, her husband might return to her.

"What are you working on?" he asked.

She hastened to cover up the sheets.

"Nothing much," she said. "A few poems. Nothing serious."

She used to write poems. He knew that about her. He had

never read them, but he used to see her tucked away in a corner of the house on weekends and during vacations back when he was little. She seemed to have let it go the last few years, though once in a while his father would bring it up to tease her. It bothered Aidan now to see the sheets, the crumpled balls of paper littering the table and porch floor. He could guess the subject of her poems and hoped he wouldn't be asked to read them.

"Well, I'm going to bed. I'm beat."

"Need me to wake you in the morning?" she asked, stubbing out her own cigarette.

"No thanks." He stooped behind her to tie his shoe. Noticing one of the balls of paper by his foot, his curiosity got the better of him, and he grabbed it, slipping it into his pocket as he stood. "Yeah, maybe," he said, changing his mind. "Only if you're already up." He turned to the house and opened the screen door. Her voice stopped him mid-creak.

"It was nice talking to you tonight, Aidan. I've missed talking to you."

He paused in the doorway, his back to hers. He knew he had to say something.

"You too," he said, and fled inside, into the house and up the stairs.

Closing his bedroom door, he took the paper from his pocket and set it on *The Odyssey* at his bedside table. It was not the rough, uneven shape of a hastily crumpled sheet, but had been carefully crushed and shaped by her hands, resistant to his opening. He went to the window. The shadows had swallowed almost everything, and a mist was settling in as the temperature dropped. He pulled the shade and turned back toward the bed. The wad of paper—a brittle egg, whole but cracked—waited. He undressed in the stuffy room and collapsed on top of the sheets, trying to bring himself to turn out the light, to bypass the paper. In the end he couldn't help himself. Finding an edge, he uncrumpled the paper and smoothed it out as best he could. It looked like the page he had seen earlier at the table: aborted lines and false starts weaving irregularly along the page, line after line crossed out, scribbled black so that the writing was obscured. Except for one line he could just make out:

Where are you waiting? Where have you gone?

He rolled the sheet back up and threw it away into some dark corner of the room before turning off the light.

EIGHT

By the time Aidan realized he was trapped, it was too late. He had lingered in his room again this morning before coming down, waiting for the telltale sounds of dishes and steps from the kitchen below, waiting for the voices of mother and daughter mixing between intervals of silence before rising from his bed. He dressed quickly, not bothering to shower. By now he knew there wasn't any point—before long he'd be grimy and hot, with chaff sticking to his sweat like it had the last few days. Yesterday he'd finished clearing out the loft, and in the afternoon he'd begun helping Donny in the upper fields with the rowen. In spite of what looked to be another scorching day, he put on jeans and a long-sleeved shirt, still able to see the remnants of the rash the chaff had made along his forearms and legs after working all day in shorts and a T-shirt. Looking in the mirror, he snorted at the clothes that made him look like Donny and headed downstairs.

But as he reached the bottom step and swung into the kitchen, he sensed something was wrong. Everything seemed in order—his place was set for breakfast, the usual smells of coffee and bacon hung in the air, Memère stood with her back to him washing dishes at the sink. Glancing out to the porch and back again, it hit him.

"Where's Mom?" he asked, trying to hide the unease in his voice. Memère stopped her washing in the sink, stood still for a moment longer than Aidan would have preferred, and turned. She didn't answer at first, but merely beckoned to his seat at the table with a smile that suggested the slightest hint of victory. She finally had him cornered. The moment he had been dreading since the night in the orchard three days ago had finally arrived. He cast a sidelong glance at the door and, for a moment, contemplated bolting. Then he sat down.

"Patrice has gone to town. She has an interview. I don't know when she'll be back," she said, setting a plate before him.

"Oh . . . ," he muttered, turning his attention to the check-ered pattern of the tablecloth. Forgetting his anxiety for a moment, his eyes snapped back up as she settled across from him at the table. "Wait. What interview?"

"Lyndon Institute. An English position just opened up."

"Institute? What is it, some sort of mental hospital?"

"Very funny. No, it's the high school. It's where you'll be going to school, you know. Your mother went there. And your father."

"Oh . . . ," he said again. He delved into breakfast, all the while aware of her fixed gaze. He knew she wanted him to bring it up, to ask the questions that he'd been fighting off for days. But he wouldn't. He refused to acquiesce. She sighed.

"By Jesus, you've done a good job, Aidan. You've managed to sneak around me, around what happened. But you can't hide forever."

"What do you mean?" he asked. She simply laughed.

"Aren't you even curious? Don't you want to know about them? Anything at all?"

"No."

"You're a smart boy, Aidan. I can see it in your eyes, in your look. You're like your mother that way. That's why you can't hide from me. All the time, you're thinking, eh? I know you want to know."

"I don't. I don't want to know. I wish I could just forget the whole thing." He tossed his fork onto the plate. He didn't feel like eating anymore.

"Ah," she said, "of course you do. The truth can be a painful burden." She sighed. "Don't think I'm any happier about this than you are. Believe me, I'd just as soon you hadn't found out. But what's done is done. Forgetting's not an option."

"Then, what is?"

"Acceptance, of course."

"Whatever," he said. His eyes flickered up to see her reaction. The response always sent his mother through the roof, and he half expected it to do the same to her, but she hardly flinched. She simply stared more intently with her wintry

114

eyes, the same half smile on her lips.

"You can be quite the little smart-ass when you want to be. 'Whatever'? All right then, whatever." She took his plate away and the cup of coffee he hadn't drunk and brought them to the sink.

"I better go," he said, getting up from his seat. "Donny'll be waiting." He lingered at the table, as if only she could release him.

"By the way," she said, her back to him once more as she stood before the sink, "have you been reading lately? The book I gave you?"

"Yeah, I've been reading it."

"How far have you gotten?"

He had read most of book ten last night. Odysseus and his men had landed on Kirke's Island. The goddess had charmed his soldiers, turned them into pigs, but he had saved them. Armed with knowledge from the gods, he had conquered her and she had taken him to her bed. Aidan had been puzzled by the affair, by the intimacy and its mild eroticism. He thought of Penelope waiting at home on Ithaka, lonely. What would she think if she knew? He reddened at the memory of last night's reading.

"Kirke's Island," was all he said.

"Ah, *bon*," she replied with a smile. "Kirke, my favorite character—Odysseus aside, of course. Good, Aidan. Keep reading."

"Right," he said, and turned to go.

"When you stop being afraid," she said, freezing him in the doorway, "afraid of them, afraid of what this means for him, I'll tell you all about it." He could tell she faced him now, but he stayed on the threshold, looking out from the porch down to the orchard, where the tops of the apple trees trembled in mid-morning breeze.

"Afraid of what this means for who?" he demanded.

"You know exactly who I mean," she said.

He pushed the screen door back all the way and was down the porch steps before he heard it slam behind him.

Aidan plopped down on a stack of rowen, taking a moment to catch his breath. Wiping sweat away, he watched Donny guide the tractor along the windrows across the field. The baler came behind in tow, eating up the rowen, its mechanism thumping away in perfect rhythm, always turning, always drumming with a beat that seemed to stir up the heavy air. Everything around him sang along to this droning pulse— birds, insects, leaves—and the air was alight with floating seeds and flies that rode this chorus of sound, pushed along by the sun's slanted rays, which lit up the particles on the air as if a mass exodus of souls had left heaven and were falling, here, to this field.

Late afternoon had worked itself into early evening and still they labored on, hustling at what seemed to Aidan like a manic pace. Donny was a slow man at rest, but when it came to work, he sprang into action with an unsettling intensity that left Aidan struggling to keep up. They had been baling all day. Donny drove the tractor while Aidan followed, picking up the bales that were dropped behind and piling them into stacks. When all the rows were baled, Donny helped Aidan finish stacking, and then the real work began. The truck was brought into the field—not Donny's old Ford, but a bigger farm truck, equally rusted, with a large, flat bed that held more than a hundred bales. The two moved from stack to stack, pitching up the bales and packing them against the wooden rails of the bed before moving on. And when the truck was full, it was back to the farm to unload the neat stack, brick by brick, onto the hay elevator, which carried the bales up into the darkness of the loft—to undo everything that had been done in the field above. Then back up the mountain to reload the truck, load after load.

The one good part about it all was that Aidan had gotten to drive the truck. After the first load was brought down to the farm and put away, Donny got up in the passenger's side.

"What're you waiting for?" he asked, looking down at Aidan standing awkwardly beside the door. He thought at first Donny was playing a joke on him. But that wasn't his uncle's style.

"I've never driven before," he admitted.

"Well Jesus Christ, no time like the present."

"I don't know how."

"It ain't a standard. You can drive it. You'll figure it out."

Aidan went around the front and climbed into the

driver's seat, tracing his hands along the steering wheel as Donny checked to make sure it was still in park before turning the key. He explained the basics—gas, brake, shifting lever—and then they were off. After a bit of jerking, Aidan managed to get it back to the field without much trouble.

"Not bad," Donny said as they pulled up to a stop.

"Don't tell Mom," Aidan warned, smiling as Donny turned the engine off.

"I guess I won't," was all his uncle said.

For the rest of the day, Aidan had driven the truck, moving it slowly up and down the field, growing more at ease with its handling, until he could guide it along with hardly a stutter. It had taken them from late morning through most of the afternoon to finish the first field, and now, as Aidan rested on the soft rowen watching Donny finish baling the last few rows, it wouldn't be long before the second field was finished. Looking down at his gloves where the baling twine had already worn a crease, he imagined what his friends would think if they could see him now. They would probably laugh at him, his face streaked with dirt and sweat, his work clothes covered in chaff. He pulled the gloves off and examined the blisters on both hands, white and swollen. *What would Dad think?* he wondered. He tried envisioning his father's reaction to the sight of him laboring in a Kingdom hayfield. Unlike Aidan's friends, he probably wouldn't laugh.

Aidan surveyed the cleared slope. How many times had his father hayed this field? Maybe he'd sat right where Aidan was sitting. No. He wouldn't have been sitting—not with a job unfinished—and he wouldn't have felt as sore as Aidan felt now. He would still be fresh. He could keep going forever.

A flash of light in the corner of his eye made Aidan turn. Along the eastern edge of the field, bordered by the gravel road running from Southlook above, he could see the bike speeding down the mountain. It was Angela. The spokes of her tires caught the sun, sparkling for a moment as she spun by. He had kept half an eye out for her these last few days up in the fields, scanning the meadow roads, but she never appeared. Until now. He raised his hand and gave a tentative wave, not certain she saw him, but she waved back. *Maybe she'll come over*, he thought, his hand still in the air. He wanted to tell her he'd tried looking for her, that he'd thought about her. He almost called out, but by the time he worked up the nerve, she was well past him, her momentum carrying her away. He watched her until she faded from sight.

The stuttering growl of the tractor as Donny hit the gas brought Aidan back, and he glanced at his watch, amazed to discover it was past six. They still had to finish gathering up the last of the rowen, bring it back, and unload it. It would be almost eight before he got home, and Memère would already be gone. That was fine with him. A breeze picked up and washed over him, turning the lines of sweat along his temples and neck into cool streaks. He shivered for a moment in spite of the heat, thinking of Memère at the basin, of the blood falling into the cold water drop by drop, and of the pale, hungry faces crowding around, the echo of their voices still calling his name.

Donny finished the last row, drove the tractor to the edge of the field, and killed the engine as Aidan hurried to pile the remaining bales. His uncle joined him with the truck, and they finished loading. When they were done, Donny disappeared into the cab, returning with a bottle of beer and a Coke. He handed the soda to Aidan and cracked the beer, taking a long swig. The bottle was cold in Aidan's hand, slippery with an icy film of water.

"Got a cooler in the backseat," Donny explained, taking another swig. He leaned back against the railing of the truck. Aidan did the same, and they both looked out across the shaved hillside, squinting against the sun lowered in the western corner of the sky.

"Gotten a lot done last couple days," Donny commented. "Just 'bout finished."

"What's left?"

"Got that big field over there," Donny said, gesturing off to the right. "Mowed it this morning before you came. I'll ted it tomorrow. Hopefully the weather'll hold."

Donny finished his beer and tipped the bottle upside down, shaking out any lingering drops before leaning back against the truck. A minute passed, then another, as they continued to gaze out at the skyline. The birds had begun their evening song.

"Pretty goddam peaceful up here, ain't it?" Donny said. "I always liked it up here. Played here all the time. Good place to get away from Dad. Used to keep going up the mountain to the top. Me, Timmy, and Patty."

"What's it like up there?"

"Big rock face. Nice view, I guess. I ain't been up there for years now. Who knows, maybe the trees have grown up over it."

Aidan tried to imagine them, two boys and a girl, running around the mountain. He could see them for a second, could almost hear their laughter, but they weren't his parents or his uncle, just three little kids. "You three play together a lot back then?" he asked.

"Christ, yeah. When we were little, I mean. Timmy, of course, was the ringleader. Used to drag us all over the goddam mountain, building forts, playing hide-and-seek, sometimes fighting, you name it."

"You'd fight?"

"Yup. Kid's stuff, you know. Patty always stuck up for me. I was smaller. She was always tough. 'Course, you probably know that. Aidan?"

Aidan was no longer listening. His gaze was fixed upon the far edge of the field, watching the two figures that had emerged from nowhere now walking down the hill. He recognized their shapes against the tree line—a tall, lumbering man in a checkered jacket drifting beside a girl in black. As they neared the bottom edge, the girl looked back for the slightest moment and seemed to beckon slightly. Then both shapes disappeared, melted into the dusk. Aidan knew where they were going and shivered again as the breeze picked up for an instant before dying.

"Do you believe in ghosts?" he asked.

Donny gave him a puzzled look, then turned away and sighed, leaving Aidan still watching the lower end of the field. He tossed his bottle up into the cab of the truck.

"I ain't never seen one, so I guess not. You?"

"No," Aidan whispered, and finished the last swig of Coke.

"Let's get the hell out of here," Donny said. "We can unload this in the morning. I'm late for milking—cows probably ready to burst by now."

"Okay."

"Think you can drive the truck back yourself? I got to bring the John Deere down."

"Sure."

"Good." He turned and headed toward the tractor parked nearby. Aidan climbed into the cab and started the engine. Gazing through the dusty windshield, he searched one last time for any sign of the shapes, but the only movement came from a pair of crows who rose from the top of a maple and glided down onto the field, scavenging for rodent victims of the mower. A bang against the door startled him, and he looked down to see Donny signaling him to turn off the noisy engine.

"Park the truck out back in the same spot. In case you're gone before I get down there, just wanted to give you this." He held a bill up to the window.

"You're paying me now?" Aidan asked, taking it.

"No. I'm keeping track of your hours. I'll give you a check for the whole week later. This is just a bonus. You worked your ass off today, Aidan."

"Thanks," Aidan replied.

"Aidan," Donny said, stepping back from the cab, "I don't know about no ghosts. But I do know the past is right here. It's all around us, but we don't usually see it." The sun dipped down behind a cloud, sending blazing streaks across the sky. Donny gestured down the mountain. "Sometimes when I'm up here, I'll look out and see Dad or even my grampa cutting hay or driving the cows in for milking. Sometimes I can remember them just like they was right here, right now. Even if there ain't no ghosts, them are close enough they might's well be."

"I guess," Aidan said. He watched the crows lift off the ground and wing their way back to the trees as Donny headed for the tractor.

"See you tomorrow," the man called back, throwing his hand up in farewell.

Aidan started up the truck once more. He unfolded the bill and saw it was a twenty. It was wet with sweat and smelled like rowen. He folded it back up, stuffed it in his pocket, and headed down the mountain.

The kitchen was empty when Aidan got home. A plate covered in plastic wrap lay at his place on the table, its contents obscured beneath the condensation. In the living room the TV blared, and a glow flickered from the darkened doorway. His mother must be in there, away from her usual evening spot out on the porch. He went into the living room. The shades were drawn, and his mother was lying on the couch. She didn't seem to notice him, and for a moment he just watched her staring intently at the screen, a bemused smile on her face. She was watching a movie, some old musical. Aidan didn't recognize the woman cavorting amid the alpine landscape, twirling through some faded Technicolor dream.

"Hey, Mom!" he called out over the elevated volume. She glanced over at him, gave him a little wave and a smile. She didn't seem startled by his greeting—she must have seen him come in after all. She joined in now with the woman in the film, matching the operatic style with her own.

"'The hills are alive . . . with the sound of music!'" she bellowed, smiling at Aidan while throwing out her arm in a dramatic gesture. He made a face and turned to leave.

"Hold on, sweetie," she said, pausing the movie, "don't go."

He turned back in the doorway. "Only if you promise to stop singing."

"Come on, now. All in good fun," she said. Sitting up, she patted the couch. He came over and plopped down at the other end with a groan. "Tired?"

"Wicked. It was a long day."

"They all are," she replied. "There's dinner for you on the table."

"I saw. Thanks. Memère gone?"

"Yup. Her usual stroll."

Aidan looked away. *If only she knew.* He wondered if she did. She didn't seem to have a clue, but he wasn't about to bring it up. "What're you watching?" he asked instead.

"*The Sound of Music.* It was my favorite when I was girl. Saw a copy for sale in the grocery store and couldn't resist. I must've seen it a dozen times when it came out."

"Great," he said.

"Hey—it's a classic. It's based on a true story, you know. The von Trapp family. They escaped the Nazis and came to Vermont, eventually. Settled in Stowe."

"Lucky them."

"Watch it," she said, tossing a pillow at him. "So how is the work going? Donny treating you all right?"

"Donny's fine. He told me today about you guys playing together when you were little."

"That's right," she said. "Your father took us on all kinds of adventures. We made the most of it here on the mountain."

"He said you used to fight."

"Your father and Donny mostly. But I did too. I was one of the boys, after all. Besides, somebody had to stick up for little Donny. He was a sweet kid. I mean, your father—well, your father was your father . . . but there was always something tender about Donny. Anyway, that was a long time ago. But I'm glad to hear things are working out between you two. I'm sure he appreciates your help."

"I guess."

"Hey—aren't you going to ask me how my interview went today?"

"That's right. Memère told me this morning. So how was it?"

"Good. I think I'll get the job—it's the last minute, and they're desperate. It was strange, though, going into the school today. The rooms, the halls, everything looks the same. It was kind of eerie. It's like every time I turned around, I expected to see . . . " She didn't finish her sentence. She didn't need to.

"No more poetry?" he asked, to change the subject.

"Not tonight." She sighed. "I don't know—I thought coming up here might recharge the batteries, but so far nothing good's come. I suppose I should just be patient."

"Maybe if you get out. Get a social life."

She snorted. "Right. How about you? Have you spoken to any of your friends? What about Andy?"

"Yeah, I've talked to him a bunch," he lied. He hadn't talked to Andy since the first call.

"Tell him he's welcome to come up for a visit. He can help you do chores," she joked.

"I'm sure." He stared away at the screen, where the

woman's face loomed large, the smile of ecstasy frozen on her face.

"What you need," she said, smirking, "is a girlfriend."

The memory of Angela appeared, floating down the mountain on her bike, glowing in the sun. He had a sudden thought to call her, then remembered he didn't have her number. He didn't even know her last name to call information.

He got up from the couch. "I'm going to grab my dinner and head upstairs, go to bed early."

"Okay. Good night, sweetie."

"Good night."

He returned to the kitchen. The music resumed as he poured himself a glass of milk. It sounded old and trembly, the way old movies always seemed to sound, and he was glad to put it behind him as he climbed the stairs to his room.

After gobbling down dinner, he took a long shower, washing all the chaff from his hair and the dust from his body. Now he felt clean and drowsy. He flopped back onto his bed and let out a sigh. He should just go to sleep.

Rolling over, his eye caught *The Odyssey* lying on the window seat. *What the hell*, he thought. He grabbed it and settled into the black armchair. He'd convinced his mother to let him bring his father's old chair up a few days ago, and after an hour of heaving, twisting, and arguing in the heat, they'd finally managed to squeeze it in. It filled the entire corner, the smell of its leather permeating the room.

Sometimes he even thought he caught a whiff of his father's cologne.

He opened the book, found his spot, and began to read. A year had passed since Odysseus and his men had come to Kirke's Island. *How could he have let so much time go by?* Aidan wondered. *How could he let himself be caught?* But now it was time to move on. Odysseus begged Kirke to be released and asked for help in getting home. Her reply brought goose bumps to Aidan's skin in the stuffy room. He couldn't go home directly, she told him. He had to sail to the ends of the earth, to the island of Erebos, portal to the land of the dead. He had to find the shade of the blind prophet Teiresias and discover his fate. She instructed him how to do it. Aidan read the lines, and then read them again. A knot began forming in his stomach as she described the ritual of summoning, described the pit he must dig, the liquids he must pour in to serve the dead, the water, honey, wine, the blood of sacrifice that would give each shade a taste of life.

His heart pounded as he lifted his eyes from the page.

The clatter of the screen door sounded from the kitchen below. He froze in his chair, listening to Memère's footsteps rising on the stairs, a slow, steady beat. He could hear her at the top of the stairway, her steps growing louder in the hall as she came closer, pacing in time to the tune of her humming, which stopped with her steps as she reached his door. He held his breath in the silence, counting the seconds, until she continued on her way to her room at the end of the hall, until the door closed behind her.

He returned to the page and kept on reading.

The men didn't take the news well when Odysseus told them, and Aidan couldn't blame them. "But," Odysseus said, "nothing came of giving way to grief." So in the end they made their way back to the ship, weeping. They looked for Kirke, but she had gone. Aidan read the last two lines of the chapter: "For who could see the passage of a goddess unless she wished his mortal eyes aware?"

He lingered over those lines, avoiding the facing page, blank but for the title of the next section: "Book XI: A Gathering of Shades." He had seen this page before. He had opened to it his first night here, marked by the pewter dagger. He contemplated closing the book, closing it forever and never speaking to his grandmother of it or the orchard again, no matter what she said or did. But he couldn't. Compelled by curiosity and the desire to find some explanation for what he'd so far failed to understand, he turned the page.

Now that he'd surrendered, he read quickly, racing across the lines as Odysseus's ship raced to the distant island, where they disembarked. Aidan trembled at the eerie familiarity of the scene as Odysseus poured the libations and spilt the blood, and the shades rose up and gathered round.

Teiresias came and drank. He not only told Odysseus the path home, but spoke of his life beyond, revealed the hero's fate. *Must be nice*, Aidan thought, *to know your future. Even if it's bad, at least you know.* Teiresias finished, and Aidan expected that to be the end—Odysseus had done what he came to do. But it wasn't finished. The blind seer said that if the hero wished to speak to any of the shades, he should let them come and drink. Just before Teiresias arrived, Odysseus had seen the shade of his mother, Antikleia. Aidan had flinched reading the passage. Odysseus didn't know she'd died; he'd been away and never said good-bye. And now he would get his chance. He would speak to her.

No, Aidan thought, *don't do it.*

Now came the moment Aidan realized he'd been dreading since Odysseus first laid eyes on her. She strode forward, drank, and recognized her son. They spoke, told the stories of his life and her death, but Aidan hardly read the words. He skimmed across them, blinking back the tears that gathered in his eyes. He hadn't cried since last November, since he'd been left standing alone in Southlook, the others filing out, his mother last of all, to go back to the dinner Memère had worked all day to prepare for hungry mourners. He was determined not to give in now. As he left the cemetery that day, he had promised himself that he wouldn't cry anymore. He had decided he'd cried enough.

And so he fought the tears, came back to the tale as the conversation between mother and son ended:

I bit my lip,
rising perplexed, with longing to embrace her,

and tried three times, putting my arms around her,
but she went sifting through my hands, impalpable
as shadows are, and wavering like a dream.

The lines blurred completely now; he could no longer hold back. He slammed the book shut and threw it across the room. It smashed into a pile of CDs, sending jewel cases clattering to the floor.

The next evening came cooler, the air drier than before. The old woman, having inspected her rows of peas and beans, having pulled the new weeds, straightened up and looked back to the house the way she always did before continuing on her way. She'd reached the edge of the lawn and had just started along the path worn in among the tall grass when her eye caught the movement of a sapling. She looked over to where he stepped from behind the tree.

"Hello, Aidan."

"Nice night for a walk," he replied.

She paused for a moment and pursed her lips. Sighing, she reached out her arm. He strode forward and took her hand, and the two passed down into the orchard together.

NINE

"You didn't seem happy to see me back there," Aidan said as they made their way toward the clearing.

Memère paused for a moment before him on the path and then shrugged her shoulders before continuing. "I didn't expect to see you, that's all. Besides, I'm not sure it's such a good idea."

"Why not? I'm not afraid," he said, trying to hide the quaver in his voice.

"What you've been through, what you're going through now—it might not be for the best."

"You said before you wanted to tell me about them."

"That's right, mister, *tell*—not show. I just wanted you to know why I do this. Since you'd found out, I thought it'd be better to at least explain."

"So why *do* you come here?" he asked as they entered the clearing.

"Well, like I said before, they're my friends. They keep me company, I feed them. We give each other what we need.

Question is, why are you here?"

"Why not?" he said, looking away. "It's something to do."

She snorted in reply. Picking up the pitcher, she wandered over to the brook and filled it just as he'd seen her do the other night. He watched her pour the water into the basin, holding out the pitcher until the last drop fell into the center of the pool.

"So how'd you learn to do this, anyway?" he asked.

She hesitated. "It's hard to explain, really," she said at last. "It happened four years ago. I was up late reading *The Odyssey* one night. Book eleven—you know the one?" He nodded, looking down. "Anyway, that night I had the strangest dream. I found myself walking through this orchard. There were voices calling to me. I couldn't hear what they were saying—they were speaking all at once—but they kept calling out. I had the same dream the next night, and the night after that. Finally I just came down here, and it happened. Without even trying, I knew what to do, as if I'd done it a hundred times before, as if the voices were guiding me. All I did was allow myself to listen—not think, just listen." She put the pitcher on the ground and reached into the pocket of her dress for the needle. "That's the thing about me, Aidan, that you need to understand. I go by instinct. I always have. I'm not saying it's the smartest thing to do, but it's all I know."

"I don't think there's any logic to the world anyway," Aidan murmured.

"You might just be right about that, dear," she said. She produced the needle and had raised it to her fingertip when he stopped her.

"You said before that they were waiting. But why?" he asked, his voice faltering. "What's wrong with them?"

She sighed. "Each of them has their own troubles, I suspect. Remember, Aidan, they were people once, and everyone's different. Everyone has their own pain, their own burden. I respect their mourning. I don't ask them questions, I only try to help them forget."

A thought struck him. "I thought ghosts only came out late at night. How can we see them in the daylight?" he asked.

His grandmother frowned. "Why wouldn't you be able to? That's the question you should ask. Forget all that garbage you learned from the movies, dear. This is the real thing."

There were so many more questions he wanted to ask, but he could tell she was eager to move on. He stepped back and watched her apply the needle. A quick stab and it was done. A moment later the drops had fallen, and the same quick breeze from the other night swept across the orchard, shaking the leaves, rustling the fabric of her dress.

"Here they come, boy," she said, gripping Aidan's hand. "This is my favorite part. I love to watch them—wild, yet so serene."

They came from behind the trees with the steady drift of

expectation, not shadows, but the shadows cast by shadow, glimmering amid the darkened green of limbs like the negative of a photo taken at noon under the sun. They seemed paler than before, and Aidan wondered if it was because he now knew their true nature or if they were simply hungrier this cooler night. He tried to steady himself, to prevent the shaking that had been building all day in the fields as he became more resigned to join Memère.

She was smiling as she watched them come, taking time to look up at Aidan with a wink of reassurance. They didn't look at Aidan or Memère as they approached or even seem to notice them. Their eyes stayed fixed on the birdbath as they gathered around it and, like before, came forward, drank, and settled down to wait until all had had their turn. Aidan watched the pool as each one bent down to sip. The water gave only the slightest stir, a movement that could just as easily have been caused by the breeze that anticipated their arrival. Still, as each one drank, the level in the basin seemed to lessen, almost imperceptibly at first, but by the time the last figure had had its fill, the liquid was nearly gone.

Stillness descended now on the clearing as Memère took to her chair and Aidan sat beside her on the grass. Minutes passed, and no one spoke. The spirits seemed lost in their own peace, digesting thought as they digested the water tinged with the old woman's blood. The silence made Aidan uncomfortable. The last time he was here, the others had gotten down to the business of chatting right away. He wondered if the quiet was due to him, if he was the source of their withdrawal. He looked up at his grandmother leaning back in the old Adirondack, humming to herself, seemingly content to absorb the silence. Her eyes flickered down on him and must have noticed his worry, for she stopped her song and leaned forward to pat his shoulder.

"It's like this sometimes, Aidan. Some nights we hardly say a word. Depends on what mood they're in. Or what mood I'm in," she added.

He scanned the collection of eight shades. He recognized most of them from before, especially the young girl in black, the one he'd seen yesterday in the field. She seemed so out of place among this group in various historical representations of rural dress. He had met her kind before, a reflection of the suburban punked-out girls he'd known back in Boston. Everyone referred to them derisively as "Goth chicks," but Aidan had always been secretly attracted to the type—they had a mysterious and stubborn edge to them that other girls lacked. This one—Eve, he suddenly remembered her name—was beautiful, with her catlike eyes and pouting lips. She noticed him staring, and her eyes narrowed as a sly smile spread across her pallid face. She winked and he turned away, feeling the blood rushing to his cheeks.

Looking around, he noticed a figure he hadn't seen before and couldn't find one he had. The man in breeches and dress coat with the long, pulled-back hair, the one he'd tried to grab, whose touch had convinced him of the ghosts' reality, was missing. In his place another man sat. He had curly hair and sideburns and wore a T-shirt with rolled-up sleeves. He sat next to the large man in the wool coat, glowering at nothing in particular.

"Who's that?" Aidan asked, pointing toward the newcomer.

"That's Bobby," Memère said, and made a little face. "He was one of the LaPoints who lived near the base of Harper by the bridge. You know that old, falling-down hole on the right just past the river?"

Aidan nodded in recognition, not pointing out how the abandoned house didn't seem much worse than their own.

"That was their place," she continued. "Most of the LaPoints are gone now. Can't say that I miss 'em much, by God. That Bobby was a stinker in life, and he's not much better now. If it weren't for the fact that he's Smitty's friend, I wouldn't abide having him here at all. At least he has the decency not to come too often."

"Christ, Eloise, I may be dead, but I ain't deaf," Bobby barked. "And who's that little bastard beside ya, anyways?"

"That's my grandson, Aidan," Memère snapped back, "and you watch your tongue or there'll be no more coming here for you!"

"Take it easy, Bobby," Smitty, the sagging logger, offered in his slow voice. "He didn't mean it, Aidan. Don't be mad."

"Oh, shut up, you miserable fat-ass," Bobby snarled, turning on Smitty. "Since when do you give me orders, anyways?"

"Oh dear, oh dear," the woman in the blue dress and horn-rimmed glasses fretted, her fingers rising to her temples. "I don't like this at all. Not at all."

"Relax, Wilma, you old fart," Bobby replied. "Smitty don't mind when I call him names."

Wilma moaned, her hands shaking about her head at Bobby's continued aggravations. A clamor broke out among the group, a feverish whisper of sound that made the hair stand on the back of Aidan's neck. He drew up against the chair. Memère sighed and looked down at Aidan.

"I'm sorry, dear. This happens from time to time. Nothing to worry about." She cleared her throat and looked over at the man in the dark blue officer's coat with a saber hanging at his side. "Jackson?" she prompted with a tone of expectation. Jackson rose to his feet and drew his sword.

"Enough," he boomed, his voice resonating with command. The order worked; all bickering ceased, and each resumed his or her place as if the outburst had never occurred. "Let's not forget we're guests," he reminded them, and they all nodded and smiled. Even Bobby's face softened.

"Where's that other man? The one I . . . touched before?"

"Daniel, you mean?" Memère said. "Oh, it's a rare occasion when he stops by. And don't worry about what happened, Aidan. It was forgotten the moment you left."

"How's the rowen goin', Aidan?" asked the man in overalls—the one who'd first called Aidan out last week.

"That's Alton," Memère whispered.

"Just about done," Aidan said, feeling shy as all faces turned toward him expectantly. "We've just got one more field to finish."

Alton sighed. "You're a lucky boy," he said. "What I wouldn't give to spend one hour in the field toutin' bales. 'Course, I couldn't hay my own christly fields even if I weren't gone now. They've all fallen to seed. The popples are taller than a son of a bitch on my side of the south face, or else there's one of them houses sproutin' up. Your uncle's got the only operation on Harper now."

Aidan nodded, not really sure what to say to the man. Marie, the regal woman from the family photo, spoke up.

"I just can't get over how much young Aidan looks like my son Maurice. He's a spitting image."

"I've often thought so," Memère concurred.

Their talk turned now to other matters, a series of mundane observations shared by Memère at the prompting of the ghosts, accompanied by simple reminiscences on their part of the lives they used to know. From time to time a shade would rise and come to the center and drink again from the pool that diminished but never seemed to disappear. Aidan wandered in and out of their conversations, no longer in fear of their presence, even when the talk was punctuated by a haunting silver laugh from one spirit or another. He found himself drifting away as the shadows lengthened and the dusk faded into deeper twilight. A coolness radiating at his side snapped him away from where he'd been staring beyond the circle out into the reaches of the orchard. It was Eve. How long she'd been at his side he couldn't say—last he knew, she'd been on the other side of the clearing.

"Looking for something?" she asked demurely.

"Not really," he replied.

"Okay," she responded in a tone of mock belief. "So, got a girlfriend?"

"No," he said, his earlier blush renewing. Eve was as striking as Angela, maybe even more so, but the two were so different. While Angela was fair-haired with tan skin, Eve's skin flashed white against her raven hair. He tried to look away, but her eyes kept him frozen in place. They were paler than Memère's, so pale they almost blended into the whites around them.

"I don't believe it," she cooed. "Too bad you weren't here when I was around," she said, moving closer as she spoke, until she was only inches away. "We could have had a lot of fun." Her hand came up, as if to caress his face, but stopped short of contact. Aidan felt his eyes grow heavy as she spoke, his gaze focusing on her purple lips, parted slightly to reveal a pierced tongue.

"Eve!" Memère's voice barked. Aidan jolted at the sound and the sight of her looming above them. Eve shrank at the admonition, her eyes wild and away, cowering like a dog caught pilfering the garbage. Aidan blinked and she was gone, back on the other side of the circle. Aidan looked across at her. She gave him a quick wave and a grin.

"It's getting late," Memère said, turning to the group. "Aidan and I must be going. *Bon soir.* See you tomorrow."

The crowd rose to their feet at her words and began leaving the clearing in ones and twos, waving a silent farewell, beginning to flicker as they made their way back into the shadows. Only Eve lingered at the end.

"Shoo," Memère cried. The girl smiled one last time and then departed with the final breath of wind. The leaves now ceased their hushing; the clearing was empty once more. Memère took Aidan's arm, and the two turned back toward the house.

"You've got to be careful, you know," Memère said as they reached the lawn.

"What do you mean?"

They paused at the edge of the garden. She let go of his arm and bent over to inspect the potato plants, breathing heavily from the walk back.

"Eve. I saw her giving you the eye. Beware a woman's charms, Aidan, even one like her. Especially one like her."

Aidan reddened at the suggestion. "Come on, Memère. We were just talking."

"No you weren't. I've been around long enough to know a thing or two, Aidan. Don't be embarrassed. I understand— she is an alluring one, that's for sure, by Jesus. Still, watch out."

"Well, she *is* the only person my age around here to talk to."

"Is she now!" Memère said. She laughed that certain

laugh that always irked him. The one he knew was directed at him, but could never be sure how to take it. "Don't be so certain. Remember what she is, Aidan. She has no age. She may seem as young as you, but she's beyond that now. Never forget it, for any of them." She leaned in closer, got down on one knee. "Hand me that over there, will you? Christly potato bugs, at it again."

Aidan retrieved an old can from the end of the row and brought it over. Taking a whiff, he recoiled at the stench.

"God! What's in there?"

"Kerosene," she said. She began plucking the little beetles from the leaves and plopping them in the can with a practiced rhythm. Aidan peered in at the bugs floating on the surface, stirring up tiny ripples with their squirming.

"So what's her deal, anyway?" he asked, trying to sound casual.

"Eve? She's a sad story, poor thing. Can't say I ever knew her when she lived on Harper. I'd see her from time to time—always alone, a black speck in the fields or in the woods. Even then she seemed a ghost. Came to an unhappy end about six years ago, and I'll leave it at that. Her parents moved off the mountain the following spring. Don't know where they went."

Her cryptic remarks made Aidan all the more curious. He tried to guess what an "unhappy end" might entail. After all, weren't they *all* unhappy? What could it be? Murder? Suicide? Illness? He closed his eyes and tried to imagine, but all he could see was her crystal beauty.

"She's a wild one," Memère continued. "More so than the others. Showed up last year. She didn't say much at first, didn't seem to want to be there. Now she comes every night, or just about. Always has that look, you know, of some kind of animal, lean and hungry, caught in a cage and looking for a way out. Maybe she's not used to what she is yet, or maybe it's her nature."

"I kind of like her," he challenged.

Memère made a brief face. "I like her too, but that's beside the point. Just don't forget what I said. Remember what she is."

She held out her arm for Aidan, and he helped her to her feet. She rose stiffly, letting out a little groan.

They marched the rest of the way up to the house in silence. His mother was on the porch, lying on the swing, her head propped up on a pillow, reading. A glass of wine sat by her on the floor, beside it a half-empty bottle. She remained engrossed as they climbed the steps. Aidan paused to watch her. Her eyes stayed fixed on the page. Memère stopped too, squinting to see what her daughter was reading. Aidan couldn't make out the title, but the cover illustration gave it away—a buxom woman swooning in the arms of a swarthy man.

"Patrice!" Memère barked. His mother kept on reading. She either didn't hear her or was ignoring her. Memère walked over and pushed back the book to read the cover.

"*Days of Passion?* What is this garbage, anyway?"

His mother finally looked up, frowning slightly. "Hey! I'm just at the good part. Go away!"

"I'm disappointed," Memère intoned. "An English teacher, no less."

"Let me have my fun. Nothing wrong with a good bodice ripper, Mama."

"Nothing right, neither," Memère replied.

His mother looked over at him. Her cheeks were flushed, and Aidan wondered if it was from the wine or Memère's scolding. Aidan threw his arms up, indicating he wanted to be left out of it.

"So, you two have a good walk?" his mother asked, to change the subject.

Aidan froze at the question, casting his eyes down, afraid of what they might betray. Memère stepped in.

"Aidan and I had a fine time. I got to show him around the orchard a bit. Let him see a little of the past."

His mother chuckled. "I spent a lot of time there as a girl. We used to play in the trees and swing from the branches. Made you furious, Mama. I remember the spankings we got whenever you caught us."

"I never spanked you," Memère snapped. "Those were love taps. And you were ruining the trees, messing with my apples."

"I haven't been down there since Aidan fell and broke his arm. Remember that, Aidan?"

"How could I forget? My arm still hurts whenever it rains."

"God, I was so scared. What's it like down there now?"

"It's all grown in," Memère said. "Since Papa died."

"Maybe Aidan can clear it out for you before he goes back to school," his mother offered.

"No, that's okay. It can stay wild. Best to leave some things undisturbed, to take their natural course."

"Since when did you ever give in? That's not like you, Mama."

"I'm old now, Patrice. People change." She turned and shuffled inside. Aidan watched his mother as she downed what was left in her glass and poured another. She looked up at him for a moment and then turned back to her book.

TEN

Aidan joined Memère the next night, and the night after, and so on into the next week. His time with the shades soon lost its eerie edge as he became more familiar with their ways. By now he knew them all by name, had grown accustomed to their quirky nature. It didn't take long. In fact, what struck him most about his time in the orchard was its sameness. Every night was like the last—the same ritual, the same conversations, the same summer sky. By the third night, as the lines of dialogue repeated once again, Aidan began to feel as if he were observing rehearsals for a play that would never be performed. Listening to their talk, he thought back to that first moment he'd seen them, when he'd wondered if maybe they were actors.

Memère didn't seem to mind. He marveled at her patience as the same questions were asked over and over, as the same observations rose in regular cycles with only the slightest variation. She always replied with an enthusiasm as sharp as the night before. She made their forgetfulness her own, and in doing so became a force as vital as the brew she fed them. All in all, Memère amazed him. She was the center of attention at these meetings. Like a conductor, she spurred the conversations on, moderating their tempo and balance. Other times she reminded him of an animal trainer at the zoo, the only one who could keep her wards at bay, induce a sense of calm with that soft voice, the same one she used when speaking to her flock of flamingoes and little gnomes up on the lawn.

Only Eve seemed immune from his grandmother's charms. She had backed off since that first evening's advance, but she never stopped gazing at Aidan with that look of hunger that he found difficult to ignore. They spoke a few times during the week, catching moments when the others were distracted. They mostly talked about music. Eve seemed to possess an encyclopedic knowledge of early nineties grunge, Nirvana in particular, that Aidan was somewhat familiar with, but not enough to keep up. She, on the other hand, didn't seem to have much interest in any other bands and knew nothing current. He didn't hold it against her. Soon, he realized, up here away from all record stores, radio stations, and friends, he wouldn't be much better.

The sameness of the gatherings was punctured one evening by a moment of drama. It was the fourth night. Aidan had noticed the day before that Esther, Alton's wife, hadn't joined in the feeding, but held back along the periphery, seated beneath an apple tree, looking at the sky as if a rain were about to fall. She didn't speak that night or even seem to notice the others casting periodic glances in her direction.

"Why doesn't she drink?" he asked Memère.

"She isn't hungry anymore," Memère replied, looking over at Alton, who nodded with an anxious smile. "She's getting ready."

"For what?"

"To move on, to let go."

Is that what this is all about? Aidan didn't like it. Why would you let go if you didn't have to? If you had a chance to be with the ones you loved, wouldn't you do everything you could to hold on? *Move on.* It sounded so final. And move on to where? That was the big question. But he didn't bother to ask it—he knew he'd get no answer. Instead he had a different question to ask Memère, one that had been weighing on his mind ever since he'd discovered her secret.

"Memère," he said, and then hesitated. "Where are all the other ghosts? Every time I come down with you, it's always the same ones. But lots of people have lived here on the mountain—why don't they show up? Aren't they hungry too?"

"Some I've known in life who are of the mountain have never come. I've never seen even a glimpse of them. Who knows what's kept them out of sight? But there have been others," she said, nodding. "Since I started, others have come. They come, they feed, they linger for a while, and then they go and I don't see them anymore. Maybe they got what they needed—a little taste and that's enough. Like Esther here. You'll see."

The next night, when Esther appeared with the others, she once again held back, now a dim figure, more faded than her friends. Aidan watched her beneath the tree, flickering in and out of sight with a snowy crackle, like the staticky image on an old TV. At one point he glanced away, only to be drawn back by a sudden brightening from her shape. His eyes widened as her figure filled with light, growing stronger by the second, illuminating the clearing. All conversation stopped, but none of the other shades looked at her. They turned their heads away toward the basin and grew still. Only Alton, who had seemed agitated all evening, turned to gaze, his pale eyes taking in the light.

"Good-bye, Esther," he said amid the silence.

Though he heard no reply, Aidan thought he saw her mouth form a farewell. It was hard to tell—the light had nearly consumed her now. A moment later her form submerged into the brightness. Then the light faded and was gone, leaving an empty spot beneath the tree.

There was a moment of calm, a stillness so perfect one might think the flow of time had frozen or simply ceased to exist. And then it passed. The conversation resumed, the shades picking up where they left off as if nothing had happened.

The next night things were back to normal. Though there was a certain comfort in the predictable quality of these evenings, there was always a part of Aidan that felt restless, that kept turning his eyes away toward the edges of the clearing. Ever since that night he'd read of Odysseus's journey to Erebos, a tiny hope had begun gnawing at the corners of his grief. Odysseus had long since left the island at the edge of the world, but a part of Aidan was still back there. And so each night for the last week, when the drops of blood had fallen, swirled, and disappeared into the basin, and the breezes had curled in among the leaves, a nervous excitement would swell within him, rising to his throat in anticipation of who might arrive as the figures emerged, only to be followed by a pang of disappointment when he wasn't with them.

Eve had guessed it, that first night Aidan willingly joined the circle. She had asked him if he was looking for something. "Not really," he had said, but as he said it he knew it wasn't true, became fully aware of the hope that he might see his father. It kept him coming. There were other reasons, but deep inside he knew this was the driving force that carried him down to the apple trees each night alongside Memère.

Aidan's quiet evenings with his grandmother and her friends were joined with quieter days of hard work with his uncle. Each morning he coasted down the mountain road a little earlier. Each afternoon he peddled his exhausted way back up a little later. His muscles had grown accustomed to the heavy lifting and repeated motion of labor faster than he had expected. The hours he spent with Donny, if not exciting, were pleasant enough, and the aspect of his uncle's personality he had dreaded—the reserved silence—became the thing he liked most about the man. Over the course of their days together, Aidan had come to admire Donny's efficiency, not just with his body, but with his words as well. Donny asked few questions and said little, but when he did, it counted.

The rowen was finished, and Aidan was spending most of his time now down on the farm. In the barn he helped Donny grain and hay the cows, clean out the stalls, scrub the milking parlor, and haul feed. Outside he helped his uncle with equipment repairs, handing him tools as needed or retrieving items that seemed to be scattered across every square foot of the farm. He also assisted with an endless list of fixes to the house, the barn, and the myriad sheds that spread out behind the barn in random fashion. Donny seemed able to do anything, whether it was welding an engine mount, fixing a broken waterline, or tending to a sick calf. He never formally taught Aidan as they worked—said he didn't have time—but Aidan learned by watching.

One afternoon Donny let him go after lunch.

"Go on," he said. "Take a break."

"But I thought you were going to show me how to feed the calves."

"I can do that some other time. Take a break. Don't want you to burn out, you know."

"Well, what are you going to do?"

"There's plenty I can do. I don't need no help today. See you tomorrow."

With that he turned and went back into the barn, leaving Aidan alone in the yard. Aidan grabbed his bike, trying to think of how to pass the unexpected time. He didn't feel like going home, so he headed down the mountain, coasting past the remains of the LaPoint place. Its broken windows exposed the inside's ruined darkness. Aidan wondered if Bobby might be lurking there. He didn't know where the shades spent their days. Maybe he would ask.

Crossing Mallard's Run, he made his way into Maxfield. The village was sleepy in the afternoon. Only a third of the parking spaces were filled, and the people on the street drifted in ones and twos, hardly speaking. He hadn't left Harper since joining the ghosts, and it felt strange to be around people and cars, even the few there were. He made a quick loop through town, stopping in the park like he had that first day he rode off the mountain. As before, the park was nearly empty. The few people there, gathered under the shade of the maple trees, paid him no mind. In fact, no one in the village seemed to take any notice of him at all. It was as if he himself were a ghost. When he stopped into one of the three mini-marts in town to buy cigarettes, the cashier, a heavy woman in her forties with flat brown hair, scarcely looked up from her magazine as she rang the pack up, took his five-dollar bill, and gave him back his change. He stayed at the counter as she flicked through another glossy page, the two of them alone in the store.

"How far is it to the school?" he wondered aloud. It

occurred to him he'd never seen it. Maybe it would give him something to do.

She looked up at him, squinting her eyes as if he stood a mile away. "Which one?" she replied.

"The high school."

"Lyndon Institute? 'Bout fifteen miles down the road."

"Thanks," he said, but she had already gone back to her reading. He left the store and wheeled circles around the small parking lot, debating whether to make the trip. He decided it was farther than he felt like going. Besides, he didn't even know what direction to go in—the cashier had neglected to say, and he wasn't going back in to ask. Instead he sped back to Harper, slowing only once he'd crossed the bridge.

Later that night, as he lay in bed listening to the electric squeak of bats catching moths outside the open window, he thought about his journey into town, about how hard he'd pedaled back to the bridge, to be on the mountain once again. It had seemed so much more solid than the town, as if it were somehow more real, though it was hard to tell *what* was real anymore. As the week drifted by, between the work on the farm and his nightly visits to the orchard, the days all seemed to blur, reducing the outside world to a faded dream, as if the universe were drowning beneath a flood, leaving him stranded on this island of a mountain. He allowed himself to be lulled by the pattern of days, stirred only by the first sighting of the spirits each night.

He thought of the lotos plant Odysseus's men had eaten, how they'd forgotten their old lives. Was he in danger of the same? No. Somewhere off the shore of the mountain, his life in Boston lay submerged, but not forgotten. Maybe it would be better to forget than to be stuck in this in-between place, like the shades in the orchard, trying to hold on to what was gone for good. At least then he could join the circle each night in peace, free from the disappointment of his father's absence.

If anyone had partaken of the lotos, it was his mother. Each day the stack of romance novels grew higher, their homogeneous titles forming a little tower on the porch. Every night the bottle of wine always more empty than full lingered by her side.

On the seventh evening he paused a moment longer than usual to watch her lying on the swaying swing, her face obscured by the paperback of the day.

"Ma?" he said. "Ma!" he said louder when she didn't look up.

"Yes?" she replied at last, lowering her book. He came back up onto the porch. Memère had gone before him and now waited on the lawn, examining one of her plastic flamingoes.

"Do you want to do something?"

"What do you mean?" she replied, as if he'd asked her to go to Mars.

"I don't know. Maybe get a movie? Or play Scrabble. You're always trying to get me to play."

"Aren't you going to go for your walk with Memère?"

"I can take a night off."

"Aidan?" Memère said, turning from her lawn ornaments with an air of expectation. Both he and his mother looked down at Memère. His mother gave a faint smile.

"That's sweet, Aidan. But go ahead. Maybe another night." She went back to her book and was already far away by the time Aidan left the porch and joined his grandmother.

"What's the matter? Getting tired of our walks?" Memère asked as they passed the garden.

"No," he replied. "It's just that . . . I don't know. I feel bad leaving her every night like that."

"I know what you mean, dear," she said, sighing. "But leave her be. She's had a tough time of it lately, just like you." She reached up and squeezed his shoulder. "Your mother will work it out. Everyone has their own way. Isn't that so?"

"I guess," he said. But it gnawed on him all the way down to the circle, even as Memère poured the water in the basin, and he found himself hungering more sharply than ever for a glimpse of his father who, once more, didn't show. For the next hour he impatiently watched the edges of the trees, practically ignoring the rote exchanges of the ghosts. Even Eve's attempted banter failed to draw him in. At one point his heart began to pound when the shadow of a man emerged from behind the farthest tree, but it was only Bobby, who gave Aidan the finger accompanied by a wide, crooked grin as he joined the circle.

Finally they broke company, and Aidan was just as glad to leave. They hadn't yet reached the lawn when Memère stopped and squeezed his arm.

"Okay, mister. No more games. You tell Memère what's going on."

"Nothing's going on."

"Bull. I've been watching you the last few nights, even if you've been too distracted to notice. I've seen you drifting off, as if you're somewhere else. I know we're not the most exciting bunch, but if you're that bored, you might as well stay home. Don't do this for me."

"I'm not bored. It's not that."

"It's your mother, then," she said, shaking her head. "I hate to see you so worried about her, Aidan."

"It's not that either. I just . . . " He couldn't find the words to tell her. But suddenly he didn't need to.

"Ah!" she whispered, her eyes widening in comprehension. "*Ton père*. You hope to see him, don't you? You think your father will show up." When he looked away and didn't answer, she let go her grip and stepped back. "Aidan, it doesn't work like that."

"Why not?"

"It just doesn't. Listen, I know what you're feeling. When I first started this four years ago, I was the same way. Pepère had been dead a year. I was so lonely. I waited for him to come, but he didn't."

"You mean you've never seen him?"

"No. I don't think so, not in the circle, anyways. Sometimes, when I'm coming back to the house, when it's darker toward the fall, I think I catch glimpses of him coming across the lawn, but I can't be sure."

Aidan thought back to the shadowy figure of the man he'd seen that first night he arrived, remembered the gait that had seemed somehow familiar. He shivered at the memory.

"But I'm supposed to find him," he said at last. He could feel tears rising in his eyes and closed them, not wanting her to see him cry.

"No you're not, Aidan. Don't even try. It's a bad idea."

"I don't believe you. You wanted me to. That's why I'm here every night, isn't it? You wanted me to learn your secret. You wanted me to join you. That's why you gave me that goddam book—you knew I'd figure it out." He was yelling now.

"No," she said faintly. She seemed to shrink before his eyes, and he saw something on her face he'd never seen before—a look of doubt. "No. I . . . gave you that story to read because I thought it might give you strength, that some part of its spirit might help you get past this terrible time." She hesitated, shaking her head slowly. "I just don't know, Aidan. Maybe, in the back of my mind, I thought there was a chance you'd make your way down here eventually, but even when you did, I wanted to believe your time with our friends might help you make peace with death, the way it has me."

"Well, you were wrong."

"I was. Terribly wrong. I forgot who I am and who you are. I'm an old woman, Aidan. That's why I can see them, I think. I'm close to death. And you are too, but in a different way. Perhaps for that very reason we can't see the ones we wish to see. They're too close in our hearts." She paused, and then spoke again with a renewed vigor that conveyed an edge of sharpness. "That's why you have to give up this notion. Nothing good will come of it. If you're meant to see him, he'll come. Otherwise, leave it be."

"No," he said. He no longer felt like crying. A calm had begun to settle in, bringing with it a coldness of defiance. "I'm not going to give up on him. He's somewhere on this mountain, I know it. If he won't come to me, then I'll go find him." He turned away. "And you can't stop me!" he called back, marching toward the house, leaving her alone in the tall grass.

ELEVEN

"Dammit!" Donny said, throwing the broken post aside. "Hit a rock. Get me another one, Aidan."

Aidan grabbed a post from the back of the pickup and handed it to his uncle. They were light, just over an inch square of pine, rough cut, and sharpened at one end with insulators—small cylinders of plastic with grooves to hold the electric wire—nailed in at the other. Setting it a foot away from the original spot, Donny pounded it in with a mallet. It sank in with three strikes.

Aidan stripped off his T-shirt, now wet with sweat in the mid-afternoon heat, and grabbed a couple more posts as he and Donny moved along the perimeter of the pasture. In spite of the heat, Aidan didn't mind the job. It wasn't hard work— pounding posts and stringing wire—and it certainly beat haying, with its constant motion and drone of machinery. They had finished three sides of the pasture and were now halfway through the last, bordering the gravel road that meandered down the mountain to the river. Occasionally a car or truck passed by, honking its greeting, drawing half a wave from Donny as it left its trail of dust behind. Each time Aidan asked him who it was, and he'd reply with "Chummy," or "That's Stimp," or sometimes, "Don't know and don't care."

"Here," Donny said, handing Aidan the mallet. "Take over for a while."

They marched to the next spot, about thirty feet away from the last post. Aidan looked tentatively at the ground before picking out a tuft of grass and setting the point of the stake on top. He paused with the mallet and looked over to his uncle, who gave a nod. He pounded down on the flattened top, feeling the pole vibrate in his hand with each strike. It resisted before sinking in at last. He looked to Donny again.

"A little more," his uncle said. Aidan pounded harder until it dropped a few more inches into the earth.

"Isn't this a long way from the barn to bring the cows?" he asked, catching his breath.

"It ain't for the milkers. It's for the heifers. And for Timmy."

Aidan knew by now that heifers were the younger cows that had yet to give birth and had no milk, but hearing his father's name took him aback.

"Who's Timmy?" he asked sharply.

"Timmy's a bull—my best one. Big, rugged bastard," Donny said.

"You named a bull after my father?" Aidan asked in disbelief.

"Yup," Donny said, and laughed.

Aidan laughed too. "I bet he loved that. Did he know?"

"I didn't tell him for the longest time. Finally I had to. I just couldn't help it. He weren't too pleased when he found out. I thought it was funny, but he didn't laugh when I told him." His smile faded. "That was the last time I talked to him," he added.

They moved once more along the edge, both silent as Aidan pounded in the next post. The last one had taken him at least ten strokes. This one was in with five.

"I don't remember the last time I talked to Dad," he said as he lowered the hammer. "I mean, I know it was that last morning. But I don't remember what he said. Or what I said. It was probably something stupid."

"Don't worry about it," Donny said. "It don't matter."

Aidan paused to think about it. Didn't it matter? Shouldn't there be some final moment to pass between a father and son, pregnant with meaning, even love? Of course, there was no way for either of them to have known the inevitable circumstances of their parting. Aidan had never thought about the inevitable until it was too late. Maybe Donny was right—by then it didn't matter. In the end, though, it came down to a simple question: If he had known, would that morning have been different? And the simple answer was yes.

He had no sooner finished the thought than the tingling started. Aidan shivered as the spidery chill once more emerged and danced across the notches in his spine. He hadn't felt it since his early encounters with the shades, and feeling it now caught him by surprise. To his relief, the sensation faded quickly, more so than before, and the accompanying noises never materialized. Putting all thought of the moment aside, he was turning to Donny for another post when a flicker along the far end of the pasture caught his eye, a flash of color against the cluster of dark spruce bordering the field. A boy had come out from the trees along the bottom side of the pasture and was now making his way along the fence line that ran up the modest slope of the mountain, sometimes walking, sometimes skipping. From the distance he was indistinct. All Aidan could make out was his auburn hair shining under the sun. Aidan dropped the hammer and stared. Donny—the stake he had been handing to Aidan still extended—turned to follow Aidan's gaze.

"Who is that?" Aidan asked.

The boy, having nearly reached the end of the far side, slipped under the fence and disappeared into the spruce.

"Who's who?" Donny said. Aidan looked over at his uncle's blank expression.

"I thought I saw red," Aidan stammered.

Donny raised an eyebrow. "Jesus Christ!" he said. "Don't

tell me you're getting sunstroke already. It was probably just a fox. There's enough of them around here."

"Yeah, you're right."

"You okay? You're looking a little peaked."

"I'm fine. It was nothing," Aidan said, picking up the mallet and taking the post Donny still held out. They moved another thirty feet to the next spot.

But it wasn't nothing. And it wasn't a fox. It was a boy—a boy with red hair. Aidan closed his eyes and saw him again, playing along the fence line. Donny had looked where he looked and hadn't seen him. It could mean only one thing. But who was the boy? Aidan looked back once more to the other end of the empty field, resisting the urge to drop the pole and run across the open space and into the trees.

"We ain't getting any younger out here," Donny murmured, rousing Aidan from his trance. Aidan pounded in the stake and they moved on.

They were nearly finished laying in the posts, moving at a steady pace, lost in their shared quiet, when she appeared above Aidan on the road. Her voice startled him from his meditation on the mystery of the boy.

"Hey, stranger!" Angela called out.

Aidan looked up the slope of the bank. Like last time they spoke, she sat perched on her bike, a sheen of sweat lighting up her skin just as it darkened her tank top.

"Oh. Hey. How's it going? Angela, right?" he said, shifting on the uneven ground in his dirty jeans and boots, shirtless, trying not to fumble his words. Once again she'd caught him off guard.

"That's right, Aidan," she said, breaking into a smile. There was something about her smile that reminded him of Eve—a certain confidence that made him shrink, a mischievousness that both frightened him and drew him in. "So what're you doing?" she asked.

"Building fence."

"Cool. Who's that?" she asked, gesturing behind him.

"That's Donny," he said, turning around to point to his uncle, but Donny had disappeared back to the truck, rummaging through the cab as if looking for something vital, leaving Aidan alone with the girl. For a moment neither spoke. She just continued to stare with that same smile on her face.

"So I've been wondering when I'd bump into you again," she said at last.

"Me too," he said. He thought about mentioning the wave they'd exchanged last week while he was haying, but he held back. *Don't sound desperate. Don't sound pathetic*, he told himself. "Having a good summer?" he asked.

"I've been keeping busy," she replied, nodding. "Besides, summer's always good. That's what summer *is*. You bike?" she asked.

Aidan paused for a moment, thrown by the non sequitur. "Yeah," he said.

"Cool. We'll go sometime. You can show me around. You

know your way around here, don't you?"

"I guess. I'm starting to, anyway. But I don't have a lot of free time. I've got work and stuff. Donny's my uncle. I've got to help him on the farm."

"Have you been up there?" she asked as if she hadn't heard him, pointing to the top of Harper.

"Not yet," he said. "Why, have you?"

"No. I want to check it out. Why don't we go sometime? Before summer's over we'll pack a lunch and go."

"Okay," he said.

"Good, then. Well, I'm headed. I'll see you around, Aidan."

"Okay," he said again. "Wait!" he called out as she fitted her feet back into the pedal stirrups to take off. She stopped and looked back down. "What's your name? Your last name, I mean. What's your number?" he asked.

"Unger," she said. "Like hunger without the *H*." She rattled off the digits of her phone number and, flashing one last smile, took off. Aidan watched her pedal away, reciting her number until she was out of sight. He felt a gentle prodding against his back and turned to see Donny holding out another stake, wearing an unusually large grin.

"Pretty girl," Donny said.

"I suppose."

"No supposing 'bout it. Ain't from around here, is she."

"Connecticut," he replied.

"The Constitution State," Donny declared. "Well, she

certainly seemed to like you."

Aidan scowled. "You were listening?"

"Well, I weren't not listening," he said, grinning again. Seeing Aidan's face, he added more seriously, "Don't worry—I didn't hear most of what you were saying. But I could tell she was interested in you, by God."

"Stop it," Aidan said. "It doesn't matter anyway. I told her I was busy. Said you were a slave driver."

"Well, I think I can manage to free you for a day or two to go, oh I don't know, biking or maybe for a nice hike," he said.

"Come on, we've only got one more post."

They were at the bottom corner of the pasture now. Aidan could just make out the sound of Mallard's Run rushing through the trees below. They finished putting in the post and set to stringing the wire along this last side. Aidan held the large coil on a dowel between his arms, releasing the line as they moved along while Donny looped it around the insulators, pulling it taut between the posts. After this they would run a line up to the farm that would carry the juice back down to the field, giving a generous shock to any heifers that might try to push through the fence.

"How's your mother doing?" Donny asked as they loaded up the truck. It had been about twenty minutes since either had spoken, and Aidan stiffened at the question. "Not doing so hot, is she?" Donny said.

"I don't know. She reads a lot. And drinks—nothing

serious, but she didn't used to. She doesn't do too much of anything, actually. I don't know. Maybe she's lonely."

"Well, I could tell that day we unloaded your stuff she was in bad shape. She puts on a good front, but I could tell. I hope you're helping her out."

"What am *I* supposed to do?" Aidan said defensively. "Besides, Memère said to just let her work it out."

Donny nodded. "Anyways, maybe I'll stop up to the house and see her sometime. You don't think she'd mind, do you?" he asked.

"I don't know. I guess not," Aidan said. He slammed the tailgate closed. "Come on, let's go."

"Go open the gate," Donny instructed. While he started up the truck, Aidan went over to a section of fence and unhooked the handle attached to a loop of wire on one of the posts. He pulled back the lowered line enough for Donny to drive through and reconnected the fence. Instead of getting into the cab, he jumped into the bed of the pickup. Donny glanced back at him through the glass. Aidan waved him on. As the truck lurched forward and began chugging up the hill, he scanned the far end of the pasture one last time. His roving gaze stopped short, his heart raced. Down in the lower corner, the little figure stood. Aidan brought his hand up to cut out the glare and watched as the boy turned once more under the fence, this time moving downhill toward the river. Then the field disappeared behind the trees as they rounded a corner and headed back to the farm.

"What a beautiful dress you're wearing, Eloise," Marie said, smoothing out the edges of her own skirt on the grass before folding her hands in her lap.

"*Merci*, Marie. I made it myself," Memère said. "Nothing fancy. Just a summer dress. Too hot for anything else."

Have I seen it before? Aidan thought. He knew this part by heart.

"Have I seen it before?" Marie asked.

"I believe you have. I made it last summer. I know how much you like it. That's why I wore it, you know."

"Well, isn't that sweet, Eloise," Marie said. "You're such a good girl." She leaned forward to inspect the flowered pattern. "That's right. I remember now."

I just love those daisies, Aidan said to himself.

"Those are daisies, aren't they," Wilma chimed in. "I just love daisies. I grew the most beautiful daisies in my yard."

"I never cared 'bout flowers much," said Alton, "but them were nice. Every day in the summer, driving down to Maxfield, we'd pass by 'em, and Esther always made me stop. 'Oh, how I wish I could grow flowers like that,' she used to say."

"They were the envy of everyone on Harper," Memère added.

"Well, thank you. I certainly put a lot of time into them. Every year when school was out and I had said good-bye to the children for the summer, I turned to my flower beds.

Weeding, digging, transplanting. How fast the days went by."

"You brought me a bouquet when my son Norbert was born," Memère said.

"And when Esther died," said Alton.

"Did I, now? I suppose I did. I used to bring flowers to a lot of people. Except that one year"—she shook her head and chuckled—"when Bobby cut them all down." She sighed. "All my pretty daisies gone."

"That weren't me," Bobby snapped. "That was Smitty."

"No it weren't!" said Smitty. A look of confusion clouded his face. "I don't think it was, anyways."

"Yeah, Smitty, you dumb-ass. Remember you put 'em all in a paper bag and gave 'em to Jennifer. Said you were sweet on her. What'd she do when you gave 'em to her, Smitty?"

"She liked them. She said they were pretty."

"Like hell she did. I was there, Smitty. She laughed at you. We all laughed."

"You told me she would like 'em," Smitty said, looking down at the ground.

"I might have said something along those lines," Bobby conceded.

"Well, Smitty may have given her the bag," Wilma scolded, "but it was you who filled it. By Jesus, you fourth graders were a handful that year."

"That was fifth grade, Wilma," Bobby replied.

"Either way, Bobby, you were a stinker," Memère said with a tone of finality.

Aidan lay back in the grass and sighed. This was the third time he'd heard the daisy story, though the part about Bobby's prank was new. He stared up through the arching limbs of an apple tree, its top leaves glowing against the leveling sun. *What am I doing here?* he wondered.

After his fight with Memère the evening before, he had skipped out last night on grounds of exhaustion. But today, after seeing the boy in the field, he couldn't help himself. There was something about the tiny figure that unsettled him, and he had spent the rest of the afternoon trying to figure out why. At first he thought it was just the normal fear of seeing a ghost, but he was past that now. He had the feeling that he was somehow meant to see him, but why? Perhaps he was a sign, some sort of omen. Regardless, in the end he decided that coming here might help calm the stirring in his mind and provide the sort of clarity he needed. And so, at the customary time, after the dishes had been washed and put away, his mother ensconced in her usual place on the swing, Aidan had accompanied his grandmother once more past the cluster of gnomes, past the foil pinwheels, past the bathtub Mary gazing down with her arms spread wide in benediction.

Memère had given him a puzzled look as he followed her off the porch.

"Didn't expect to see you again," she said a minute later as they crossed the border of the lawn.

"Well, I'm here, aren't I? You want me to turn around?"

"Suit yourself. Just tell me you've given up that foolish idea. The one we spoke of? You have, haven't you?"

"Yes," he mumbled, walking behind her on the path.

"Good boy."

But he hadn't forgotten. If anything, the desire to find his father had only grown stronger since that night. The only frustration was knowing where to begin. What was he supposed to do? Comb the entire mountain? The orchard seemed like a good place to start, but even as the desire intensified, the hope of finding him here was dying. He thought of asking the shades, but he guessed they wouldn't say, if they even knew. Besides, those kinds of questions would tip off his grandmother. She would know he hadn't foregone his quest, but had instead just begun it. Maybe he needed a different approach. Maybe he needed to dig around somewhere else. All he knew was that far from settling his mind, coming here tonight had only deepened his frustration. He should be elsewhere—anywhere—searching.

"Aidan, did you hear?"

"I'm afraid we've lost the boy," Jackson said.

Memère nudged him with her foot and he sat up. "Yeah?" he said.

"How was your day, Aidan?" Marie asked.

"Fine. Nothing too interesting," he said. "Donny and I fenced in one of the lower pastures down by the river for the heifers. And one of Donny's bulls."

"I had a bull once," Daniel said from across the circle. He

sighed, his color fading. "It was the death of me," he added.

"Poor Daniel was gored by a bull," Memère reminded Aidan.

"Got me right in the thigh. They brought me back to the house, but by the time the surgeon arrived, it was too late. There was so much blood. Be careful of them, young man. They seem docile, but they can turn on you when you least expect it."

Aidan nodded.

"What else, Aidan? Tell us," Alton said.

In his mind's eye Aidan again saw the little figure skipping along the fence line, wandering alone. He considered telling them of his vision, but he held back. Then another face came to mind.

"I met a girl," he blurted out. "Well, I met her once before. But I talked to her again today." A murmur of excitement rippled around the circle. Eve sat up from where she'd been reclining on the other side of the clearing, her eyes narrowing.

"Did you now," Memère said, raising her eyebrows. "You didn't say anything about it at dinner."

"I forgot," he replied.

"Tell us about her," Jackson invited.

"Is she pretty?" Smitty asked.

"Yeah, she's pretty, I guess. Her name's Angela. She just moved to Harper, lives on the other side of the south face."

"I know who she is," Eve snapped. Aidan stared across at

her. Her pale eyes smoldered back at him, her dark lips tightened at the corners.

"Do you like her, Aidan?" Daniel asked.

"She seems nice enough."

"Oh, young love! I remember it so," Wilma chimed in.

"You never married, Wilma," Alton said.

"When you spend your days with boys and girls, you see enough of it. Besides, I may not have married, but I loved once," she whispered. She seemed to fade slightly as she spoke, the edges of her form blurring.

"Come on, you guys," Aidan broke in. "It's nothing like that. I don't even really know her that well. Besides, she's probably not even going to be around much. She doesn't go to school up here."

"If you need any advice, Aidan, let me know," Bobby said, flashing a grin. "I used to be a ladies' man. Ask anyone."

"I remember the girls you used to go around with," Memère challenged. "They weren't exactly the respectable type. Little sluts, more like it."

Smitty guffawed, his shoulders rising and falling beneath his woolen coat. Bobby shot him a menacing look, and his laughter died.

"You got to take what you can get, Eloise," Bobby retorted. "And I took."

"Whatever," Aidan said. "Look, the point is there's nothing going on. We may go for a bike ride or something like that, but it's nothing serious. Okay?" He knew his voice was rising, taking on an edge they hadn't heard before, but he couldn't help it. They all lowered their heads and looked glumly at the ground, except for Eve, whose eyes still bore down on him, her expression unchanging. He tore up a tuft of grass and scattered it before him. Memère patted him on the shoulder.

"There, there, Aidan," she said. Aidan resisted the urge to shirk her touch. It was bad enough to be embarrassed by a bunch of dead people, but to have his grandmother patronize him the way she did the others, to treat him like he was just another ghost, made it worse. There was a long silence. Several of the shades came to the center for another drink. The sun had set now, and the tops of the trees were dark against the afterglow of twilight.

"That's a beautiful dress you're wearing, Eloise," Marie observed.

"Yes, those daisies are simply beautiful," Wilma cooed in the shadows.

Aidan sighed as he tore up another handful of grass, ripped it in half, and tossed it away.

Returning from the orchard, Aidan and Memère paused at the sight of Donny's pickup in the driveway. His uncle had said he might stop up to see his mother, but Aidan hadn't expected it to be so soon. As they drew closer to the house he saw Donny and his mother sitting on the swing at opposite ends, talking. When his mother noticed them, she rose and stepped forward, leaning against a post at the edge of the porch. Coming to the steps, Aidan glanced up at her. Her eyes looked red and slightly swollen. He hovered at the base of the porch as Memère came up beside him and Donny stood to join them.

"Donny!" Memère said. "Always nice to see you."

"Eloise," he replied with a nod.

"What've you folks been up to?" she asked.

"Took a little drive," Aidan's mother said. "I wanted to get off this mountain, and Donny was kind enough to oblige. Just got back a little while ago. Been talking about old times."

"I see," Memère said.

"Well, I should be going," Donny said. Aidan's mother stood back to let him by. As he passed by her he stopped and brushed away the white chips along her arm and shoulder. She started at his touch, before looking down to see the flakes fall to the floor.

"Got paint stuck to you," he said.

"That stupid post," she said. "The paint is old. Everything is old around here."

"You're not," he offered.

"I'm getting there," she said with a quick laugh. She gave him a hug. "Thanks for the visit, Donny."

"No problem," he said, and headed down the steps. Memère and Aidan separated to let Donny go between them.

"See you tomorrow, Aidan," his uncle called back.

"Right," Aidan said. "Same time?"

"Same as always," Donny replied, getting into his truck. The engine growled to life, shaking the rusted body as it idled. Aidan watched his uncle turn and cruise down the driveway. The muffler gasped and rattled in the distance long after the truck had disappeared.

TWELVE

The water rushed around Aidan's legs as he took his first steps into Mallard's Run, and he gasped at its unexpected chill in the heat of late July. It lacked the iciness of the Atlantic on the outer Cape in early summer—those waters had always numbed him, sending needle pricks along his legs and feet—but it was cold enough to give him the slightest head rush. It had rained last night, and the river was swollen and fresh, noisy in the joy of its renewal. Fishing pole in hand, he took another step, tentative on the rocks, and watched the water surge against his legs, leaving tear-shaped pockets on the downstream side as the separated waters rejoined into a single flow.

He was crossing here in the shallows, the water safely below his knees, in order to go back up the river to a deeper pool, broad and quiet against the white noise of the rushing sections above and below it. The other side of that pool, the side he was heading for now, was more open, with a pebble beach free of the trees that had threatened to snare his line. He knew there were trout in that pool. There had to be. If he were a fish, that's where he would live—down in the dark, away from the golden colors of the shallows under the sun.

He reached the other side and began picking his way back upstream, his Tevas leaving runnels that darkened the stone. He was off the mountain now, had crossed the border and was looking on from the other side. To his right he could just make out the peak of Harper through the birches and poplars that lined the far edge of the river. He thought of everything that lay between him and it, everything he knew was there and the one thing he hadn't found yet but was sure existed.

It had been a frustrating week. He'd finally grown tired of hoping for his father to appear in the circle of shades and had decided to stop waiting and start looking. Even if the search was fruitless, at least he was doing *something*. Each day he had stolen hours to seek out his father, sometimes in the morning before showing up at the farm soaked with dew, sometimes in the afternoon before coming home for supper. To avoid suspicion, he still joined Memère each night in the orchard. There were moments when he didn't mind being there—the quiet observations and simple recountings of his days offered a distraction—but inevitably he found himself itching to be somewhere else, imagining his father's shape across some distant field, always far away and faceless.

Whenever Aidan closed his eyes and tried to bring him closer, the figure would dissolve. Nevertheless, he was always there in Aidan's mind no matter where Aidan was—in the orchard, in the darkness of the barn, even in his dreams. It had gotten to the point where Aidan would sometimes think he saw him as he searched along the mountain, a flicker that brought a rush of hope, but then he would blink his eyes and his father would be gone, and he would know it was just his wishing.

He had been everywhere and found nothing. He had even made his way several times to the lower pasture, which lay only a few dozen yards behind these trees, in the hopes of once more seeing the boy. Maybe he would know something, provide some clue—at this point, it was the only lead he had. But the boy was never there. Nothing seemed to be working.

At least his mother was doing better these past few days. He was so distracted by his search he didn't notice it at first. Soon, though, he began to see little signs of change. She was brighter in the morning, more animated at supper, and spoke with a timbre he hadn't heard in the months since his father died, maybe even before that. At night she didn't lie back on the porch swing, but sat up as she read, the customary glass and bottle still present but hardly touched.

The other night, coming out on the porch with Memère as they set out for the orchard, the scent of her perfume made him pause. He looked down at her. She turned from her book and smiled.

"You look nice tonight," he said. "Did you get a haircut?"

"Yeah, I was in town this morning. Figured I might as well—it was getting too long anyway. You like it?"

"I guess. It's the same one you always get."

"It's a little shorter," she replied.

"What are you dressed up for?" he asked.

"I'm not dressed up," she said. "I just got tired of sitting around in the same old clothes every day. I just felt like something different."

"Okay."

"Memère's waiting. You better go," she said. She waved him on and went back to her reading. He bounced down the steps and caught up with Memère. She had gone ahead and was repositioning her gnomes into a new configuration.

"*Mes petits garçons.* Cute little buggers, aren't they?"

"Adorable," he quipped. She shot him a look. "Have you noticed Mom lately?" he asked as they headed down across the lawn. "She seems different."

"I suppose. And if you ask me, it's for the better. For a while there I was trying to decide who would win the prize for gloomiest offspring. You were winning at first, my dear. Then you got better, and she pulled ahead. Now you're both better. I chalk it up to my loving care."

"Yeah, that's it," he said sarcastically.

"Hey. There are different kinds of love," she replied, "and different ways of being kind."

He supposed she was right. He knew she was right about

his mother. It *was* good to see her coming out of her rut.

He knew for sure yesterday that things were different. He had left Donny's early, had combed the growths west of the farm before coming home an hour before supper, slipping into the house while Memère was picking wax beans in the garden. He was in his room when a knock on the door startled him from where he sat reading in his father's chair. The door opened and his mother poked her head in.

"Hi," he said, putting down his book. She came into the room and sat down on the bed.

"You busy?" she asked, her hands clasped in her lap, fingers locked together.

"Not really. Just reading."

"*The Odyssey?*" she said, leaning forward to glance at the title. "Heavy stuff."

"I suppose. Memère gave it to me."

"One of her favorites," she said with a laugh. "Used to read it to us kids at night before bed. I always thought it was kind of weird, her obsession with that book. Then I read it in college, and it seemed even weirder. Like I said, heavy stuff. I can only imagine what you would've done if *I'd* given it to you."

"I would've read it," he said defensively.

"Either way, it's nice to see you two connecting. You're probably closer to her by now than I am. She always preferred the boys. Said they were easier." There was a pause before she spoke again, and when she did, her voice was quiet, tentative. "I was wondering if you could help me out."

"Sure. With what?"

"I was thinking it might be a good idea to go out in the barn and sort through some of your father's things. And our things too. We should figure out what we need and what we don't. I was thinking about having a yard sale sometime in August, before school. The longer it sits out there, the more it'll smell."

"Okay," he whispered.

"It's supposed to rain again tonight. I don't think anything's gotten wet yet, but I don't trust that roof. There's nothing worse than mildew. Besides, it's been out there long enough. I don't see any point in waiting."

"You're right."

They walked out to the barn, which sagged against the house, and threw open the double doors, sending afternoon light into the recesses of the room. The pile of boxes still clung to the side wall, where they'd stacked them a month ago. They were dusty already, and the cobwebs had breached the edges of the pile. A few of the boxes were stained where drops had seeped through leaks in the ceiling. They both stood in the doorway for a moment looking at the pile. Then his mother strode forward and began opening boxes. He joined her, and they set to work sifting and sorting. They put all the boxes containing her books in a separate pile. Most of their clothes had already been taken in earlier, but they found their winter things and put them in another pile. Quite a few of the boxes held his father's clothes. His mother came across the first one, slicing through the packing tape with a razor and pulling out a sweater.

"I gave this to him for Christmas two years ago," she said. "He never wore it."

"Yeah, he did. I saw him wear it a few times."

"You want it? Why don't you take his clothes. They're nice clothes."

"They don't fit," he said. "They're too big."

"Maybe you'll grow into them. We'll bring them in. We can put them in the spare bedroom upstairs. You can go through them later if you'd like."

"All right."

They continued sorting through the boxes, his mother moving faster the further along they got. The things neither of them wanted or needed they set aside—dishes, flatware, vases, framed prints—everything went into its own pile to be tagged and sold. It made him uneasy seeing all these objects out of context. It seemed as if they were going through some other family's things, and he felt somehow guilty, like an intruder, like a robber.

At one point he picked up a small box. He had expected it to be full of books and was startled by its lightness. It was more solid than the others, its cardboard a thick brown, devoid of any markings, anonymous.

"What's this?" he asked, showing it to her. She looked at it a moment.

"You can set that aside—that's my stuff. Just a few papers and things. Put it over there. I'll take it up in a minute."

He set it down where she pointed, then went back to the pile. Soon everything was sorted. All that remained were a few objects too big to have been boxed up, mostly his father's toys.

"Put the golf bag in with the yard sale pile," she said.

"You want to sell his clubs?"

"Your father always hated golf. He pretended to like it, but he hated it."

He heaved the bag over his shoulder and dropped it next to a box of china. The clubs rattled as they hit the ground.

"What about these?" she asked as he came back over. She handed him a couple fishing poles and a tackle box. "You don't really fish, do you?"

"We used to," he said. "I used to. With him."

"Well, do you think you'll use them now? I'm sure we could sell those pretty easy around here."

He gazed at them for a moment, light and balanced in each hand. "Yeah," he said suddenly. "I'll use them. I want to keep them."

"Okay. Just checking."

When they had finished sorting, they carried the boxes of clothes and the other things they wanted to save into the house and placed them in the empty bedroom upstairs. The yard sale pile they wrapped with a blue plastic tarp. They left the heavy boxes of books in the barn covered with another tarp. She told him she'd go through them separately later.

"I'm glad that's done," she said as they swung shut the double doors. "Nice to have it taken care of."

She makes it sound like everything just disappeared, he thought. He watched the shadows close in on the covered piles as the doors came together. *All we've done is stick it someplace else.*

But he wasn't about to tell her that. Nor was he about to question her good mood. Lyndon Institute had called earlier in the week to let her know she'd been hired. Maybe that was it. Or maybe she was just moving on. New job, new place—everything was different, but in some ways nothing had really changed. Regardless, it was one less distraction. He could stop worrying about her now and focus on his search.

In spite of his anxiety about reopening the remnants of their old life, a part of him had hoped that going through his father's things would give him some kind of epiphany, present a clue or feeling of direction. It hadn't. All he'd been left with were sore arms and a couple fishing poles.

And so this morning he had decided he needed a break, if only for a few hours. After breakfast, seeing the poles leaning in the corner of the kitchen, he decided to go fishing, get down to the river and clear his head. Donny had given him the day off, and his mother had left for the day. Even though it was Saturday, she wanted to get into her classroom and start getting organized before school. Memère was puttering around somewhere outside. He grabbed one of the poles, checked the line and reel, and then rummaged in the tackle box, pulling out a few lures he thought he might use. He put them in an Altoids tin, which he stuck in his pocket. Then he hopped on his bike and coasted down the mountain, steering with one hand, grasping his pole with the other, past Donny's farm, past the newly fenced-in field with its small herd of heifers and the bull standing stocky and firm in the middle of the pasture, all the way down to the bridge. He tucked his bike under the abutment and began fishing his way upstream against the current.

The waters quieted now as he reached the pool. Slinking across the pebbles to the edge of the water, he unhooked his lure from the eyelet and made a tentative cast up toward the head of the pool, where a small waterfall rushed down between two rocks, feeding the pool with a frothing swirl. His initial casts had been clumsy—it had been a couple years—but he quickly got back into the rhythm of it, and his release now was smooth. He reeled in, feeling the Panther Martin vibrate with an even speed as it spun, invisible beneath the surface. He had already been fishing for an hour and had caught nothing. He had had a few tiny strikes downstream, but his reflexes were slow and he hadn't been able to set the hook in time.

His first cast into the pool brought no results, so he cast again, and then again. Over and over he cast, dropping the lure into every corner with no luck. Maybe he was doing something wrong. He tried to imagine what his father would advise. They had fished this river and the surrounding lakes together in past summers, and his father had always caught at least a few trout. Even in the most unlikely places, the shallowest pools or riffles, he could draw a strike. It was the only thing his father really got excited about on the rare occasions they came up to the Northeast Kingdom and—when Aidan stopped to think about it—was one of the only things they'd ever really done together.

Early on, the trips were disasters. Aidan was young, just learning to cast, and his father was impatient. The results were usually tangled lines, snagged hooks, and lots of yelling and crying. When Aidan got a little older, things went a little more smoothly, though there was always tension as he bristled under his father's constant corrections. Then there was the squeamishness. Aidan refused for the longest time to bait the hook—the idea of impaling the squiggling worm was more than he could handle, and his father scolded him for it.

"If you want to be a fisherman, you've got to be willing to do these things yourself," he'd say.

"Why can't I use a lure like you?"

"I told you. You're not old enough yet. You don't have the skill. Now just hook the worm."

"I don't want to. You do it," he'd reply, and each time, grumbling, his father would.

Aidan remembered the first time he caught a trout. He was ten. It wasn't anything big—maybe seven or eight inches—but it felt huge at the time as he jerkily reeled it in, his rod tip bobbing. He brought it in close and then pulled the trout out of the water, so that it hung suspended in the air, writhing and spinning at the end of the line. He froze in amazement, watching it twist and sparkle in the sun, while his father shouted behind him to swing it over onto the bank before it could free itself. At last he swiveled and heaved it into the bushes, where his father pounced on it and, after a momentary struggle, unhooked it and brought it over, beaming. Holding it by the lower jaw, his father dunked it in the river to rinse off the sand and leaves and then presented it to Aidan. Aidan stared at it in wonder. It seemed small in his father's hands, its gills working against the air, its body shivering with spasms every few seconds.

"Okay," his father said, "now you've got to break its neck."

He'd seen his father do it plenty of times, grasping the upper lip and pulling back the head in a fast, firm motion that left only a momentary quiver. It never occurred to him he'd have to do it himself—until now.

"Can't we just put it in the bag?" he pleaded.

"You can't do that, Aidan," his father scolded. "It'll just suffocate. You don't want it to suffer, do you? Do it fast. It won't feel a thing."

Aidan hesitated. "Let's just let it go."

"Come on! It's your first trout. Don't you want to show it to Pepère?"

"I don't care," he said.

His father turned and tossed it into the current with a flick of his hand. Aidan watched with a sudden pang of regret as it hit the water and disappeared. His father leaned down and took the pole from Aidan, reeled in the line, and gave it back to him.

"Go up to the house," he ordered. "If you can't do the job, you've got no business being here."

"What about you?" Aidan asked.

"I've got more fishing to do," he said. "Let me know when you're ready to learn to do it right." He briskly strode upstream, leaving Aidan standing on the bank.

Aidan did eventually learn to do it right, though it took him a long time to get used to the motion of killing, to not shiver whenever he felt the crunch of the spine beneath his fingers.

His line was slack now, floating on the surface of the pool. He realized he'd stopped reeling and had let the lure sink all the way to the bottom. Afraid it might get snared on some rock in the depths, he twitched the line and had begun reeling in again when a sudden yank snapped the line taut and the tip of his pole bent into a heavy arch. The line whined as it pulled away from the reel, drawn out by the strength and weight of the trout. With trembling fingers he tightened the drag and then began to reel in, lifting the rod tip to apply more pressure. "Stay on, stay on!" he whispered as he played the trout back and forth across the pool. Finally he saw it, emerging from the darkness, huge beneath the surface as it struggled into the shallows, fighting against the line.

With a final heave Aidan brought it up onto the shore. It contorted for a moment across the pebbles before going still, as if trying to make sense of the alien world it found itself in, gathering strength for a renewed battle. Before it could flop again, he pinned it against the ground, marveling at the size. It had to be well over a foot long, thick in the belly, its gold and red speckles bright against the dark skin. Its underside glowed a deep orange. It was a native trout, not one of the stocked fish with their pale white bellies. He had seen bigger fish before, but none so big in this river. *How long has it lived in this pool?* Aidan wondered. He picked it up, feeling its weight in his hands. Its gills pulsed, its mouth opened and closed gently. Holding it underneath with one hand, he took the other and curled his fingers beneath the roof of its mouth and pulled back, wincing. Its top teeth bit into his hand as he applied more pressure. He had to yank back as hard as he could in order to finally break the solid back of the trout. It gave one last shudder and then went still.

Holding it by the jaw, he splashed his free hand in the water and brought it out, examining the pricks along his fingers where the trout's teeth had just broken the skin. His heart was still pounding, and in his adrenaline rush he felt no pain. He looked back down at the trout. Blood had begun seeping from the gills, running down the sides of the fish and dropping dark onto the rocks. For a minute he just stared at the trout in awe, watching the tiny rivulets of blood brilliant in the light filtering down through the high leaves, mixing with the sunset tones of the belly. A shiver broke him from his stare. As he bent down to rinse off the trout another flash of color caught his eye, and he turned to look downstream.

The boy was standing twenty yards away, where Aidan had crossed, staring into the water, his auburn hair bright even in the shade of the trees.

"Hey!" Aidan cried out. "Wait!"

At the sound of Aidan's voice, the boy looked up, then turned and disappeared into the trees.

Leaving his pole, Aidan scrambled across the rocks lining the bank, trying not to slip in his sandals, still carrying the trout. He made it back to his crossing point and scanned the far bank, breathing hard and trembling. The boy was nowhere to be seen. He rushed into the river and waded toward the other side, trying to keep his eye on the spot he'd last seen the figure. Halfway across he lost his footing. He plunged into the water, gasping as he struggled to get upright. When he got back on his feet, the trout was gone. He searched the ripples below him, finally spotting it a dozen feet away. It floated on its back, its fins spread wide by the flow, revolving downstream. He let it go and pitched back toward the bank, half swimming, half crawling in the current until he reached the other side and dragged himself onto the shore.

With water dripping onto his face and into his eyes, his clothes stuck fast to his body, and his Tevas squishing under him, he plunged into the woods, pushing aside the branches and twigs that slapped against him, stinging his skin. He came out on the other side—nearly running into the electric fence he'd helped put up last week—and frantically searched the field, squinting against the sun. Aside from the Holsteins, the pasture was empty.

Then, there he was—halfway across the field, right in the middle, standing next to the bull, reaching out as if to pet it.

"Stop!" Aidan screamed. The bull raised its head, pricking up its ears at his cry, but the boy moved on again, skipping toward the far side. He watched him get farther away, desperate to follow but afraid to take the shortest way across, which would bring him near the bull, now plodding toward him. Cursing, he moved laterally, following the fence line to the corner of the pasture, then turned uphill, trying to keep his eyes on the figure. By the time Aidan was halfway up the side, the boy had reached the far end. As Aidan hurried along the outside of the fence, wading through the grass and pricker bushes that scratched and clawed at his legs, he saw that the boy had stopped just at the fence, still on the inside, his back to Aidan, standing motionless, as if he was waiting. As Aidan rounded the last corner and bore down—now only thirty yards away—the boy ducked under the fence and disappeared into another set of trees.

Aidan followed the boy in a meandering line all the way up the mountain. At times the figure would seem to flicker and almost disappear; sometimes he would disappear entirely behind a tree or around the corner of a bend. Aidan would stop, double over in exhaustion, try to catch his breath and resist the urge to give up. Then the boy would appear again, swinging from the low-hanging limb of a tree or leaping between the rocks that lined the side of a meadow road. Aidan no longer dared call out to him—every time he did, the boy only picked up speed and got farther away. There seemed to be no pattern to the boy's wanderings except for an indirect but always upward course. At one point they passed near the farm, then they were in sight of Memère's house, then they were above it. At times Aidan would see the boy far in the distance, and at others he would seem so close that Aidan was sure he could catch him with one good burst of speed. But he never could. Each time he tried, the elusive shape would slip away into a cluster of pines or down over a bank.

Aidan finally lost him for good in a huddle of white birches far up the face of Harper. Tracing the figure to the isolated copse, he had felt a surge of triumph, but as he stumbled into the shade of the trees, gasping as he leaned against a smooth papery trunk, he found that he had lost him once again. He waited for several minutes to catch his breath, wiping the sweat from his forehead and neck, hoping the boy might appear, but the grove remained empty. Finally, his legs and arms scratched and bloody from the chase, he passed through to the other side. Caught up in the pursuit, he had forgotten where he was, but coming back into the sun, he suddenly knew. To his right, the familiar line of ridges spread out 180 degrees. In front of him lay Southlook, its gravestones resting in uneven rows.

He turned around and stumbled down toward the house.

The sun disappeared behind a dark band of clouds racing in from the west as he made his way back. The air was heavy, and in the distance he thought he could even see brief flashes of lightning in the purple clouds. *It will rain again tonight*, he thought.

He suddenly remembered he'd left his bike and fishing pole down at the river. They'd have to stay there until tomorrow—he was too tired to go get them.

A strange noise caught his attention as he crossed the last field above Memère's. At first he thought it was thunder, but as he continued down the hill it grew louder and sharper. He realized it was coming from behind the house.

Pop! Pop! Pop, pop, pop! The sound of gunfire echoed up the mountain.

He broke into a run, letting his momentum carry him on legs wobbly from exhaustion. Coming up on the side of the house, he pitched around the corner into the backyard and stopped. His mother was standing near the house facing the backyard, both arms extended before her, a pistol in her hands.

Bang! Bang, bang! Bang, bang, bang!

Aidan plugged his ears and followed the direction of her aim. At the far end of the back lawn stood a bench lined with plastic gallon milk jugs. As the gun crashed, one of the jugs jerked and leaped off the bench, water exploding from both sides. It had barely hit the ground when the one next to it followed suit. His mother moved on down the line, taking out three of the five containers before emptying the clip. Aidan strode toward her as she popped the clip out and clicked open the action, a wreath of blue smoke curling around her.

"What the hell are you doing?" he called out.

"Hi, Aidan," she said, bringing a hand up to wipe her eyes. Her eyes were red and puffy. He could tell she'd been crying. "Good Lord! What happened to you?" she asked, looking at the scratches on his arms and legs. He ignored her question.

"What's with the gun?" he demanded.

"It's a Browning. Nine millimeter. You like it?" She offered him the handle, barrel pointing toward the ground. Frowning, he shook his head.

"It was your father's," she said, sighing. She placed the pistol on the arm of the Adirondack chair beside her and began pulling cartridges from an open box on the seat, snapping them one at a time into the clip. "I had stuck it in a box and found it this afternoon."

"I've never seen it before," he said.

"Of course you haven't, sweetie. We hid it. Your father hid it. I had forgotten all about it until we packed up the house."

"Since when do you shoot?"

"I used to shoot a lot. Your father and I both did—mostly

when we were dating. It was one of the only things I was better at than him. Used to drive him crazy." She shook her head. "I always liked shooting. Good way to blow off steam."

"Is that what you're doing? Blowing off steam?" he said, gesturing toward the shattered plastic remains of the jugs.

"No. I just wanted to try it out. It's been a while," she said.

"You're crying," he said.

She wiped her eyes again. "I'm not crying. It's the smoke—gunpowder always irritates my eyes." She paused and gave him a look. "Aidan, does this bother you?"

"I don't care. But I can't imagine Memère likes it, what with the noise and all."

She laughed. "Your grandmother's a better shot than I am. Who do you think I learned from?"

"You're both crazy," he muttered. He pushed by her and went back around onto the porch.

Bang! Bang! Bang!

He sighed and sat down on the swing. The sky was overcast now. He could see Memère down in the garden, her back to him as she hunched over a row. His foot kicked something underneath the swing, and he looked down to see an open box. It was the small, sturdy box his mother had had him set aside yesterday. Picking it up, he stood and glanced through the windows of the kitchen into the backyard. His mother was still out there, blasting away.

He sat back down and held the box on his lap. Pushing aside the flaps, he gazed in. On top were a leather pouch and a small case that contained a gun-cleaning kit. He set them aside and peeked back in. The rest of the box was mostly letters. His hand hovered for a moment over the box. Finally he began picking through. Most of them were addressed to his mother here on the mountain, sent by his father from UVM, in Burlington. A few were ones she had written to him in return. Aidan looked back down at the garden—Memère was still bent over, pulling weeds. Heart pounding, he pulled out one of his father's letters and opened it. It felt so strange to see his father's handwriting, the tight and angled letters so oddly familiar. For a moment he just stared at the page, absorbing the lines as a single block, like some abstract design. The letter was short. He read quickly.

May 13, 1980

Patty—

What's up babe? Things are fine here. I've been working my ass off this week but exams are almost done and pretty soon I can put the semester behind me. I've been thinking about what you asked me and I'm sorry but I'll have to pass. I didn't even go to my own prom. Besides, I'm in college now. It'd just be too weird. Why don't you take Donny instead—he could use a night out with a hot chick. Ha, ha. Anyway, I know you'll understand.

Once again, I won't be coming home this summer. I've got a place on Church St. with a couple guys. I know you

wanted me to, but I just can't handle the idea of working
for the old man. You know I can't stand that sonofabitch,
especially after senior year. I've got a better idea—you come
here. There's plenty of jobs and you can stay with me. Don't
worry—you're a big girl now, you can handle B-town.
Besides, you'll be coming here next fall anyway. Why not
get a leg up? Let me know and I'll come pick you up.

Love, Tim

Aidan folded the letter and returned it to the box. There were plenty of others, but he didn't feel like reading any more. He wondered how his mother had felt first reading the letter. He wondered if she'd joined his father like he'd asked.

He continued pawing through the box. At the bottom, buried under the letters, was a small pile of photos. He pulled them out and started flicking through. They were older shots, some of his parents dressed in outdated clothes, and others of people he didn't know—friends of his mother's probably. Then one photo caught his eye. He did a double take, dropping the box, sending the letters and pictures scattering across the floor.

It was an old photo, small and square, its colors nearly faded. In the picture were three little kids. The girl was in the center, both arms around the shoulders of the two boys on either side. All of them were laughing. There was a haunting familiarity to their faces, and despite the distorting filter of youth and the blurriness of the image, he knew who they were. Turning the photo over confirmed it: "Timmy, Patty, and Donny—1970" said the unfamiliar script.

But it wasn't the crinkling smiles or the dissonance of time that made his head spin and his hands shake as he stared. It was the image of that one boy on the left, that boy next to his mother and his uncle, that boy with the auburn hair.

Bang, bang, bang, bang, bang!

The shots rang out again, making him jump, jolting him from his shock. He stuck the photo in his pocket and scrambled to his knees, shoving the fallen letters and pictures back into the box. Glancing up, he saw Mémère rising to her feet. He returned the leather case and cleaning kit to their proper place on top, closed the box, and tucked it back under the swing.

THIRTEEN

Creeping past a pile of rusted, forgotten sap buckets and into the edges of the sugar bush, Aidan glimpsed through the pillars of maples spread out across the mountain slope. The sun would be setting soon, and it was dark in the shadow of the nearly unbroken canopy suspended above the trunks. He froze for a moment to watch the murky figure drop over a rise and disappear, then renewed his stalking with a practiced motion, picking one foot up and placing it down softly before lifting the other. Last autumn's leaves, yellowed by winter, quiet in decay, afforded him almost the same silence of his prey, making no more than a papery whisper as he stole across them.

For the last ten days, he'd been following his father. It had begun at the river with the little boy on the bank and had now led him here to the sugar bush high up on the mountain, east of Southlook, in the far corner of the settled face of Harper. But somehow he felt that it wouldn't end here—it would just go on and on, as if it had always been this way. Ever since seeing that photo of the three of them, ever since realizing the strange boy was the one he'd been seeking all along, it seemed like he was journeying through a long, glass tunnel, his vision fixed on the ever-fleeing figure at the far end, with everything around it a blur, driven on by the questions burning in his brain. They accumulated like logs tossed on a fire, each new doubt, each new fear, catching fire from those beneath it, fueling his desire.

Foremost in his mind was the mystery of form. Over and over he wondered why his father appeared in the shape of his childhood self. The other shades Aidan had met in the orchard were static, seemingly frozen as they were just before death. Why should his father be any different? More disturbing was the fact that now his father's ghost was changing. During the first days of the pursuit he had seen his father only a few times, and each time his father was the little boy in the photo, equally blurry, flickering in and out of sight, appearing for a few minutes at a time. But then the figure began to change, growing taller and losing the red tint of the hair, which had now faded to the more familiar brown. These last few days his father had taken on the shape of a man. His boyhood clothes—the cutoff jeans and green T-shirt—were now replaced by a long, dark overcoat, his neck wrapped in a black scarf that made Aidan sweat all the more as he followed the shade through the final days of July. It was the kind of coat his father had worn to the office, the kind he'd worn those winter mornings when he dropped

Aidan off at school before heading into Boston. Aidan wondered if it was the one he'd had on that last cold night in November.

The only thing that didn't change was the ghost's constant retreat. It seemed that no matter how fast Aidan moved, the figure was always ahead of him, sometimes near, sometimes far, but always before him with his back turned. There were moments when Aidan even wondered if it was really his father at all. But then he would see the familiar stride—driven and sure—or some recognizable gesture, like the flicking back of the hair, and Aidan would know that it was him.

What caused his father to morph each day as he wandered up and down the mountain? What was the source of this bizarre evolution from boy to man? His father seemed so restless, first as a little child, and even more so now as a man, no longer skipping and playing along the fieldstone walls but striding with eager steps. The more Aidan followed, the more he began to fear for him. What if he was in some kind of pain? But that couldn't be—his father had always been so sure, so confident in his success, had always epitomized in Aidan's mind everything a happy man should be. All Aidan wanted was the chance to finally catch him and hold him, discover the reason for his appearance and maybe even help him, if only his father would let him.

These questions pushed him on, and he spent every moment he could out looking. Even when he wasn't wandering, he found himself thinking constantly about the search, running over and over in his mind images of the shifting ghost, planning new routes, trying to make sense of his failure.

It was starting to catch up with him. Donny first said something a few days ago. Aidan had begun helping with the morning milkings, showing up at six o'clock to pitch grain to the cows and clean out the stalls while Donny moved up and down the line of Holsteins with the vacuum hoses that pumped the milk back to the bulk tank in the parlor. The early hours didn't bother Aidan—it allowed him to leave earlier, gave him more time to search. That morning, though, a hand shaking his shoulder startled Aidan. He turned to see Donny frowning.

"What's the problem?" his uncle said, shouting above the hiss and drone of the motorized pump.

"What do you mean?" Aidan cried back. His uncle pointed at the ground by Aidan's feet, and Aidan looked down to see his rubber boot covered in a pile of grain that had fallen from the scoop dangling in his hand. "Oh," he said.

"Goddamit!" Donny said. "Are you on friggin' drugs or something?"

"Don't be crazy."

"Well, that's the fifth time I've caught you zoning out in the last three days. You better mind what you're doing, or you're gonna get hurt. A barn ain't no place to fool around."

The next day his uncle's prediction came true as, once again, Aidan lost track of the moment remembering last night's search, lulled by the susurration of the pump and constant lowing of the cows. Not paying attention, he had gotten too close to the rear of a particularly edgy Holstein in the midst of being milked and had startled her. He didn't know what he had done to spook her. All he knew was that one moment he was seeing his father dashing across the upper meadow, and the next he was lying on his back in a pile of steaming manure gasping for air. Donny rushed over and helped Aidan as he struggled to his feet, shaken but not seriously hurt.

"Christ, she kicked you good," his uncle observed.

"Yeah," Aidan panted, trying to wipe the manure off as best he could.

"Maybe she knocked some sense into you."

"Let's hope," Aidan said.

His uncle frowned and shook his head. "Go home, Aidan," he said.

"What?"

"You ain't no use to me like this. Last thing I need is for you to end up with a broken jaw. Or worse. Your mother'd have my hide."

Aidan left, sore and somewhat embarrassed. Still, it gave him the rest of the day to search. After that he began ditching work, showing up to help Donny with chores and then conjuring up some excuse to leave. In spite of the scolding he'd given Aidan earlier, Donny had been unusually upbeat lately and didn't give him a hard time. It had gotten to the point where, these last two days, Aidan stopped even bothering to make excuses.

He had even begun skipping out on Memère in the evening, forgoing the orchard ritual. He used Angela as an excuse, telling both Memère and his mother he was going over to her house, though in truth he didn't know where she lived. He hadn't even called her. He knew he should, a part of him wanted to, but every time he picked up the phone, something kept him from dialing—a fear of entanglement, of anything that would distract him from his quest, even something pleasurable, especially something pleasurable—and he would find himself staring at the pad of numbers as if they were hieroglyphics, listening to the distant dial tone before finally hanging up. Both Memère and his mother seemed pleased enough by the lie that they let him go without question, and he would hop on his bike and coast down the driveway, then, ditching his bike, turn off onto the path he'd planned for the night as soon as he was out of sight. He preferred searching in the evening. It was cooler, and there was something about the potency of dusk that made him feel more hopeful. Like tonight.

Weaving through the maples, he came to the top of the rise where he'd last seen the figure and scanned the slope before him. It was quiet in these woods, with no wind to rustle the leaves like in the orchard. The only sound was the song of the thrushes calling to one another in watery notes between the trees. Then—there he was, below Aidan, to the right, hands in his pockets, shoulders hunched as he ambled along.

Aidan slipped down the incline and headed toward the spirit. The enormous grove, long abandoned by the sugarers, was interlaced with a faded network of roads, and Aidan turned onto one as he pursued the dark shape ahead. He hurried faster now in the hope of catching up, springing over the long, dead trunks that had fallen into the road, more-slender maples that hadn't grown fast enough to reach the sun and had been killed by the other trees. One trunk had fallen from higher up, all the way across to the other bank to form a bridge, and when Aidan rose from ducking beneath it, his father had disappeared. He stopped and waited. At this point, he knew from experience, the figure would return.

Telémakhos had it easy, Aidan thought. *He had Athena to help him out.* At first Aidan had thought of the young man as a sort of kindred spirit, but in many ways their journeys were so different. Early in the epic Telémakhos discovered his father was alive but had no idea where he was. Aidan's father, on the other hand, was dead, and Aidan knew where to find him—he just couldn't catch him. Aidan was still reading each night and was closing in on the story's end. Odysseus had returned to Ithaka in disguise, and Aidan couldn't help but feel a little envy as he watched the hero and his reunited son conspiring together, preparing to slaughter the suitors who had violated their home. Last night Aidan read in awe as Penelope—the ever-faithful wife who had struggled for years, holding out on the hope her husband would return alive—descended to the hall to question the disguised Odysseus. There he was, right before her in the shape of an old beggar. Though she gave no sign of recognition, Aidan suspected she knew. Perhaps she remained silent to protect him from the suitors, or perhaps she kept it hidden from herself because the knowledge was too incredible to bear.

The shade reappeared once more from behind a maple. It turned and began to drift downhill. Aidan left the road and headed after it, coming in at an angle.

Crack!

He hadn't noticed the fallen limb half-buried by the leaves until his foot was already through it. The sound rang through the woods like a rifle shot, and he froze in horror. For a moment the woods went completely dead. The thrushes' song ceased, and everything was still but for the ghost, which seemed to pick up speed before vanishing over another bank. Aidan sighed and began to follow, when a blur of movement to the side made him pause again. He looked back to his right. Far away through the trees he saw the black shape standing where he'd passed earlier. His father had pulled this trick before—disappearing and reappearing a moment later at a distant spot—and Aidan turned in the new direction.

But something was different as he picked his way back to the road and started toward the ghost. The dark figure wasn't running away. It just stood there, almost as if it was waiting. It was still far away, but as Aidan closed in he could see it begin moving toward him on the road. His heart began to pound, and he picked up speed. *This is it*, he thought. *This is the moment.*

Aidan was only fifty feet away when he stopped. The figure continued toward him, but as it came closer Aidan could see something was wrong. The black clothes clung tight to the shape, different from the long drape of the over-coat his father had been wearing, and the shade was too short, with black hair.

It was Eve.

She stepped closer into view and stopped twenty feet away, and Aidan could see that familiar grin stretched across her face, playful and inviting, her pale eyes narrowing into slits.

"No!" he hissed. "You're supposed to be him."

Her mouth seemed to shape words, but no sound emerged. He looked frantically around. Had he been chasing her all along? If not, how long had she been following him? If his father got away because of this . . . but no, there he was—a dark-coated flicker among the trees below. Aidan looked back at Eve and glared. Her smile faded, her lips parted.

Abandoning stealth, he tore off running down the slope.

Bobbing between the trunks, Aidan raced down the hill after his father's ghost. It flitted from tree to tree, disappearing behind one maple only to step out from another farther ahead. Every few moments he glanced behind him to see Eve still following him, never moving but somehow never far away. The slope was leveling off, and Aidan could make out a building ahead through the trees. He ran out of the maples and into a clearing in time to see the shade duck through the open door of an old sugarhouse, its windows broken, its faded boards warped and stained with mold. Aidan stopped for a moment to catch his breath. His father was cornered.

He ran up to the doorway and dashed inside.

The building was empty.

Aidan scanned every corner of the shack, but the shade was nowhere to be found. All that remained were some pitted buckets and an old boiler pan, rusted and leaning over a wood stove. The stove door was open, revealing a bed of white ashes.

He kicked a sap bucket, sending it skittering among the leaves that littered the floor, and left.

The sun had set; twilight had overtaken the forest. He peered through the growing darkness, but his father was gone, and inside Aidan knew he wouldn't see him anymore tonight. Even Eve had disappeared. Apparently she, too, had given up the chase. Maybe she wanted the same thing he did—an opportunity to connect, a moment of intimacy between the living and the dead.

He left the clearing and continued south. He was near the bottom edge of the sugar bush and, following the road, it didn't take long to leave the woods behind. He set out for the house with heavy steps.

Why was his father avoiding him? Or if he wasn't, then what was he running from? There had to be something Aidan didn't know about, some trouble from the past, some dark secret that pushed his father from place to place, that pushed him from one form to another. It had to be something besides Aidan himself, some other reason why his father refused to come to him, to answer his calls. If he'd learned anything since moving up to the Kingdom, it was that there was more to his father than he'd ever known, or at least had ever bothered to think about. He was beginning to wonder if he had ever really known the man at all. It seemed like he understood his uncle better than he ever had his father. And why shouldn't he? He'd probably spent more time with Donny in the last six weeks than he had with his father in the last six years. Maybe this was what had kept driving him out into the fields and woods each day for the last two and a half weeks.

If there was some secret, he would find it. Then, and maybe only then, he could reach the ghost. He couldn't interrogate Memère—she would quickly figure out his reasons for probing. He would have to ask his mother and Donny. If anyone would know, they would.

He picked up his pace now, hurried home in the dying light.

Aidan went in through the back door and paused. Everything

was quiet. There were no lights on anywhere, and dusk had reduced the kitchen to shadows.

"Mom?" he called out, turning on the lights.

When there was no reply, he pushed through the screen door onto the porch. His mother's car was not in the driveway. Turning to go back inside, he jumped at the sight of his grandmother seated on the swing.

"Hope I didn't startle you too much," Memère said.

"You just come from the orchard?" he asked.

"I've been back awhile now. Didn't stay long tonight," she said. Her voice sounded strange—precise and oddly formal, as if the words carried the weight of some important matter—and he suddenly felt nervous.

"Where's Mom?"

"Looks like she's out. The question is—where have you been?"

"Over to Angela's. I told you before," he said, sitting down on the porch steps with his back to her.

"Oh yes, Angela. She stopped by—you just missed her. We had a nice chat, though."

A sick feeling rose from his stomach. He desperately tried to think of some excuse, but it was too late. For a moment the only sound was the ambient call of the crickets. He wondered if she was waiting on purpose, taking pleasure from his squirming, relishing her advantage.

"She's a nice girl," she said at last. "Lots of spirit. Said she saw you a couple weeks ago and hadn't heard from you yet.

Wanted to know if you'd like to get together and go hiking. I took the liberty of saying yes for you. I trust you don't mind."

"What?" he shouted, turning around to face her where she sat silhouetted against the kitchen lights.

"She's a nice girl, Aidan. A real looker, too. Not often around here will a chance like this come your way."

"You shouldn't have done that, Memère."

"Why not?" she snapped.

"Because it's my business," he snapped back. "Besides, I've got other plans."

"Other plans, eh? That what you call it?"

Aidan withered. So she knew. Of course she'd figure it out.

"I told you before to stay away from her, young man. She may be beautiful, but there's a darkness to her that chills even me sometimes."

"What are you talking about?" he demanded. She had just made a date for him with this girl, and now she was telling him to stay away? Besides, Angela was anything but dark. Then it clicked; just as his grandmother spoke, the image of the pale girl approaching him in the sugar bush flashed through his mind.

"Eve!" Memère cried, rising from her swing and looming over him. "She hasn't come to feed for the last few days. I know you've been with her, Aidan, so don't lie to me. I don't know what kind of a hold she's got over you, but you'd be smart to break away from her. You're a young man with natural urges, so I don't fault you, but whatever she's offered you, it isn't real."

Aidan jumped to his feet to face her, horrified by what she was implying. "I haven't been with Eve," he exclaimed. "I don't want anything from her!"

"Then explain yourself, mister," she demanded. "Where have you been?"

She wanted to know? Fine—he would tell her. "I've been looking for *him*!" he shouted. "I've been looking for Dad!"

She went still at his words. In the dim light Aidan could see the shock creeping across her face. "Of course," she whispered, more to herself than him. "Why didn't I guess that? You said you wouldn't, but I should have known the temptation would be too great." She sat back down on the swing and sighed. "I thought we had agreed it was a bad idea, Aidan. It's a fool's errand. You're doing yourself no good trying to chase after something that isn't there."

"But I've seen him, Mémère!" he said, coming over and kneeling before her.

"What?" she exclaimed, taking his hands. "Where? Tell me."

"All over the mountain. I've been chasing him for more than a week now."

"How do you know it's him?"

"I *know*. I know it's him. I've seen him."

"Amazing," she whispered.

"But he won't let me near. And he keeps changing. First he was a little boy. Then he began to grow. He keeps getting older. Why does he keep changing? What's wrong with him?"

"I don't know," she said slowly, shaking her head. She repeated the words, as if amazed by the novelty of the admission. "I don't know. But I don't like it, Aidan. I don't like it at all."

"What does it mean?" he asked again, choking back the anguish rising in his voice.

"I don't know," she repeated more forcefully. "But I suppose it makes sense. Your father always was a restless man. Never could sit still."

"There has to be more to it than that," he replied. "There's got to be something that happened to him. Maybe when he was growing up? Something bad?"

"I liked your father, Aidan. And I always felt I understood him pretty well—certainly better than his stubborn ass of a father ever did. Christ, once he and Patrice starting dating, he spent more time here than down on the farm. But I don't know of anything that ever happened. If there were any skeletons in the closet, he kept them hidden. As for him leaving the Kingdom, I think he just wanted something different. Probably felt like he didn't belong here, that he was made for bigger things. He wouldn't be the first. Or the last."

"I just don't understand," he said. "I don't understand *any* of it!"

She sighed again and squeezed his hands. "I know you want answers, Aidan, but I can't give them to you. I'm just an old woman content to spend these quiet evenings with her friends, happy enough with what they offer, happy enough to give what I can. There's nothing more to it than that. There shouldn't be."

"Maybe that's enough for you, but I want more," he said, gazing down at the weathered hands clasping his own.

"Perhaps that's the trouble."

His eyes snapped up at her words.

"Maybe your father's here *because* of you. Maybe *you* summoned him."

He pulled his hands away and stood up. "So this is my fault? I'm the reason he's out there wandering? Suffering?" he demanded.

"Well, you may be suffering, but you don't know he is. And I'm not saying you did it on purpose, dear. But maybe underneath, from out of your pain and desire, you brought him back to this place. Let me ask you something—have you ever asked yourself why you're chasing him to begin with? What it is you want from him?"

Aidan fought back tears. The image of Odysseus trying to embrace his mother's shade, his arms each time closing on air, rose in his mind. "I don't know. I just want to be able to see him again, to talk to him. We never got to say good-bye."

"Good-bye? That's all? Come on, Aidan, there's more to it than that. I don't think you want to say good-bye. You want more—you said it yourself."

"Oh really," he snapped. "Then, why don't *you* tell me what it is I want."

"I won't, Aidan. You need to figure it out for yourself. I'll just say this—if you really want to say good-bye to your father, then you'll stop chasing him all over this christly mountain. Until you do, you'll have no peace and neither will he. Let him go, Aidan."

The glow of headlights appeared in the yard. Aidan turned to watch the shifting light brighten.

"Don't forget tomorrow," Memère said. "Six-thirty at the end of Parrish Road. Angela will be waiting. And Aidan . . . "

He looked back to her in the murky light of the porch.

"Best to put aside the dead and start thinking about the living."

What about you? he thought, but said nothing.

A moment later the Honda crept into the driveway and settled to a stop. His mother killed the headlights and the yard returned to darkness. She emerged from the car and came toward the porch, humming to herself. Aidan recognized it as his grandmother's tune. He strode to the edge of the porch steps and folded his arms. She stopped at the bottom and looked up to where he stood waiting.

"Where have you been?" he demanded.

"At the movies. There wasn't anything worth renting, so I decided to catch an early show."

"Well," he snapped, "I'm glad somebody's having fun around here."

"What's your problem?" she retorted. When he didn't answer, she turned to her mother, who shrugged her shoulders.

"He's a little distracted," Memère said.

"Things not going well with that girl? What's her name—Angela?" his mother asked.

"Go to hell," he muttered. "Both of you." He turned around and marched into the house. He could hear his mother yell for him to come back. He paused in the stairway at her cry before continuing up to his room.

FOURTEEN

"So where's the trailhead?" Angela asked as they stopped to rest.

"I don't know. Maybe there isn't one," Aidan replied, trying to catch his breath.

"The neighbors said there was. Or used to be."

They had met near her house, at the corner of her road, and biked all the way up to Southlook, where the main road ended. Leaving their bikes behind, they had passed the cemetery and headed through the upper pastures and groves to the edge of the thick woods that girded the summit. They moved at a steady clip, with Angela leading the way. She was in incredible shape. As he stood gasping, Aidan noticed she'd hardly broken a sweat and stood at ease in her khaki shorts and slim red tank top, the same one she'd worn that first day he saw her. Her hair was different, though, not compacted in a bun but hanging loose to the tops of her shoulders. She noticed him watching and smiled, pulling her hair back as if she was going to put it in a ponytail, before letting it drop down again. He turned and looked away.

A small stand of poplars blocked much of the view from here, but he could make out the early evening sun through the branches. A breeze shook the limbs, shimmering the leaves that blocked the sun, setting off a tremor of sparks. He looked back to see her busily scanning the edge of the tree line for an opening that might show some path to the summit. He returned his attention below and began peering into the groves and across the fields. He was looking too, but not for any trail. All the way up the mountainside, he had been casting glances left and right, searching for the now familiar shape of his father. He had tried not to. He had tried to focus on what Angela was saying as they traveled together, but he couldn't help it. He surveyed the landscape below him. There was no movement, and he'd seen nothing on the way up. *Where is he tonight?* Aidan wondered. Maybe he was back in the sugar bush. That was where he'd seen him last.

Cold drops on the back of his neck broke his attention.

"Hey!" she said. He turned back to see her holding out a plastic bottle.

"Sorry?"

"I asked if you wanted some water." When he hesitated, she thrust the bottle closer. "Don't worry. I don't have cooties."

"I know," he said. He grabbed the bottle and took a long drink. Crystals of ice slushed together as he tilted the bottle back, and the coldness gave him a momentary head rush.

He handed the water back.

"That's good," he said.

She peered at him, her eyes narrowing the slightest bit as she examined his face. "Is this too weird for you?" she asked after a moment.

"Is what too weird?"

"Well, you never called me. You hardly said a word on the way up here. And let's face it—your grandmother basically set this up. I just want to know if you're cool with this."

"Of course I am."

"Look, all I'm saying is, well—don't do me any favors, okay?"

"Don't be silly," he said. He suddenly forgot everything and stared, as if seeing her for the first time. She was beautiful in her doubt. "Come on, let's see if we can find a trail," he invited. They turned together and headed for the woods.

"I think I saw an opening over there," she said, pointing toward a section of fir. They reached the perimeter where some branches parted to reveal a faint path. One of the trunks was marked with a splash of blue paint, a faded patch that showed they were on the right track.

"Well, at least we know *somebody's* been here before," she said, motioning to the blue blaze. She set out on the trail, and he followed.

They picked their way up the slope, brushing through the ferns that slanted across the path. It was dark in these woods; the thick branches of the evergreens shaded the trail so that the sky was hardly visible. As they made their way up, the twisting track steepened and began to meander through a series of switchbacks. The path was easy enough to follow even without the trail blazes, but Angela had eased off her earlier pace. Aidan wondered if she was slowing down for him.

"So your grandmother's pretty cool," she said, glancing back as she strode ahead. "I had fun talking to her."

"I can only imagine what she said," he snorted.

"She told me a few things," Angela replied, more quietly. She suddenly paused in the middle of the trail, and he bumped into her, coming up behind. She pushed back her hair again. "She's not like other old people," she said. "I mean—she doesn't even seem old. She looks it, but she doesn't act it. She's full of life."

"Yeah, she's something else."

"My grandmother—the one still alive—isn't anything like her. She's just sort of bitter—about everything. It's like she's just hanging around, marking time. I feel bad for her."

"That's no good," he agreed.

"I know. Life's too short." She turned and set off again. "So are you guys close?" she called back.

"Memère and I? I guess you could say that. We didn't use to be, when I was younger. I didn't see her too much—we only came up a few times a year. Truth is she used to scare me a little when I was a kid."

"Her? I can't imagine."

"Don't let her fool you. She may seem sweet on the surface, but she's tough. She has a different side to her."

"Everybody does," Angela replied.

They continued on now in silence. The trail grew even steeper and began winding around rocky protrusions as they moved closer to the top. The curve of the mountain slope disoriented Aidan. There were times when, rounding the corner of a switchback, he thought they were just about there, thought he could make out a clearing through the dwindling spruce and yellow birch, but each time it turned out to be an illusion, and the path lingered on. She had picked up the pace again, as if drawn by the promise of the summit, and he began falling behind. At one point she looked back and, seeing him struggle, stopped and waited for him to catch up. As he drew up she sat down on a boulder and let him rest.

"I think we're almost there," she said.

"God, I hope so," he gasped. "I didn't think it was this far."

"It is deceiving."

"I'm more out of shape than I thought," he said, bending over to catch his breath, then gestured toward where she sat, composed.

"Sports," she explained. "Everybody at Andover plays sports. I work out a lot too. I like the release. Keeps me from losing it, know what I mean?"

"I guess," he said.

"You work out too," she offered. "On the farm."

"It's not like this. Not usually, anyway. It's more of a slow, steady burn. Or burnout, depending how you look at it."

"At least it's useful," she replied. "You like working with your uncle?"

He straightened up, wiping the sweat from his face with the bottom of his T-shirt. "Donny's a good guy," he said, nodding. "He's a hard worker. 'Course, I think he's crazy doing what he does, trying to keep a farm together. Smartest thing would probably just be to let it die. Get out while you still can."

"Oh, I don't know," she said. "There's something to be said for what you guys do. I just think it's cool—working with the earth, being close to nature, and all that."

He laughed. "It's not that romantic. Not when you're knee deep in shit, anyway."

"Come on—there must be some parts about it you like. Otherwise, why bother?"

He thought about haying, about looking out over the upper fields in the evening when the land was smooth and rolling against the hills, and the dandelion seeds floated on the air. He thought about his uncle plying the tractor across the field with the baler in tow. He thought about his grandfather doing the same, and *his* father before that, and about what Donny had said, about the past being everywhere around them. Then Aidan thought of his father, the man who had hated everything to do with the farm, wandering alone in the woods.

"Let's go," he said. He brushed by her and took the lead. "So what about you?" he called back as they continued on the trail. "What do you do all day?"

"I read, mostly. Summer reading list from school."

"I thought you weren't going back," he said.

"I haven't decided yet," she replied. "I'm still deciding. But I figure, since I bought the books, I might as well read them."

"Anything good?"

"Sure. They're all good. Today I read *The Old Man and the Sea*."

"You read the whole thing in one day?"

"It's Hemingway. It's short."

"I know. My mom's an English teacher."

"Cool. Good book, isn't it?"

"Actually, I haven't read it," he admitted, laughing. "I was supposed to. But I never did."

"Well, you should," she scolded, giving him a push from behind. "It's about this, well, this old man, a fisherman, who goes out in this dinky boat desperate for a catch, for something, for anything to keep him going. He finally latches on to this massive marlin way down deep, and the thing drags him all over the gulf for days. Part of him knows he should just cut the line and let it go, but he can't. He's a stubborn bastard, and that fish is all he's got, basically." She spoke quickly, the words tumbling from her mouth in a rush of excitement as she hurried behind him on the trail.

"So what happens?"

"I'm not telling. Read it yourself. You can borrow it."

"Thanks, but I'm already reading something," he said.

"Oh yeah? What?" she challenged.

"*The Odyssey*. It's an epic."

"Yeah! We read that last year in English. Awesome book."

"It's pretty good," he admitted, "for poetry."

"Damn right. Great characters. I like Kalypso the best."

"Kalypso? She's one of the bad guys! She keeps Odysseus trapped on her island for years. It's her fault he didn't get home sooner."

"Yeah, but she saved him in the first place. When his boat got trashed and all his men drowned, she saved him. And she only kept him there because she loved him. Besides, she cracked me up. Like when Hermes comes and tells her she has to let Odysseus go, remember? She gets mad and totally calls the male gods on their hypocrisy. You know, how it's okay for them to have flings with mortal girls, but as soon as a goddess takes a male lover, they all flip out. Somebody needs to stand up to those guys once in a while, don't you think?"

"I guess you've got a point."

A minute later the trail took a sharp hook almost straight up around the squat tower of granite that turned out to be the summit. It rose above the stunted trees that gathered round, desperately gripping the meager soil for whatever sustenance they could get. Bare but for a boulder or two deposited by some capricious glacier long ago, the flattened top was weathered clean.

For a moment, after stumbling onto the platform, neither spoke. They just turned in circles, taking in the 360-degree view. The south-facing side had a sense of the familiar—Aidan could see the usual line of ridges, the village down in the hollow, and even a glimpse of Memère's house below through the trees. It was strange, though, to view the common sights from the perspective of this height. They were so much smaller from here, and the elevation opened up whole new rows of mountains in the distance. He recognized the farthest set in the west—the Green Mountains, with Camel's Hump toward the south, Jay Peak up north, and Mansfield in between. The east was a different story. There the Whites in New Hampshire stood massive and close, sharp, almost new in comparison with the weathered Greens in the west. He recognized Franconia Notch amid its line of peaks—the gap through which he'd come to this mountain six weeks ago. That was the last time he'd passed that way. It seemed like forever. He tried to imagine himself as he was then, traveling north through the Notch with his mother in the U-Haul, oblivious to what lay ahead, and wondered if he was even like that boy anymore. Maybe they were strangers. Maybe they were more alike than ever.

"Jesus," Angela said in awe.

"Yeah," he agreed.

He plopped down on a west-facing shelf of granite. She sat down beside him. For a few minutes they just watched the sun as it brooded, swollen and gold, above the Green Mountains. Aidan had watched plenty of sunsets throughout the summer, but this one seemed different. Normally the sun made a hasty retreat down over the hills, but tonight it lingered, as if time had stopped altogether. He cast a sidelong glance to his left, where Angela sat with her arms wrapped around her curled-up knees. Beads of perspiration had emerged along the edges of her hairline, and a single trickle of sweat traced a path down her temple and past her ear before curving along the outer edge of her cheek. It caught the evening light and shone like a vein of silver.

"Your grandmother told me, Aidan. About your father's accident. About what happened to him," she said, looking away to the hills.

He groaned and picked up a rock beside him. It was gray and indistinct, neither round nor square. He tossed it over the edge of the cliff and waited for the sound of its landing, but there was none.

"I just wanted to say I'm sorry. That's all."

"Thanks," he replied, trying to muster a smile.

"I can understand why you wouldn't want to talk about it."

"Thanks."

"But if you want to, that's okay too. I wouldn't mind."

"There's not much to say, really," he replied, knowing it was a lie. There was a lot to say—he just couldn't say it.

Not without sounding crazy.

Nodding, she reached into her pack and produced a pair of apples. "I brought apples," she said. "You want one?" She put one in his hand. It was a blend of rose and gold. He bit into it, breaking off a crisp chunk that held just the right tartness, and raised his eyebrows in a show of approval as he chewed. "Braeburn," she said. "They're the best."

They proceeded to eat in silence, taking their time with the fruit, each lost in their own thoughts.

"I miss him so much," Aidan murmured, and then froze, startled by the words that had just fallen out of his mouth, words he had been thinking but hadn't meant to say. He hated the sound of them, not because they weren't true but because they were true, because they sounded so simple and stupid.

"Of course you do," she replied. The brightness, the touch of flippancy, was gone from her voice, replaced with a tenderness that made her seem older somehow.

"I just—I just wish we could be a family again."

Angela reached over with her hand and placed it against the small of his back. But he hardly felt it; he was too stunned by the latest revelation. Like the previous admission, it had slipped from his mouth—a half-formed thought that rose like some murky bubble in a pond, bursting at the moment of its surfacing. He suddenly thought about all his efforts over the past two weeks, the constant urge to reconnect with his father, the exhaustion of the chase. "What is it you want from him?" Memère had asked him last night. He wondered now if this was it, if this was what pulled him out each day—the chance not to make contact or say good-bye, but to start over. And if he could bring his father in, reign him into the orchard circle, Aidan could bring his mother in as well, just as he had been brought in, and neither of them would have to be alone anymore.

Looking up, he noticed the sun had begun to drop—time had resumed. A high breeze passed over in a wave, cool on the mountain, but the goose bumps had already appeared on his arms.

"I can't even begin to imagine what you've had to go through," Angela said, interrupting his thoughts. He looked over at her. Her brow creased in concern, as if she was worried about having insulted him.

"Thanks. It's good to hear that," he replied. Far from being a cold dismissal, it was the best thing anyone had said to him yet about the death. Until now the myriad words of consolation—no matter how well intentioned—had always fallen short because they couldn't possibly capture the experience of loss.

"Not everything is bad," she offered. "You've got other things to turn to."

"I guess. But sometimes it doesn't seem to matter. Everything can be going well, and it just takes one bad thing, something terrible, and everything else is ruined. Not *even* ruined—just not there at all."

"I know what that's like," she said.

He snorted. "You? No offense, but no one should be as happy as you are."

"I am happy," she agreed. "Or at least most of the time. Happy enough." Her face seemed to darken, and she hesitated, as if searching for the right words. "I haven't always been," she said, looking down. "In fact, for a while there I was more than just unhappy. It's a long story, but basically a year and a half ago I tried to, well, you know—off myself."

To hear such an admission from her stunned him. "How?" he blurted out.

"Pills," she replied matter-of-factly.

"Christ, what happened?"

"Fortunately, my knowledge of pharmaceuticals was pathetically inadequate for the task. I had my stomach pumped and got a nice little rest in the hospital."

"I just can't believe it," he said.

"Sometimes I can't either. It was just so weird. I mean, it's not like I had a bad childhood or anything cheesy like that—it just came out of nowhere, like a tree fell on me or something. 'Clinical depression,' the doctors said. A pretty mundane diagnosis, if you ask me—kind of disappointing, to tell the truth. If you're going to come down with a mental illness, it may as well be something interesting, like schizophrenia or even obsessive-compulsive disorder, for chrissake. That's a joke, by the way," she said, laughing at the look of shock on his face.

"Well," he offered, "you're better now, at least."

"Yeah," she sighed, and then laughed. "It's amazing what a ton of therapy can do."

"You mean that stuff really works?"

"It helps—if you let it. It can only take you so far, though. You have to want it. For a long time I didn't. I wallowed in the dark. I even considered trying *it* again."

"What made you change your mind?"

"It's hard to explain." She paused a moment, thinking. "It's like *The Odyssey*, I guess. Like with Kalypso—Odysseus has the chance to stay forever on that island with a beautiful goddess. And he can be immortal. That's a pretty tempting offer. But he doesn't stay—he leaves it all behind to go home to his wife, not knowing what's there, only knowing his wife is growing old and that she'll die someday and so will he. Why? Because in the end reality is always better than fantasy—that's what that whole story is about. That's what my teacher said, anyway, and I think he's right. And I had to make that kind of choice. I had to decide whether to escape or stick around and deal with the pain and hope to make it through. I'm glad I made the right choice."

"Me too," he said, glancing over at her. She was looking away now, staring ahead to the horizon, shading her eyes as if searching for something in the distance. The trickle of sweat was gone, evaporated by the breeze.

He stood up and stretched. "We'd better go. The sun will be setting soon. It'll be dark in the woods."

They picked their way off the summit and headed into the trees. Aidan's legs felt a little wobbly as they trotted down the trail, but it was a relief to be going in the other direction, to let gravity pull him along. They didn't talk on the way, but moved together silently through the encroaching dusk, focusing on the winding path. The trail that had seemed so long going up soon ended, and they stumbled out into the field just in time to see the sun slip over the hills.

As they made their way back down through the meadows to Southlook, Angela spread her arms out. "Check out that sky," she said. The high cirrus clouds had picked up the color of the sunset and glowed with an array of pinks and oranges against the blue.

"You really do like it up here, don't you," Aidan commented.

"I do. A change of scenery is always good. That's one of the reasons why my parents moved us up here, I think. They never said it, but I'm sure they thought it would help me."

"Well, I guess they were right."

"Totally. Except at night. I don't like the nights up here."

"Why not?"

"It wasn't bad at first," she said, hesitating, "but the last few weeks I haven't slept well. I keep having these awful dreams. I'm trapped somewhere in a deep well or someplace like that. Everything's dark, and I feel just the way I did before, like nothing's changed. I hear this girl crying, and I think it's me, but not me at the same time—you know how dreams can be. Then I wake up, and for a moment I still hear the crying. I know it's just in my head, but it's kind of creepy all the same. If it weren't for the fact that I don't believe in that crap, I'd swear the house was haunted."

Aidan slowed at her words, coming to a halt as she finished. Noticing he'd dropped behind, she stopped a little ways ahead and turned back to face him.

"Who owned the house before you?" he asked.

"I don't know. Some couple, I think. When we came up to look at the place, the realtor was kind of vague. He didn't say much about them. Just said they'd wanted to find someplace different. Hadn't lived there in a while—the place was empty. Why?"

"No reason," he said. But as they continued he couldn't help but think of Eve, of the story Memère had told him.

They reached Southlook a few minutes later. As they picked up their bikes, Aidan looked out across the sloping fields and groves. The familiar urge crept in on him once more. There was still some daylight left, still some time to make a quick pass across the mountain, and maybe he would be there. Aidan turned to where Angela waited on her bike.

"If you don't mind, I think I'll take the back way home," he said. "I know a shortcut."

"All right," she replied.

"I had a good time tonight," he said. "Maybe we can do it again."

"I'd like that. Call me. You have my number. Or your

grandmother does, at least," she added with a sheepish grin. He laughed and rolled his eyes. As she turned to go he stopped her.

"Angela," he said. "Don't worry about the dreams. Dreams can't hurt you."

"Right," she said. She waved good-bye and sped off down the hill.

Aidan watched her disappear before turning west along the meadow road, the image of her still in his mind. He pedaled with a sense of lightness, an elation that felt so foreign, like a distant memory creeping back. He hit the brakes and skidded to a stop. A voice inside spoke up. *Why do you need to look tonight—it was a good night, why end it with disappointment? You won't find him, and even if you do, you won't catch him*, it said. For a moment he considered turning around. Maybe he could catch up with her. A flock of blackbirds, calling through the air, swept overhead, winging their way in his direction toward a nearby copse. As he watched them fly another voice spoke up, urgent and distinct. *You need to go*, it said. *Maybe this will be the night. Everything's going right—this is the time. If you turn back now, you'll miss your chance.* He released the brakes and pedaled on.

He headed toward the upper pasture he'd hayed with Donny that first week he worked for him. Two different times he'd picked up his father's trail there. He followed the faint road around the corner of an outcropping of pines, and for a second time skidded to a stop. The blue rusted Ford sat parked on the edge of the field below. He wondered what Donny's truck was doing there and scanned the rowen for a sign of his uncle. It had grown back up over the last month, but not far from the pickup he saw where a blanket, spread out beneath two people, had formed a pocket in the foot-high grass. He dropped his bike and crept down through the trees for a better look, eager to see who his uncle was with. Coming to the edge of the pines, he froze, clinging to a trunk.

Donny was on his back. Next to him was his mother, lying on her side, her hand resting on his chest.

Aidan gasped as she leaned over and kissed his uncle.

All the lightness he'd felt upon leaving Angela, all the energy and hope that had spurred him on, drained from him in an instant. He turned and stole back to his bike, stumbling and numb. He mounted and fled, back the way he'd come, pedaling furiously along the meadow road, oblivious to the stiff pain in his legs, back to Southlook, not stopping but turning, plunging down the mountain road, feeling only the wind roaring in his ears and against the tears streaking across his temples. He nearly dumped his bike rounding the corner of the road leading up to the house, but he didn't care, he didn't feel afraid, he didn't feel anything as he flew into the yard, threw his bike against the side of the porch, and stumbled to his room.

FIFTEEN

By the time Aidan came downstairs the next morning, the heat had already begun. It rode in through the back windows of the kitchen, sliding in on the rays of the sun that had crested the top of Harper an hour ago, feeding off the heat of breakfast cooking on the stove. Memère turned from the sink and opened her mouth to speak, then stopped, seeing the look on his face. She came forward, holding out a cup of coffee. Aidan waved it off, brushing by her and out through the screen door onto the porch. His mother was at the table, sitting before the open pages of the *Burlington Free Press* with a mug in one hand, a cigarette in the other.

He strode to the edge of the porch and gripped the post. The paint chips bit into his hand as he stared south. A haze stirred up by the morning sun dulled the sky's blue and masked the far ridges, draining them of their color. Already he was starting to sweat. He gripped the post harder when she spoke.

"Paper says a real heat wave is settling in," she said.

"That's okay—when winter hits, we'll be grateful for the memory of these days."

He turned around to face her, leaning back against the post. She smiled at him before taking another drag. He walked over, grabbed a chair, and, pulling it up to the table, sat down across from her. She raised the pack lying next to the ashtray and shook it in the way of an offering.

"No thanks," he said. "I quit."

"Oh," she said with a look of surprise. "Well, good. That's good, Aidan."

"Besides," he snapped, "what kind of a mother would encourage her son to smoke?"

She frowned at the accusation. "I'm not trying to encourage you, sweetie. I just figured—why pretend?"

"Good point. Why pretend."

"So," she said brightly, ignoring his tone, "how was your date? Mama says she's a nice girl. I'd like to meet her."

"It wasn't really a date—we just went for a hike. But yeah, she's a nice girl. Very honest, very mature."

"Well, you'll have to invite her over to supper sometime," she said, going back to her newspaper. He leaned back in his chair and folded his arms. A trickle of smoke drifted across the table, and he twitched at the odor. For a minute they sat in silence.

"Oh, by the way," he said, leaning forward, "I just remembered last night—happy anniversary."

She paused, still gazing down at the paper, then stubbed

out her cigarette and wafted away the remnants of smoke before looking up.

"August first, right?" he challenged. "You didn't forget, did you?"

"No," she whispered. "Well, you know how it is in the summer. You lose track of the days."

He jumped up from his chair, startling her. Leaning over the table, he grabbed the edges of the newspaper and flipped it to the front page. He stabbed his finger down near the top. "See," he cried, "right there—*August first*."

Following the line of his finger to the page, her eyes filled with tears. A single drop fell onto the sheet, spreading out and darkening. She wiped her eyes once to check the flow.

"Well, I'm sorry, Aidan," she murmured. "I'm sure you can understand why this might not be the easiest time to remember right now."

He wouldn't let her get away this easy. "I'm sure it isn't," he quipped with all the sarcasm he could muster, "what with your new boyfriend, and all." Her eyes shot up to his, frantically searching for a sense of what he knew.

"What are you talking about?" she said.

"I saw, Ma," he said, choking on his words. "Last night. I saw you in the field with Donny."

"Oh God," she groaned, and covered her face. At last she lowered her hands and looked at him with red eyes. "I didn't mean for you to find out this way. I meant to tell you, Aidan."

"How long has this been going on?" he demanded.

"Not long. Two, three weeks," she said. She seemed confused trying to explain, as if waking from a dream. "It just . . . happened. I wasn't planning on it; neither was your uncle," she said, shaking her head. "I wanted to tell you, Aidan. So many times, I tried, but every time—"

"You couldn't because you knew how I'd feel about this. About how *he'd* feel," he shouted, his voice straining. "How could you, Ma?"

"What do mean?"

"How could you do this to him?"

She looked baffled for a moment. He could see her trying to steady herself as she realized what he meant.

"Your father? You mean your father," she whispered. When she spoke again, her voice grew louder and angry, and her eyes filled once more with tears. "He's dead, Aidan!" she cried. "He's dead! He's not coming back. Can't you understand that?"

You're wrong! he wanted to tell her. *You can't do this to him. To me.* He wanted to scream out the truth, tell her everything. *After all the work I've put in, all the time I've spent trying to pull him in, you've been ruining it all along!*

He turned away, fuming. He could feel his entire body stiffen into a single clench. He wanted to scream, punch the post, hurl a chair, do *something*. He looked back at her with dark eyes. She drew another cigarette from the pack. With a shaking hand she flicked the lighter a few times, but it refused to flame. She gave up and threw the lighter and cigarette down on the table.

"You don't understand, Aidan," she said at last. "I'm just so tired of being alone. Donny's been a comfort, a good friend. He cares about me." She paused, seeing the look on his face. "Don't think this has been easy for me. Some days I'm so happy—happier than I thought I could ever be again. And then I think of you and your father, and it fills me with guilt."

"You should feel guilty," he snapped from across the table. "You haven't even gone up to see his grave yet, have you? He's up there, you know. He's waiting."

She shut her eyes.

"I know why you're really doing this. You want him back, don't you? And if you can't have him, then you'll have the next best thing—his brother. Admit it—that's all this is about."

"No!" she cried, withering. Then she hesitated, dismay washing over her. "No," she said more weakly, "that can't be. I have feelings for Donny. I just . . . I don't know."

He could see the doubt beginning to creep across her face. He seized the advantage.

"Well, you can try to replace him if you want, but don't expect me to play along. I already *have* a father."

A movement in the doorway caught the corner of his eye, and he looked up to see Memère standing behind the screen door.

"Aidan!" she barked. "*Ici!* Your breakfast is ready."

"I don't want your goddam breakfast!" he bit back as she

240

came out onto the porch with a frown. He glared at both women. "I don't want anything—from either of you!"

He jumped down from the porch, snatched up his bike from where he'd thrown it last night, and tore off down the driveway.

The next three days flashed by like a dark dream. After their fight Aidan spent most of his time out of the house, away from his mother and Memère. He could hardly stand the sight of his mother at this point, and as each day went by it only grew worse. Every time he passed her, all he could do was remember her back in the field with his uncle, bedded down like a pair of thieves on the run. For her part, she had completely withdrawn. She herself had become a ghost, pale and pained, red eyed, numb, drifting through the hours of the day. He came back from his wanderings every night to the glow of the TV illuminating the curtains of the living room, and as he pushed through the screen door he was confronted with the now familiar barrage of *The Sound of Music*. Each time he paused in the kitchen, dimly lit by a single fluorescent tube over the sink, and grit his teeth at the same cheery songs warbled by the distortion of time. He glanced into the living room to see her laid out on the couch, her face bathed blue by the screen. She never looked at him. He refused to feel sorry for her. *Let her punish herself*, he thought. *She deserves it.*

Even Memère seemed to keep out of view, tucked away in her bedroom or the garden, or filling the feeders with endless pails of seed that the birds took away to their hidden places. The three of them became like strangers, unaware that they shared the same house, each indifferent to the others' solitude. Aidan expected it from his mother, and he expected it from himself—they had been living this way practically ever since his father's death. But he hadn't expected it from Memère. All summer she had been the common link between them, taking care of their needs. On second thought, he supposed it made sense—she had her shades to turn to, her other friends to feed. He figured she still made her way down to the orchard each evening, but he hardly cared anymore. He hadn't been down to the orchard for over a week now. Part of him missed the company of the ghosts. But every time he started to wonder how they were doing, what they were up to, he would remember that he already knew. They were the same; they would always be the same. That was what death was for them—brief moments of the same interrupted by stretches of nothing.

Life was starting to feel that way for him. Since the confrontation with his mother, he had thrown himself back into the hunt with full abandon. Nothing else mattered. From morning to night he crisscrossed Harper, poking into each one of its meadows and copses, but every path was a dead end.

Like yesterday, when he'd stumbled across an old stone wall running through a pasture, falling apart in places, boulders tumbled to either side. He had caught sight of his father gliding along the wall as it passed from the field straight into the trees that had since grown up around it. He followed the ghost into the woods, picking his way across the line of stones cutting straight ahead into the shadows like the spine of some prehistoric beast. The ghost melted away where the wall ended, the rocks petering out inexplicably amidst the trees, leaving Aidan staring at nothing but the remains of a truck. It was an old-model pickup, rounded with curves, like the kind he had seen in black-and-white movies while flicking through the cable channels late at night. Only the shell still stood, rusted and full of holes, an exoskeleton spiked with saplings that poked up in different places. Trunks surrounded it like prison bars, leaving it nowhere to go even if it could have gone.

Over and over he covered the same ground with the same degree of failure. But the search had a different edge to it now—more desperate, more exhausting. He felt agitated walking through the fields and grew fearful each time he saw his father's ghost. The shade had appeared less frequently these last few days, and when it did, it too seemed agitated. It tramped faster and farther ahead than before, a dark blur that flickered out of sight more frequently, changing directions so often he grew dizzy trying to keep up.

Worst of all was the heat. His mother had been right—a wave of August heat had settled in to stay, bearing down with a vengeance, and the sky had taken on an ugly tone, a hazy glare that always threatened to break out into storm but never did. It maddened him. Each day he staggered more under its weight, fighting to keep up the pace, feeling his strength drain away. Each day the ache in his arm grew as the humidity deepened and dark clouds brooded on the horizon, fighting with the sun, rolling in swiftly with the promise of release, then retreating with no more than a low rumble or two, leaving the air more saturated than before.

But today will be different, he thought, looking at the sky. *It will break today. It has to.* How could it not? Thunderheads were piling up in the distance, turning the western sky into a vast, angry bruise, mushrooming giants that had grown tired of threatening and were determined now to let loose.

Coated since morning with a film of sweat, Aidan made his way uphill, traipsing under the arching maple limbs whose shade offered no protection from the heat, pushing his bike along the dirt road, too tired to pedal against the afternoon. He had decided to follow the winding main road up to Southlook and renew the hunt from there. It was where he'd had the most luck, if he could even call it that. He had spotted his father's ghost just once this morning. It had led him into a cornfield down by the river, a brief chase that left him stranded amid a maze of tasseled stalks that had leaped to shoulder height in the past week, the only living thing that seemed to prosper in the heat. The pursuit had lasted a mere ten minutes—just enough to keep him going, a slim offering of hope to prevent him from giving up, but no more than that.

Coming around the corner, Aidan paused at the sight of Donny's truck. It was pulled off the road a little ways over at the edge of where the maples ended and a field began, a small clearing of land that Donny didn't own, but whose owner let him hay for free. Donny was leaning against the Ford's bed, his back to Aidan, looking out into the field where the massive Holstein bull stood grazing. Earlier today, when Aidan passed the field he'd helped fence in a few weeks ago, he'd noticed it was empty and wondered where the heifers and bull had gone. He figured Donny had moved them back to the farm. Now it seemed something else had happened.

He hesitated. His uncle hadn't spotted him yet—he could just turn around and go back down the mountain undetected. Donny was the last person he wanted to see right now, but the thought of turning back seemed cowardly. Why should he be the one to give way? He wasn't the one who had betrayed his father. He was the one who had been wronged; he was the one who had a right to be angry. As he stood hesitating, his uncle turned and caught sight of him. Donny showed no emotion as the two exchanged glances; he simply stared with dark eyes, then turned away. Aidan started to continue up the hill, then changed his mind and headed for the truck.

Dropping his bike at the edge of the road, he strode up to the pickup and knocked on the tailgate. Donny made no motion but continued to gaze ahead, ignoring him.

"What's going on?" Aidan asked, pointing into the pasture. "What's he doing up here?"

Donny glanced briefly at him. For a moment Aidan thought he wasn't even going to answer, but then he spoke in his usual slow way.

"Goddam fence broke. Spent all morning chasing them friggin' heifers up on Parrish Road. Still can't find one of 'em. Matty called at lunch. Told me where to find him," he said, tossing a quick finger at the bull.

"Oh," Aidan replied weakly.

"Timmy!" Donny barked. The bull lifted its head and snorted, but didn't move. "Christly thing usually comes to me. Heat's making him stubborn, I guess."

"It's hot," Aidan observed.

Donny grunted. "Yeah, it's hot. Especially when you're trying to round up a bunch of goddam heifers by yourself." He turned and looked at Aidan. "Could have used your help this morning. Could have used your help all week," he said. He looked away again. "But I guess you wouldn't care about that."

Aidan felt a wave of guilt rise up. It quickly turned to rage.

"You know why I haven't showed," he retorted.

His uncle turned and glared. "That's right," he said. He snorted. "I suppose you're happy, Aidan—you got what you want. Your mother won't see me now. Won't even friggin' talk to me."

"You had no business being with her," Aidan challenged.

Donny turned toward him. Aidan stepped back. "Who

are you to tell me my business?" his uncle demanded. "You don't even know me."

"Yes, I do," he replied, steadying himself.

"No, you don't. You live in your own little world. You're just like your father was. What anyone else feels don't matter. All that matters is you!"

"Is that what this is about?" Aidan shouted. "Getting back at him?"

Donny's face twisted in anger. His fists clenched as he stepped forward. But then he checked himself and turned away. He went over to the cab and grabbed a thick length of rope from the backseat, slamming the door shut.

"Your father's got nothing to do with this," he said evenly, tying a quick slipknot. "I've loved your mother since I was a kid. Can't remember a time I haven't."

Aidan was silent for a moment. "I didn't know," he said at last.

"Well, now you do. Not that it matters anymore, least not to your mother. I can't compete with no ghost. I'm a goddam fool for ever thinking I could."

He knew his uncle meant only the memory of his father, but Aidan paled at the words.

"I got to walk this dumb shit back to the farm," his uncle barked. "Throw your bike in the back. You can make yourself useful and drive the pickup down. If it ain't too much trouble, that is," he added.

Aidan nodded and numbly walked back to the road.

247

Returning with his bike, he paused by the truck to watch his uncle. Donny was before the bull now, rope held out, speaking in low tones. The bull balked at his approach, tossing its head and stepping to the side. Donny spoke sharply and drew closer, reaching out to place the loop over its head, when the bull made a quick turn, lowering its horns. The charge caught his uncle by surprise, and Aidan watched in horror as the bull flipped the man effortlessly onto the ground, bearing down with a bellow.

"No!" Aidan screamed, dropping his bike and leaping forward, unsure what to do.

Donny threw his arms up and rolled desperately in an effort to get away, but the bull pressed on, butting his head against the fallen man several times before finally pulling back. It stomped the ground and bellowed again, shaking its head in agitation. Donny scrambled to his feet and hobbled toward the truck, holding his side.

"Goddam son-of-a-bitch . . . " he snarled, a string of curses flying from his mouth all the way back.

"Are you okay?" Aidan cried, striding out to meet him. He could see a long scrape across his uncle's arm.

"Get back to the truck!" Donny ordered. He marched over to the cab and snatched his rifle from the rack hanging in the rear window. Aidan came over to see him rummaging in the glove box. He pulled out three cartridges and loaded them into the gun with shaking fingers.

"What are you doing?" Aidan gasped.

"Shut up!" his uncle growled. He closed the action and limped with determined steps back out to where the bull stomped and snorted.

"Don't do it!" Aidan cried after him, but Donny ignored him.

Aidan stood frozen, watching as his uncle pulled the rifle up and drew a bead on the bull, which now stood silent about a dozen yards away, its ears pricked forward. For a moment Donny paused. Everything was frozen. No one moved. The only sound was a low rumble emanating from thunderheads in the west. A second later it was replaced by the crashing report of the rifle as Donny pulled the trigger. The bull flinched, tugged back as if startled more by the noise than any impact. Donny yanked the bolt and loaded another round. The empty shell that ejected from the rifle glittered, spinning in the sun as it fell. Donny fired again, and again the bull jerked. Looking dazed, it hovered shakily on its legs for a moment before finally buckling to its knees, then collapsing with its legs still under it as if settling down for sleep.

Donny lowered the rifle and stumbled back to the truck. Aidan stared in shock, saying nothing as his uncle drew near. The man paused, seeing the dismay on his nephew's face, and glanced down at the ground for a moment.

"You saw what that bastard did," his uncle fumed, ejecting the unused cartridge. Aidan could see he was breathing hard. They both looked back at the bull. Aidan could just make out the two small holes—one along its neck, the other in its white chest—from which runnels of blood had begun to flow. "You can't have an ugly bull around. There's no sense in it! The christly thing was too old anyways," he said at last, his voice quavering. "He was no good to me. I was going to get rid of him sooner or later."

Aidan didn't reply—he just continued to stare at his uncle's plaintive face. Finally Donny turned away. He looked back at the bull for a moment. "Goddamit!" he shouted, throwing the rifle down.

He limped around the front of the truck and jumped into the cab. Aidan stepped aside as his uncle gunned the engine, backed into the road, and tore off in a cloud of dust.

Aidan remained after the sound of the Ford's engine had faded, still staring at the bull lying in the grass, too dazed by the sudden turn of events to even want to move. The animal hadn't stirred from its last position; he guessed it must have died quickly. Another faint roll of thunder broke his gaze, and he looked over toward the west. The purple clouds that were piled high loomed closer, and only now did he realize the sun had fallen behind them, though the sky above him was still a hazy blue. The storm that had been threatening for the last three days would finally arrive.

SIXTEEN

The brook had faded to a trickle from the recent heat, but there was still enough water to fill the container. Aidan stood up, carried the dripping pitcher over to the center of the clearing, and emptied it into the basin. The liquid swirled and splashed around the edges as it filled, quickly settling until all that marred its surface was a pattern of widening rings as Aidan let the last drops trickle from the pitcher.

The water looked silver beneath the darkening atmosphere. Leaning over the pool, Aidan's face was no more than a dim shadow against the sky, his reflection blurring for a moment as a drop of sweat fell from his forehead and broke the surface. He stood back and set the pitcher down beside the chair before casting a nervous glance around the empty clearing. His heart was pounding, though whether it was from a fear of being caught or from what he was about to do he wasn't sure.

Screw them. Screw all of them.

Leaving the field earlier, he'd ridden numbly back to the

house and had retreated to his room, sick from the heat and from the image of the dead bull stuck in his head, its blood still staining the grass when he closed his eyes. Desperate for a distraction, he had tried reading for a while, but an hour later gave up.

It wasn't bad at first. Penelope had proposed a contest: whoever could string her husband's old bow and shoot an arrow through the rings of twelve ax heads would win her hand. Still in disguise, Odysseus gathered with the suitors in the great hall for the challenge and watched in amusement as they all took turns struggling in vain, unable even to string the weapon. But the contest of the bow was over, and the slaughter had begun. Aidan read as Odysseus and his son began the systematic butchering of all the men who had tried to steal his life away, but after a few passages Aidan shut the book. He'd had enough killing for one day.

Agitated, he had paced in his room. Then, looking out the window, he stopped. The dark clouds had drawn closer in the last hour. He could see them where they loomed above the trees in the orchard. An idea crept into his mind, driving away his agitation, replacing it with a cold anger. With it came a determination to put his fruitless wanderings aside and, like Odysseus, take matters into his own hands. He was tired of chasing his father, tired of his devotion to an ungrateful spirit. If his father wouldn't come to him, he would make him come. And nobody could stop him.

Snatching the tiny jackknife from his tackle box on the

porch as he left the house, he'd stolen down across the lawn, taking a furtive glimpse back to make sure he hadn't been seen before ducking onto the path.

Now, in the orchard, the air was heavy and still, the only sound a distant rumble from the nearing storm as Aidan pulled his father's old knife from his pocket.

He opened the blade and held it up, turning it back and forth before him. It was worn thin from years of sharpening. As if in anticipation of the deed, a breeze picked up and shook the boughs of the apple trees, casting them white as the wind revealed the underbelly of the leaves.

He had only a moment's pause, wavered only slightly at the expectation of pain before steeling himself and drawing a quick line across his finger with the knife, feeling the thinness of the blade as it burned across the skin. For a brief second the wound was clean, nothing more than a sliver of parted flesh before the blood welled up, rising faster than he had anticipated, sliding down the side of his finger and into his palm, a steady stream. He thrust his hand over the basin and watched the blood as it dripped into the water, blossoming into little clouds of red that dissolved into the pool.

The breeze died, and everything went still. Aidan's heart sank. For a moment it seemed as if all the air had been sucked out of the clearing, leaving a vacuum of sound. Then it picked up again, vicious and cold, stronger than before. The hairs on the back of his neck stood erect. A thrill washed over him as the charged air swirled around the clearing.

Come on, Dad. I know you can.

Alton's head poked out from behind a tree. He emerged into the clearing, followed by Eve, Smitty, then Bobby. Wilma followed. Jackson, Marie, all of them, even Daniel, appeared and crowded toward the basin, looking around as they came, confused but eager.

"Stand back," Aidan shouted. "It's not for you!"

They didn't listen. They leaned down, lapping hungrily at the liquid, looking at one another with excited glances.

"That's good stuff, by Jesus!" Bobby called out, coming in for another drink.

Euphoria swept over the group. The wind strengthened. Aidan looked on, helpless as the shades began clamoring over the pool, trying to push each other aside to find a place around the crowded basin. He shivered at the babble of their voices, at the sound of their laughter.

This wasn't how it was supposed to be. They were supposed to take their seat around the circle, converse in quiet tones. Instead they shoved and squabbled, giggled and twitched. Aidan watched in horror as Alton's shimmering form danced a jig. As for Eve, she refused to leave the basin, guarding her spot warily, scooping the liquid with a cupped hand, shuddering as she drank and eyeing Aidan with a grin. He looked away, unable to watch.

It was the final betrayal. Donny, his mother, Memère, all of them had turned on him, and now even the shades seemed determined to undermine his will.

"Don't drink it all," Aidan pleaded, looking back. "Save some for him."

He glanced beyond the intoxicated group, desperate for a glimpse of his father, but he saw no sign of him. Instead a crowd of other shades now swarmed into the clearing, spirits he'd never seen before. Men, women, even children flowed toward the basin. The jabbering intensified as the pool diminished. They began crowding around him, reaching out with hungry looks.

"No!" he screamed. Turning in dread as the circle tightened, desperate for a way out, he gasped, all thoughts of his father forgotten. Their pleading voices were now inside his head, drowning out his own.

"Leave me alone!" he screamed over and over, sinking down as they hovered over him, some of their faces sad and searching, others leering and intent. He closed his eyes and covered his head with his hands.

"Get back!"

Aidan opened his eyes and looked up to see Memère as she burst into the circle, swinging her walking stick before her, scattering the shades. Still clamoring, they frantically pulled away as she rushed at each of them. Then she snatched up the pitcher, ran to the brook, filled it, and returned, dumping its contents into the basin with such force that nearly all the liquid, including the fresh water, splashed over the sides and onto the ground.

It was as if she'd just poured the water on a flame.

Immediately the shades began settling down. Most of the newcomers faded from sight. The rest retreated toward the edges of the clearing.

Memère looked at Aidan. Already the fire she'd shown a moment ago was fading. Her face bore a blend of anger, sadness, and fatigue, and he glanced down at the ground, still too numb to talk. Shaking her head, she turned to the shades that remained and began speaking in quiet tones. Aidan rose and stumbled up the path toward the house, the voices of the shades still calling out to him in his mind, as if they would never cease.

Aidan sat at the open window and let the breeze wash over him. The curtains flickered and curled as the air rushed in from the darkness, cooling off the room.

Fleeing back to the house, he'd raced upstairs and locked himself in the bathroom—washing the cut on his finger with shaking hands, still shivering from the shades' touch—and then sequestered himself in his room, not coming down when Memère called for supper. She called only once from below, then let him be. He wasn't hungry anyway—the heat in his room and the memory of the afternoon had left him queasy.

All he wanted was to forget—to forget his failure in the orchard, to forget everything that had happened over the last three days. And so, as night approached—made earlier by the dark and swelling clouds—he'd settled into the window seat to watch the storm.

It promised to be an impressive show. As the minutes ticked by, the wind gathered in strength, and flashes of lightning illuminated the lawn and trees below. The thunder had grown louder and more frequent to match the lightning, though the storm was still far enough away that he couldn't pair a particular boom with its parent flash. There was no rain yet, but he knew it was only a matter of time as the mass of clouds moved in. He listened for it, hoping its sound would combine with the thunder and wind to drive away the shades' voices still echoing in his head.

A flash of lightning lit up the yard. He sprang to the screen.

His heart began to pound waiting for the next flash. He gasped as it came again. It lasted less than a second, but it was enough for him to see the man standing down on the lawn in the circle of gnomes, the long black coat drawn in tight, the collar up around the neck, the scarf suspended in the wind. Aidan leaned against the window frame and closed his eyes in disbelief. *It can't be*, he thought. *He's never come this close. He's never come at night.* He took a few deep breaths and turned back to the window. Thunder rattled the panes as he stood frozen, waiting for the lightning. It came again, a whole series of flashes that lingered for more than a second— time enough for him to see his father still standing there, time enough for him to watch the man begin to turn his head toward Aidan's window before disappearing as the lightning faded.

Aidan leaped from the window seat and dashed for the bedroom door, tearing it open and starting out before turning back to slip on his Tevas with trembling hands. Nearly tripping down the stairs, he paused in the kitchen, catching sight of his mother in the living room. "Raindrops on roses and whiskers on kittens . . . " The music wafted through the doorway, competing with the thunder outside. He took off and burst onto the porch. Hesitating at the top of the steps, he shielded his eyes to block out the kitchen lights and waited for another flash.

"Don't do it, Aidan. Don't go."

He jumped at the sound of his grandmother's voice and whirled to see her sitting on the swing, her hands in her lap. "Stay with Memère," she said.

"You see him? You see him, don't you," he cried.

"Stay with me. Don't go."

She rose from the swing and joined him at the edge of the steps. Drops of rain began to fall, hitting the porch roof with heavy thuds, large drops that blew into their faces and splattered against their arms. They both stepped back as the drops fell faster. The wind shuddered the treetops in the yard, and the leaves roared.

"He wants me to follow him!" he said, shouting above a peel of thunder.

"You don't know what he wants," she said, leaning in close to be heard above the storm. "Maybe he doesn't even know, eh? You only know what you want. Now you listen to

Memère. I spent all afternoon cleaning up your mess down there. The least you can do is stay."

"But it must have worked," he cried back, pointing across the lawn. "See how close he is? I *must* have brought him in. Besides, you fixed things, didn't you? Everything's back to normal."

"You have no idea what you've done," she said, shaking her head. "I did the best I could, but I'm not sure it was enough. Something's not right, Aidan. There's a darkness out there, it's all around us—I can feel it. Just stay."

When he hesitated, she grabbed his arm and squeezed.

"If you won't do it for me, do it for her," she said, gesturing toward the glowing windows of the living room. "You see her in there," she scolded, "watching that same goddam movie over and over. Forget him. Go in there and help her!"

"You do it!" he shouted back, pulling his arm away. "You told me before to forget about the dead and pay attention to the living—maybe you should take your own advice. You care more about those stupid ghosts down in the orchard than either of us."

"You know that's not true," she barked hoarsely.

"Well, I can't make her do anything. You're her mother. You go in there!"

"I've tried!" she cried out. "She won't listen to me, Aidan. Nothing I say works. She's just pulled away."

Aidan turned back toward the yard. The rain was driving down in sheets now. A chain of lightning streaked across

259

the sky, and in its light he discovered his father was gone. His heart sank, until another flash revealed him again. In the flickering light Aidan could see the figure drifting across the lawn toward the orchard.

"I've got to go!" he hollered to his grandmother, and took off down the steps. "I'll help her tomorrow," he shouted back. "I'll talk to her. We can do it together!"

Aidan didn't wait to hear her reply but tore off into the storm, shielding his face from the battering rain as he hurried across the lawn down to the path in pursuit.

He bounded through the grass, trying not to slip, trying not to lose the trail in the dark. The lightning continued to streak, a steady barrage of white like the strobe lights he'd seen at parties, and the thunder was louder now, cracking in waves so sharp he could almost feel them. He caught glimpses of the dark coat, frozen at each flicker, but always farther ahead at the next burst. He sped up, empowered by the storm, by the surge of adrenaline that rose with each booming crash, by the hope of sudden opportunity. His father was heading for the orchard, for the basin.

He stumbled onto the edge of the clearing to see the figure standing before the pedestal. The basin was overflowing from the downpour, and under the millisecond flashes the streaming water was reduced to a steady line of individual drops falling in stop motion through the air.

"Dad!" he cried out. "It's me. It's Aidan!"

The man raised his head and turned toward Aidan. A

massive bolt streaked in a long arc across the sky. Aidan caught his father's profile for a moment, caught one eye before the light went out again. When the next flash came, his father was gone.

"No!" he screamed.

Another streak, and now his father was on the far side of the clearing, heading into the apple trees. Aidan dashed after him, holding out his arms to push aside the boughs that sprang out of the dark, bounding through the tall, untrodden grass. He stumbled downhill through the row of trees and reached the bottom edge of the orchard. Beyond stood thicker woods. He hesitated. But as he saw his father disappear between the cedars he suddenly remembered what lay on the other side. He knew where his father was going— back to the farm, back home. He went after him, crashing into the tangle of branches, slowing down to get his bearings with each burst of lightning, catching glimpses of the dark shadow weaving ahead between the trunks.

Aidan emerged from the woods a few minutes later to the familiar shape of the hay barn in the back of the farm, lit up by a battery of flashes. He saw his father beyond it, ducking into the doorway of the milking barn. Aidan ran across the clearing and into the sagging building. The lights in the front yard glowed through the dirty film on the windows. Looking around in the half-light, he could see the rows of Holsteins in their stalls, could smell their breath and hear them lowing, nervous from the storm. He cut through the barn and hurried out into the front yard, trying to catch his breath. Aside from the hulking wrecks of tractors and Donny's old Ford, the yard was empty. The movement of a shadow caught his eye, and he looked up to see the figure through the rain as it darted into the house.

Aidan walked slowly across the yard, his sandals squishing in the muck, trying to steady his nerves as he approached the house. He didn't know what he'd find inside, but he knew the hunt would end there. It had to.

He entered the mudroom, quietly opened the door, and went into the kitchen. The blood was pounding in his ears so hard he barely heard the thunder or even the sound of the TV blaring from the living room. The lights were on in there. He tiptoed up to the threshold and peered in. Donny was stretched out snoring in his recliner, fast asleep in spite of the storm and the volume of the late-evening news. Aidan glanced over at the staircase that rose to his right in two sections in time to see the dark pants, the dress shoes, and the bottom of the black coat disappear upstairs. He mounted the steps on shaky legs, reaching the second floor just as the legs disappeared once again up the next staircase to the attic. He slipped down the short length of the hall, lightning flashing in the window, and climbed the last flight of steps, which ended at a door.

He stood before the door, trying to muster up the strength to open it, suddenly terrified at what he might find behind it, and angry at his fear. After all his chasing, why should he hesitate now? Still, he paused, his fingers frozen on the handle. As the thunder and lightning raged, he knew why he was afraid. Why did it have to be this way? Why couldn't it have happened in the field, in the light of day?

He finally turned the handle and pushed the door aside. A large window occupied the far wall of the attic. The bright light out in the yard shone through, and in the frame of the light stood the silhouette of his father, his back to Aidan. Aidan took a step forward, then another, breathing faster as he approached. He was over a third of the way across the floor, silently closing in, when the floorboards suddenly groaned under his weight. He froze, terrified of revealing himself too soon. A peel of thunder rattled the windows. The shadow turned to Aidan and raised its arms. *This is it!* Aidan thought, his heart pounding. Abandoning stealth, he hurried to cross the remaining distance.

A sudden flash of lightning blinded him. A thunderclap followed it almost instantaneously, and the outside light flickered, then died as the power went out. When the next strike flared, the window casing was empty.

He cried out in alarm and shot to the window, only to find nothing. He couldn't believe it—after all this his father had run out on him again.

Then the lightning flashed once more, a whole series of strikes. Aidan gasped. His father stood before him in the glass, facing him, appearing just the way he had that last morning Aidan saw him before the accident. As the man lifted his eyes, Aidan thought he saw him peer out in confusion, followed by what Aidan was certain was the briefest flicker of recognition. Aidan reached out to touch him, pressing his fingers against the glass.

The power suddenly returned, and as the yard light came back to life the man's image faded from sight, leaving only Aidan's reflection in the glass.

"No!" he screamed, and punched the window in rage.

The glass shattered from the blow and sprinkled onto the floor, and the wind howled in through the jagged hole, blowing gusts of water into Aidan's face. For a moment he just stood there stunned, oblivious to the rain, until a sharp pain in his hand roused him. He looked down to see a shard of glass embedded between the first two knuckles of his fist. He yanked it out and threw it aside. A flow of blood ruptured from the cut and ran along his hand, mixing with the water to curl around his wrist and splatter on the floor. He pressed his other hand down on the cut and swore, trying to apply as much pressure as he could.

A movement of shadow on the right caught his eye, and he turned in joy, forgetting his pain. His father had come back! But as he turned his blood froze—a different shadow had emerged.

Eve.

She stepped out into the light of the window and slunk toward him like a cat, beautiful and terrible, almost incandescent as the lightning illuminated her form. Bending down silently before him, she dipped a finger in the dark pool and

grab hold of. He had no idea which way was up, no sense of direction, and he began to panic. The single urge to escape seized him. He tried to scream, but the sound was lost in the void, eaten by the darkness.

Then a voice called out from the edge of the abyss, far away and faint, a voice that stopped his spinning and slowed his plunge. He couldn't tell whose voice it was or what it said, but he let himself be drawn by the distant murmur. He felt himself rising now, like a diver out of air breaking for the surface, and as he grew closer he discovered the voice wasn't solitary, but a gathering of voices—his mother, Memère, Donny, Angela, all the people he cared for—mixing together in a single sound.

He snapped open his eyes to see Eve before him, her lips still joined to his. With his last bit of strength, he tore away and fell back against a pile of boxes before dropping to the floor.

"Not this way," he whispered, looking up at her, struggling to stay conscious, shivering from the ice still lingering in his limbs. She didn't reply but merely gazed down on him in sadness, the lightning flickering against her face.

A blast of light struck him as the attic bulbs flashed on. He squinted against the brightness, shielding his eyes with a bloody hand.

"Aidan!"

Aidan looked up. Eve was gone. His uncle now appeared in her place, crouching over him as he shook uncontrollably.

"Jesus Christ, what are you doing here? What happened?" his uncle said.

"Don't want to die," Aidan gasped through chattering teeth.

Donny reached down and examined his hand. He sighed and shook his head. "You ain't gonna die," he scolded gently. "Come on. Let's go."

Aidan barely heard him. He just kept whispering the same words over and over as Donny helped him to his feet and down the attic steps. After that everything became a blur. At one point he was dimly aware of his uncle before him in the bathroom, tending to his hand while he sat there shivering and numb. Donny didn't speak as he cleaned and bandaged the wound. He asked no questions as he led Aidan into the room next door, removed his soaking clothes, and helped him into bed. The last thing Aidan remembered before sinking to sleep was the dark silhouette of his uncle paused in the doorway.

"Don't worry, Aidan. Go to sleep," he said, then closed the door and left.

SEVENTEEN

Aidan awoke to silence. Looking through the bedroom window, he could see a blue sky free of clouds. For a second the memory of yesterday seemed like a dream, like it could only have been a dream. But as he rolled over, the pain in his hand brought everything back: the bull, the failed summoning, the storm, his father's visage in the glass, the shattering window, and—worst of all—Eve. He held his hand up and examined the pair of suture strips pressed between his first two knuckles like a bridge, holding the cut together, the last oozings of blood along it now dried black. His hand was stiff and sore, but the superficial pain was nothing compared with the grief of last night, of watching his father fade before his eyes, or the even deeper coldness of the kiss that had settled into his bones, a coldness that still lingered.

As he looked around, it took him a moment to realize where he was. It was his father's room. He'd been in here only once years ago, but it looked exactly the same as it had then, as it had for years. The room was mostly empty, but a few artifacts remained, leftovers from the day his father fled: rock posters on the wall—Boston, Neil Young, Aerosmith—old bands his father had listened to in high school; trophies capped with golden cows and blue and red ribbons from the Caledonia County Fair lining the shelves and gathering dust; a pair of work boots still askew in the corner beneath the curled and faded wallpaper, a pellet gun beside them. The remnants of a rejected life. His father had let him peek in once as a kid during one of their rare visits to the farm, had ushered him in like an annoyed curator at closing time.

"It smells funny in here," Aidan remembered saying. "It smells old."

"It stinks," his father said.

"Can I have that poster?" he asked.

"No."

"What about the BB gun?"

"You don't need it. It's all junk. Leave it be."

With that, he'd shooed Aidan back out and closed the door. Who knew how long it had remained shut? Not even Donny's ex-wife, Sherry, had apparently dared to clean out the vacant room.

Donny had hung Aidan's shorts and T-shirt over the back of a chair. They were still damp, but Aidan put them on anyway and went downstairs. No one was around. He plopped himself down at the kitchen table and just sat there, still feeling numb from last night. A few minutes later Donny entered from the mudroom, smelling of barn, having just finished the morning chores. He nodded to Aidan as he came in, took off his boots, and threw his hat down on the table.

"You want some tea?" he asked. "I'll make you some tea," he said when Aidan didn't answer. He put the kettle on and toasted some bread before sitting down. Both sat silent while the water heated. When the whistle blew, Donny made the tea, put it and the toast before Aidan, and sat back down.

"Almost brought you to the hospital last night. Didn't know as you might need some stitches," he said. He glanced over at Aidan's hand lying on the table. "Looks all right, I guess."

Aidan nodded.

"You were in a real state last night, by Jesus," Donny said. "Sleepwalking?"

"Something like that."

"Don't want to talk about it, do you?"

"Not really."

"Fine with me," his uncle said. He paused to take a sip of tea and looked into Aidan's eyes. He opened his mouth to speak, then stopped. He tapped his fingers nervously on the table. "Aidan," he said at last, "I don't want to be your father. I ain't never tried to be."

"I know," Aidan replied.

"But that don't mean I can't be something. Whatever it is, we can work it out."

"Okay," Aidan said weakly.

"But you need to know . . . " He hesitated and glanced

down at the table. "What I'm trying to say, I guess, is that I thought about it all night, and I need to tell you. I ain't giving up on your mother." He looked up intently. "I know you don't like the idea," he added hastily. "Christ, I don't blame you, after everything. But I just can't do it, that's all. I told you yesterday—I've always loved her. It's as real as can be. You two have been through a hell of a lot, don't think I don't know that. But maybe something good can happen still."

Aidan listened to the words coming slowly from the man across from him, words that seemed as though they were being squeezed out, formed by the deepest pressure of sorrow and love, tumbling onto the table like diamonds.

For a long while he didn't respond. His uncle looked on with anxious eyes. "You're right, Donny," he said at last. "You shouldn't give up on her."

Donny breathed a visible sigh of relief. "Thanks, Aidan. That means a lot," he said. "As for the farming, I've thought about that, too. I know how Timmy felt about it—I feel that way too at times—and I don't want you to get caught up in it. Anyways, if you don't want to work with me no more, I'll understand. I just want you to know I've enjoyed having you with me on the farm this summer. You're a real hard worker."

"Thanks. But I don't want to quit," he said. He suddenly remembered what Angela had said on their hike. "I like the work. It's useful."

"Good then," Donny said, nodding.

"Just tell me one thing, Donny," Aidan said.

"You name it."

"About Dad. I need to know—why did he leave? Why did he take off so suddenly the way he did? Did something happen with Grampa? I just want to know the secret."

Donny shook his head. "Ain't no secret about it. They fought a lot, specially that last year. It got ugly at times. 'Course, I was caught in the middle of it. After a while I hated 'em both."

"But *something* must have happened," Aidan pressed.

Donny sighed. "There ain't always a big dark secret in life, Aidan. You're looking for something that just isn't there. Farming's a hard life. It takes its toll, even more so when there's no mother around to tend to all the things that really count. Sometimes them little disappointments that add up over a lifetime are just as bad as one big upset, maybe worse. Who knows why your father decided to leave the way he did? He never told me. Maybe he thought it was the only way. In the end, he got out and I stayed, and I've spent half my goddam life wondering which one of us was the coward."

"Neither of you," Aidan said.

Donny nodded and, snatching his hat, rose from the table. Aidan joined him. Bringing his dishes to the sink, he noticed a fishing rod leaning in a dark corner by the refrigerator. He went over and picked it up. The rod was graphite, feather-light in his hand, and the new reel spun easy. The price tags were still on both.

"Mind if I borrow this?" he asked.

"Go for it," Donny said, pulling on his boots. "I ain't never used it. Sherry got it for me last Christmas. Only nice thing she ever gave me," he added with a grin. "There's lures in a tackle box in the mudroom. Knock yourself out," he said, turning to leave.

"Where you going?" Aidan asked.

"I got a bull to bury," he said, and shut the door behind him.

With a flick of his wrist Aidan dropped the lure into the far side of the pool and slowly reeled in. The water was high and loud after last night's heavy rain, tumbling over the submerged rocks. It had turned a creamy brown, a torrent of stirred-up sediment that obscured everything. He knew his chances of catching a trout in the murk were slim, but he didn't care. He had come to cast not catch, to lose himself in the act of reeling and the clamor of the water, to put himself back together and take stock of things. Walking down through the pasture, he had heard the river call to him from afar, murmuring like the stream of voices that had saved him from the darkness last night. Now, with each cast into the cloudy stream, he could feel himself falling back into place, piece by piece.

From time to time he cast furtive glances downstream where the little boy had appeared at the far water's edge only a couple weeks ago. It was there his chase had begun. It was a hunt that still continued, and maybe it would never end—unless he let it. He didn't know what to think anymore. Donny's words at breakfast hadn't offered the resolution he'd been seeking. Until this morning he had been holding out on the hope that he could unlock the mystery of his father's past, but now it seemed there was no mystery, or if there was, it was forever buried. Maybe the disappointment was a blessing. Maybe it held the answer, or at least a reason for him to turn away. But how could he give up on his father? How could he abandon him after all his efforts? Last night's vision was a sign he was getting closer, the last step before fulfillment.

What fulfillment? He suddenly stopped reeling and lifted his head at the question. What did he really want from his father? He had asked that question before, had recognized the hope that he could rope his father's spirit into the orchard circle. But then what? So consumed by the search, he had never thought it through. Yes, they could be together. But did he really want his father to be a shade like the others? He had grown to enjoy the company of all of Memère's friends, had found solace in their presence. But they had been reduced by death, had grown forgetful of what it meant to be fully in the world. His father, at best, would be no better. What kind of relationship would that be? If his father's death had made Aidan realize anything, it was that their relationship in life was, in its own way, shallow—not through any malice or intention, but through the natural course of their busy lives. But no matter how much time they spent in the orchard together, it would never be better. If anything, it would be worse. It would keep Aidan from ever coming to terms with what his father really was—an echo of the man he used to be.

He remembered again his father in the window last night, again saw his image fade away. This time, though, as it dissolved back into his memory another figure rose, revealing a different face. He saw his mother now, looking pale and dazed, as she'd looked lying on the couch all week, as she'd looked most of the summer, aside from that brief spark of life. These past weeks he'd fostered an indifference toward her struggling that slipped at times into condescension. She was weak, passive. He was strong, seizing the initiative. He was *doing* something about his anguish, channeling his sorrow toward the achievement of a goal.

But what had it come to? What had his efforts brought him? More pain, more heartache. Pure folly. In giving himself over to the quest, he had lost a part of himself along the way, had nearly lost all of it last night. And in pursuing a fantasy, he had lost all sense of what was really important.

Casting again into the pool, he realized that he was no better than his mother was. He wasn't on a different plane. They traveled on the same road of grief, only in different directions, miles apart but still connected.

There was a sudden twitch on the line. At first he thought it was just a snag, a small branch of leaves that had been blown into the river by the storm, but as he started to reel in, the tip came alive to the trout's struggle. He couldn't believe his luck. Perhaps it was the lightness of the rod or the rawness of his nerves—either way, as he brought in the line an electric joy surged from within, shutting out the worry in his mind. The water was too thick to see anything as he played the trout toward the bank, but he was sure it was a decent size—maybe as big as the one he'd lost before.

With a final tug Aidan pulled the fish out onto the bank. It fell into the bushes and began thrashing in the leaves. Dropping the rod, he swept down on it and, pushing aside the ferns, laughed at the sight of the six-inch trout. He wet his hands before removing the hook embedded in its bottom lip, and for a moment just held it. The little silver trout lay calm in his hands, working its gills to a rhythm only it could hear. In spite of its fragile beauty, there was a toughness to it, a pulse of raw vitality that captivated him as it lay there oblivious to its fate.

Inserting his finger along its upper jaw, he began to apply the pressure of his thumb against the neck, when a pain in his knuckles stopped him. He looked down at his hand. One side of a suture strip had come loose in the water, and the cut had reopened along that edge to a trickle of blood. For a moment he watched it flow. Then he turned back to the river and lowered the trout into the water, felt the thrill of movement as the trout jerked once against his palm and was gone. He rinsed his hand off quickly in the water and, standing up, dried it with his shirt and reattached the strip as best he could.

He stared into the river, watched the coffee-colored surge laugh along the rocks. Suddenly he knew what he had to do. He picked his rod up, hauled in the line, and headed for home.

Aidan hiked up the driveway with eager steps, but as he drew near the house he could tell something was wrong. Memère was rocking an anxious rhythm in the swing. When she saw him, she jumped up, pacing with an urgency he had never seen in her before.

"Where have you been?" she scolded as he approached.

"Fishing," he replied. "I stayed over at Donny's last night." He drew up to the porch. "What's wrong?"

Her face grew worried. "You're mother's gone, Aidan."

"Well, where is she?"

"I don't know. She was here earlier reading letters. I went down to the garden, and when I looked up later, she had disappeared."

"She probably went for a walk," he said, mounting the steps. Then he saw the open box on the far side of the swing and went over to retrieve it. "When she comes back, we'll all sit down and—"

Reaching for the box, he froze. He saw the letters, he saw the cleaning kit, he saw the leather case. But the case was open. The pistol was gone. He looked again. He reached down and rummaged through the letters, but it wasn't there.

He stood back and turned to Memère. She paled at the look on his face.

"Dad's gun," he said in response to her silent question. "It's missing."

"Go, Aidan," she pleaded, and took hold of him. He winced as her fingers dug into his injured hand. "Go find her!"

Aidan felt sick seeing his grandmother this way. He felt the coldness from last night returning, paralyzing his movements, numbing his brain. He tried to make sense of it all, put all the pieces together in a way he could comprehend, but nothing clicked. It was the same disconnect he'd felt that night last November when his mother had woken him with the news of his father. Suddenly he was back in his old nightmare again.

"Where?" he asked.

"Her car's still here," Memère said. "She's somewhere on the mountain for sure."

He tried thinking of all the places she might be. She had been reading his father's letters. Where would she go if she wanted to be with him? Where would he be waiting? Suddenly he knew.

"Southlook," he whispered.

Aidan sprang off the porch and headed toward the corner of the house. "Call Donny!" he cried back.

He ran alongside the house and cut into the backyard, passing by the shards of blown-up plastic jugs from a few weeks ago. He tried not to glance at them as he plunged into the tall grass behind the lawn.

He tore up through the woods and fields toward the cemetery. *Faster! Faster! Hurry!* he screamed to himself, trying to ignore the fire that had ignited in his lungs. He felt like he was running in slow motion, struggling in vain to match the rhythm of his racing pulse. How could it have come to this? How could he have watched her struggle and fade and done nothing to stop it, have even hastened it with his own selfish designs? What if he was too late?

She won't do it, he told himself. She wouldn't leave him the way his father had. Then he remembered again her lying on the couch with that distant gaze, fixed on some point far beyond him. Maybe she had already gone long before today, the opposite of a ghost—an absent spirit whose body remained, empty but alive. And he had done nothing to bring her back, having been too lost himself.

It was a sick joke with devastating consequences. Just one more in a series life had decided to play on him for no particular reason, like the Greek gods of old unmaking mortals, turning on a capricious whim. Moments ago he had been coming home to tell her it would all be okay, that he could learn to live with the idea of her and Donny together, that deep down maybe he even liked the idea. And he would relinquish the chase, give up his father's ghost. Like Odysseus, he would let go of the fantasy and accept reality with all its pain and intermittent joys. And both he and his mother could accept death and move on with their lives and hope to make it through.

He bounded through the last field before the meadow road that led to Southlook, lifting his legs high to avoid tripping in the rowen. Here he was, taking the tour again, like he had in years past with Pepère, as he had all summer in pursuit of his father. But this wasn't a tour. It was a race whose finish line he dreaded to see, afraid of what he might find.

Leaving the field, he hit the road and sprinted down the final stretch toward the cemetery. Before he knew it, he had rounded the last bend in the lane. Southlook lay before him. He scanned the graveyard as he ran. A momentary panic seized him—the place was empty. But as he proceeded the angle of the gravestones shifted slightly and there she was, sitting calmly in the upper corner before her husband's grave. She sat motionless, blending into the stillness, just another sepulchral statue. He felt a wave of relief, slowed his pace to catch his heaving breath, and headed for the entrance. He wasn't too late.

Pausing at the gate, he tried to think of what to say to her, tried to summon the words to bring her back. Suddenly, under the blue sky of an August day, he felt death everywhere around him. He could taste it as he had tasted it yesterday afternoon in the orchard, as he had tasted it last night on Eve's lips, bitter and cold.

A pulse of movement to the left interrupted his thought. From the corner of his eye, a dark mass appeared from nowhere. He closed his eyes and took a deep breath. He was afraid to open them. He knew what he would see.

After a moment he couldn't hold back any longer. Slowly turning, he opened his eyes and gasped in shock. Having already guessed the truth changed nothing.

His father stood ten yards away, gazing at him with heavy eyes. He still wore the black coat—pulled tight around him as if against the cold, hands buried in the pockets, collar up—and appeared just as he had last night, with slightly graying temples and a full, though now pale, face.

For a moment Aidan could only stare in astonishment at the crisp image. For weeks he'd hunted his father, always at his back, following the shade's fickle movements from a distance. And now here he was—before him and waiting. It was as Aidan had always imagined it would be during the exhaustion of the chase—a moment of calm where they would recognize each other as father and son, for he was sure his father saw him now. As if in answer to his thought, the man pulled one hand from a pocket and held it out to him. Aidan wondered if it was extended as a greeting or in summons. At that moment he hungered for his father more than he had all summer, more than he ever had before.

Instinctively Aidan started toward the figure. After a couple steps, though, he stopped. He clenched his fists and drew a sharp breath, struggling with the desire to join him. Glancing back to his mother, sitting alone before the black marble headstone, her raven hair shining under the high sun of noon, he hesitated. He had already decided he would give up the chase. How could he change his mind now? How could he leave her? He would end up making the same mistake again, only now when it really mattered.

He closed his eyes, feeling a wave of anger sweep over him. Why was his father doing this to him? How could he just show up like this, of all times, of all places? Didn't he care about Aidan? About her?

Aidan turned back to the shade where it still stood, frozen, waiting. He gazed into his father's eyes, dark pools that ate the light, drawing it into a well of infinite sadness. Suddenly he remembered what Memère had told him, how maybe *he* had brought his father back, that it was his own hunger that kept them both pushing across the mountain, locked in an endless chase. Looking deeper into his father's eyes, he realized she was right. There *was* desire in the man's face.

But it wasn't Aidan's. It was his own—an aching sense of hope that Aidan would do the right thing. For all of them.

Aidan took a deep breath. He raised his hand and waved good-bye.

A long moment passed. Then his father nodded and echoed Aidan's gesture. Aidan thought he could see the faintest smile cross his father's face, or perhaps it was the look of relief. The shade turned and headed up across the pasture toward the summit.

Aidan watched for only a moment before running to the

gate. He dashed down the center lane toward the far end, where the row of Dunkleys rested, and cut in, pulling up as he reached his mother. Kneeling at her side, he touched her shoulder.

She started at his touch, as if waking from a dream, then turned to him with a pained smile, her eyes red from crying. The gun rested between them on the grass. Its silver plating caught the sun and cast particles of light along her cheek. He picked it up and gingerly set it down behind him. As she watched, her eyes brimmed with fresh tears.

"I just couldn't do it," she said, looking away.

"I'm glad."

"I'm sorry, Aidan. To have put you through this . . . "

"Don't be. We'll put it behind us."

He sat down beside her on the dark grass and plucked a single blade. It pulled out cleanly. He bit off the white bottom tip; it was tender and sweet. He chewed it slowly as they huddled together and the minutes passed.

"So much pain. I just wish I could know when it will end," she said at last. "Sometimes I feel like it never will."

"Maybe it won't. Maybe it's not supposed to—not completely, anyway. But I don't think it always has to be this way."

She nodded. A minute passed. She reached out and touched her husband's name on the stone. "I should've come here sooner."

"But we're here now. Both of us. It's a start," he said.

She wrapped her arm around his arm and leaned her head against his shoulder. They sat there for a while before the stone, feeling the sun on their backs, listening to the electric trill of a red-winged blackbird calling from a nearby post. He looked over at Grammy Dunkley's grave. Beneath her name and dates lay the line chiseled in a spidery script, an old country epitaph—*In the midst of life we are in death.*

His mother suddenly laughed. Aidan glanced back at her.

"I was just remembering last summer on the Cape. Marconi Beach. Your father in the surf, riding the waves."

Aidan laughed too. "That big wave. He didn't see it. It flattened him, ripped his bathing suit clean off."

"He just stood up," his mother continued, "walked right up the sand to his towel, naked as the day he was born. Everyone laughed. He didn't care."

They lingered another minute.

"I guess we should say good-bye," Aidan said at last. He rose and helped her to her feet, keeping hold of her hand. "Memère's waiting," he said, bending over to retrieve the pistol. "Donny, too."

She gave him a questioning glance as he straightened. He nodded in reply. They turned back to the grave and took one last look at the polished marble, the cut letters sharp and distinct. She walked up to the stone and touched the top for a second, then they turned and passed back down the row together.

Leaving Southlook, Aidan gazed one more time up

through the fields. In the distance a black speck moved steadily through the last clearing before the thick woods took over. He watched it until it disappeared into the path that led to the top of Harper Mountain.

EPILOGUE

The whisk rattled against the stainless steel pail. As Aidan stirred, the powder dissolved, turning the water a yellowy cream. He poured the mix into a bottle and screwed on the nipple.

"You want to do it?" he asked, handing the bottle to Angela.

"Sure," she said, brightening at the offer.

They knelt before the calf straining against its rope, made eager by the formula's scent. Tilting the bottle, Angela hesitated for a moment as she maneuvered the tip toward the calf's mouth. The calf, however, had no compunctions. It seized the hovering nipple and began drawing with rapid pulls, rolling its eyes with excitement as streams of milk dribbled down its chin.

Angela laughed. "She's hungry!"

"They always are," he replied. He reached up to scratch a patch of black against the white neck and noticed the scar between his knuckles. By now, at the end of August, the cut had healed to a faded pink line. Still, when he clenched his fist, a remnant of pain lingered. He turned back to watch her feed the calf, an unbroken smile across her face. "So, are you bummed about tomorrow?" he asked.

"No. I'm kind of excited, actually. A little nervous—new school and all."

"Me too. You'll be the only person I'll know."

"We'll take them by storm," she said.

"I just hope Ma won't be too tough on you. Advanced Senior English. Sounds like a bear."

"No sweat," she replied, raising the bottle higher so the last drops could be drained.

"She's beautiful," Angela murmured as the calf finished.

"Isn't she? Donny gave her to me last week. Says she'll grow up to be a prize milker. Kind of cool."

"Totally. So what'd you name her?"

"Angela," he said, and grinned.

They gathered outside around the picnic table for dinner—Donny and Patrice on one side, Aidan and Angela on the other, with Memère seated on a chair at the table's head. As afternoon slid toward evening, they enjoyed supper together.

"Well," the old woman said as they finished their meal, "I've had enough, I guess. Time for my evening walk." She rose from the picnic table. "Thank you for the excellent supper, Donny. That chicken was just right."

"My pleasure, Eloise," he replied.

She gave her good-byes and headed across the yard toward the milking barn.

"Memère!" a voice called out. She paused in the doorway and turned just as Aidan reached her.

"You want me to go with you?" he asked.

"That's up to you, dear," she said, "as always."

Aidan looked over his shoulder and across the yard. She followed his gaze. For a moment they watched the three of them at the table on the lawn—Donny and Patrice on one side, Angela on the other. Even from here they could hear their laughter.

"I think I'll stay," he said at last. "Don't want to miss dessert, you know."

She reached up and traced a hand across his cheek. "Good idea," she said. "I'll see you back at the house."

"Right. Say hello for me."

"I certainly will, dear."

Aidan gave her a quick smile and jogged over to the table. When he looked back, she was still standing in the doorway. She waved to him, then dipped into the shadows and was gone. He turned back to the table to where his mother was cutting up the pies.

"Apple or rhubarb, Aidan?" she asked.

"I'll have both," he replied, and lifted up his plate.

ACKNOWLEDGMENTS

I'd like to thank George Nicholson, my agent, and Susan Rich, my editor, for their enthusiastic response to the idea that became this book. I'm especially grateful to Susan for her talent in guiding me through the process of revision.

I'd also like to thank John Barksdale for his thoughtful feedback. And special thanks are due to my former teacher and colleague Burt Porter, not only for his input on this story, but also for teaching me the craft of writing in the first place.

Lastly, thanks to my wife, Erica, for her edits, insights, and encouragement.